THE SECRET LIFE OF GIRLS

THE SECRET LIFE OF GIRLS

CHLOË THURLOW

Published by Xcite Books Ltd – 2011

ISBN 9781907761904

Printed and bound in the UK

Cover design by Zipline Creative

For Hanif – who taught me everything and more

Chapter One

THE FIRST TIME I had a wet dream was a summer night when I'd gone to bed exhausted after one of those tedious talks with Mother. Something had been welling up inside her for weeks and it had been a relief when it finally came spilling out.

'Something awful has happened, Bella. Awful,' she said. 'I can't even tell you.'

'Mummy?'

She took a deep breath and composed her features.

'Daddy put all his money into that, that ... business and ... he lost it. Everything. If it wasn't for Simon I don't know what we'd do.'

Simon was Simon Daviditz and he had been a regular visitor since Daddy died. At the funeral he was holding Mother's hand but I remembered his eyes that day considering me across the grave as if I were a piece of bric-à-brac at the flea market he wasn't sure whether or not to invest in.

Mother started sniffling. 'We have to do something. We have to,' she cried. 'You won't even be able to go to your new school. It's all gone, gone.'

She dabbed her eyes repeatedly with a handkerchief while I sat there feeling cross. I was going to the finishing school of Saint Sebastian the Holy Martyr to re-do my A levels and I really didn't like my plans not turning out as planned.

I left her to make her phone calls and went to bed. I fell into a deep sleep and the sun angling through the lattice windows woke me with a sense that life was starting anew and I should stop worrying about poor Daddy.

My T-shirt was up around my neck and my hands like

1

explorers in a foreign land were moving over my breasts, my tummy, my hips and down between my legs. It was sticky there as if honey had been spilled over my thighs and I had the odd thought that in the night someone had been packing my bags and I was about to begin a long journey.

There was a white dress draped over the chair. I pulled it over my head and slipped barefoot into the garden. Plump insects buzzed and hummed among the flowers. Red butterflies spiralled like dancers in the updrafts of air rising warmly from the lawn. The cat stopped, stared as if he'd never seen me before, then sauntered off to his place in the apple tree where he would watch for birds.

Sylvester was a killer and nothing gave him more pleasure than dragging wriggling, half-expired game into the house where he would display his spoils on the white tiles of the kitchen floor.

I had thought I was alone but heard Mr Lawrence softly whistling in the shed. The gardener was what Mother called a local yokel, which meant he was subnormal and she could tell unkind stories about him over the phone to her friends. I had always thought of Mr Lawrence as old and only when I entered his domain that day did I realise that he was the same age as Mr Daviditz, about 40, loads older than me, but younger than Mother.

He was preparing cuttings, trimming them with a knife with a worn shiny blade. He glanced up, nodded as he relit his roll-up, then continued whistling. In the air was the tang of cut grass, wood polish and the moth ball smell of old Jake, the Labrador, sitting immobile like a black statue beside the bench. Tools with wooden handles hung from brackets with a sense of calm and order, and ranged along the shelves were jam jars full of nails and screws.

Through the small windows the light moved in dusty sheets and I had a feeling I was in one of those old French films Daddy would often be watching late at night when I woke from a bad dream and couldn't get back to sleep again.

My underarms were damp and perspiration rolled like glass beads over my skin. I watched absorbed as Mr Lawrence positioned the cuttings in the tray, his movements slow and steady as if he was enjoying the job and was in no hurry to get it done. He made a hole in the black earth with his thumb, selected another stem, and pressed the soil sensuously back in place. He had wide, strong fingers that fondled the fragile shoots with the same delicacy you need to sew on a button or write someone's name on a birthday cake.

He took another puff on his cigarette then left it balanced on the side of a silver tin. There was a spray gun on the bench and when all the cuttings were standing in neat lines he misted the tray with several short, sharp tugs on the trigger. I had moved closer than I meant to and the spray was cool on my hot cheeks.

For as long as I could remember, Mr Lawrence had avoided looking in my direction but now his dark eyes made me flush as they met mine. There was a faint smile on his lips as he moistened my face, my neck, and he kept on jerking the trigger on the spray gun, soaking the top of my flimsy dress. My breasts had begun to tingle and my nipples like the green shoots in the seed tray seemed to burst into life and were trying to burst through the fabric.

Mr Lawrence moved round the bench. He aimed a long jet of water down my spine before returning the container to the worktop. He ran one hand slowly over the bumps of my back and cupped my bottom. With the fingers of his other hand, he rubbed the tips of my nipples in a circular motion that made the breath catch in my throat and warm dribbles began to run down the insides of my legs. The earth on his fingers stained the dress in two perfect circles around my breasts. He moved his fingers over my swollen lips and, one by one, I took them into my mouth.

I had forgotten to put on any knickers and his other hand was stroking the tense bare flesh of my bottom. His fingers slipped into the sticky pool between my legs and I often wonder what may have happened next, the next in this case being the door bursting open and Mother standing there with the light behind her like the monster that woke me from my dreams.

'Bella. Bella. You. You ...'

She crossed the shed in one long stride and hit Mr Lawrence

3

across the face with such a hard slap it left four white stripes on his cheek.

'You animal. You oaf. Get out this minute!'

Jake must have wondered what all the fuss was about and stood there with his pink tongue lolling from his mouth. Mr Lawrence stroked the dog's head. He stared boldly back at Mother and the look they exchanged I would think about later that day.

Mother turned to me. 'What would your father say? What would Mr Daviditz say?'

After the momentary shock of Mother's appearance I did the only thing I could do. I ran back through the garden and into the house crying and didn't stop until Mother became bored and said she didn't care what I did or who I did it with as long as we kept it from Mr Daviditz because he was a solicitor and a Christian and a man who wouldn't tolerate that sort of thing.

'Bella, you have to know, you're very ... Mediterranean,' she said, as if the word had the taste of a stale olive. 'You're the type.'

'The type?'

'The type men are going to interfere with.'

'You think so?'

'Look, I really can't deal with you as well as everything else,' she said. 'Don't you get it, your father lost everything. There's no money, no new school, no future. Nothing.'

I turned and looked into her eyes. 'Everything's going to be all right,' I told her.

'You don't understand anything.'

'That's what you think,' I said and she pretended not to hear.

We became quiet and watched Sylvester through the french windows. Simon Daviditz was coming for lunch and I was thinking about what I was going to wear.

I kissed Mother on the cheek, something I rarely did, and bounded three at a time up the stairs.

I put on the first CD I laid my hands on and sang along to the music as I peered into the wardrobe. One thing I had learned is you have to dress for the occasion. I opened the drawers and went through my blouses and T-shirts, tight jeans, hipsters, cargo pants, flares, little halters, long pants, hot pants; it's all so very difficult. I took off my clothes and studied myself in the long mirror.

My breasts were round and full and stayed propped up by themselves. They were lovely and I really couldn't resist touching them. My hips and bottom were small like a boy's and my thighs that tingled still didn't quite touch when I stood straight. Daddy was an Italian and, like him, I have brown eyes, honey-coloured skin and thick dark hair I'd always worn in pigtails, even when I knew it had become old fashioned for a girl of my age. Just as my breasts had started filling out, so silken threads as fine as angel hair had formed in a triangle that was now dense and soft, a little nest below my bikini line.

I'd read in one of Mother's magazines that for a woman, less is always more and so a bikini must be perfect. I had a yellow one with red flowers that was a size too small and, when I put it on, I looked like a girl who didn't know she had grown up and looked more girlish from not knowing it. I turned to look at my rear. My shoulder blades stuck out and my bottom that I'd thought belonged to a boy had grown perfectly round and now belonged to me. I had wanted to be a boy for as long as I could remember but sensed there was a lot more to being a girl.

I ran the tips of my fingers over my pink nipples. They prickled as if from pins and needles. I turned for a sideways look and really had to blink several times and look again. Mr Lawrence had tricked my breasts into growing a whole half size bigger since he'd tried to plant me in one of his pots.

Mother says I'm immature. Perhaps I am. I still behave like a girl but my inspection that autumn day revealed in the mirror all the angles and curves, all the pouts and pleats, all the magic and mystery of a woman.

Wow!

I took my hair out of pigtails and combed it over my shoulders, turning the ends under. I studied the new style, then changed it back again. Daddy had once told me that although I was growing up I shouldn't be in too much of a hurry. Latin men understood these things and I suppose it was the Latin in me that had awoken that morning.

My gold crucifix was hanging over the side of the dressing table. I put it on, squirted perfume in the air and stood in the shower as it rained over me. I was about to leave the bedroom when I heard Mother opening the door. Mr Daviditz had arrived. I waited until he was in the drawing room, crept down the stairs and out through the kitchen to the garden. I had my iPod, a towel and a bottle of sun cream which I set down on the lawn where the apple tree obscures the view from the french windows.

'Bella, Simon's here,' I heard Mother call in her sugary voice and I rushed off like an eager puppy to greet him.

'Ah, Bella, *bella* as ever,' he said.

He thought this was awfully clever and had said it before.

I was breathless from all my running about, my heart was beating like a drum and, as he lowered his glasses, his eyes fell piously to the gold cross throbbing in the dark hollow between my breasts.

Mother's expression made it clear that she intended telling me to go and put on something more fitting, but was so relieved by my warm display she decided to let it drop.

Mr Daviditz was dressed in white trousers and a dark green polo shirt that welled in a soft balloon over a woven brown leather belt. He had lots of fine pale hair of which he was clearly very proud, red cheeks, damp hands and a wispy moustache that he fiddled with incessantly. He was carrying a bouquet for Mother and broke off one of the blooms for me. I put it between my teeth and skipped off back to the garden.

Sylvester bolted up the tree and sat there cleaning behind his ears. I covered my front with cream and slid the ear pieces into my ears. I tried to calculate how long it would take before Mr Daviditz came but grew tired of the game and just listened to the music. I had made a point of being unkind to Simon Daviditz since that day at the funeral but, according to Mother, abrupt mood swings in teenagers are the result of hormones and perfectly normal.

My skin was just beginning to get that tight feeling that comes when you stay too long in the sun when a shadow brought a welcome relief. Mr Daviditz carried a drink complete with a straw and ice cubes that tinkled against the glass.

'A spritzer,' he said like a conspirator.

He knelt down beside me as I drank: fizzy water with white wine and quite repulsive. I sucked long and hard on the straw.

'Delicious,' I said.

'Yes,' he said and paused. 'Yes, indeed.'

'I can't reach my back, would you?' I gave him the sun cream and his hands were shaking as he took the bottle.

I turned over and loosened my top. He spread the cream over my shoulder blades, his cautious hands moving slowly across my back, down my arms, around my waist, one leg, then the other. He pulled each one of my toes, then moved with greater confidence back up my legs.

He began massaging the base of my spine, each downward motion peeling back my bikini bottom as if he were paring a ripe apple just fallen from the tree. As if by friction, with each movement I eased the weight from my hips. For some reason I had started thinking about Mr Lawrence and it only occurred to me now that he had the same eyes as Daddy, the same as me.

'That feels lovely,' I said. 'You have such soft hands you should have been a doctor.'

'I did consider it. Then the law got me.'

I gave an encouraging laugh. 'What a pity, you could have examined me all over when I was ill,' I told him.

He was gasping like an old train as he carried on working his palms up and down, up and down, and before I died of boredom I activated his secret plan by eliminating the pull of gravity. I raised my hips clean from the ground and, with one more tug at the elastic, Mr Daviditz had my bikini briefs down around my knees.

I lowered myself to the towel and wriggled like a freshly caught fish.

He dribbled sun cream on my back and began fondling the two moons of my bottom. I waited for that moist feeling to come but it didn't happen this time and I imagined Mr Daviditz didn't have the touch. He finally spread my cheeks with trembling fingers and we remained motionless as if time were suspended and I thought this strange little man was clearly obsessed to be kneeling there in that uncomfortable position peering inanely up my bum.

'Lunch,' I heard Mother sing out from the kitchen, and I couldn't help laughing as Mr Daviditz fell backwards and hit his head against the tree. Sylvester leapt down from the branch from where he'd been watching, hissed and ran off.

'Deary, deary me, look what's happened.'

Mr Daviditz jerked the red-flowered briefs back in place before lurching to his feet. I turned and I was unable to conceal my breasts as I reached for my top. I looked coyly up into his eyes. Mr Daviditz seemed so intense it was as if we'd just been to another funeral and I thought old people took things which were only a bit of fun far too seriously.

'Come on,' he said. I took the hand he offered and he studied my face as if written in my flushed cheeks were clues to his own destiny.

'Thank you,' I whispered before he could say anything and it occurred to me that, not one, but two men had interfered with me that day and if I'd kept a diary it would have given me something to write about.

Mother watched us making our way back across the lawn. There was a look in her eyes, the same look she had given Mr Lawrence when she slapped his face, but now that look was for me.

'Bella, you're not a child. Do get dressed,' she said.

I did, demurely, in a kilt and white blouse. Mr Daviditz at lunch was very attentive to both Mother and his moustache and, while he practically ignored me, I sat there studying Mother's vile collection of teapots arranged on the shelves. I skipped pudding and wandered through the rooms looking at paintings and ornaments, the family snaps in silver frames, the polished beams on the low ceiling.

Ickham Manor was my house, left to me in a trust, and now that Daddy was dead I wanted everything to remain the same. I sat at the piano but my mind just couldn't focus on Mozart and I gave up trying. I settled in the alcove at the end of the drawing room and flicked through an old picture book with a girl and a pony on the cover.

The story was about poor little Lizzie Dripping who wanted to ride her pony at the gymkhana, but the pony had a tummy upset *just like people*. Lizzie had washy blue eyes, a yellow ponytail poking out of her riding hat and was so exceedingly dull all she could do was sit and cry until the pony felt so irritated by her it got better. Lizzie went to the gymkhana and won a pink ribbon. I had read the book a hundred times when I was little, but now it made me want to go to the bathroom and yuck up the spritzer.

I scrolled down to the new Dallas McTee on the iPod and was just about to stretch out on the floor when Mother and Mr Daviditz appeared looking awfully pleased with themselves.

'Reading, that's a good sign,' he said.

They sat together on the sofa. Mother is an English blonde with the blue grey eyes of the Atlantic and was wearing the same intense look as Lizzie Dripping.

'We've got something to tell you,' she said.

Mr Daviditz's cheeks were redder than ever as he took her hand. 'I've asked Hester, your mother, to be my wife,' he announced.

There was a long silence while we all waited for someone to speak. I noticed the nerve in Mother's neck throb with a moment's impatience.

'Are you happy?' she finally asked.

I studied them both and wondered if they were going to have children.

'Oh, yes,' I said. 'Very.'

Mr Daviditz looked relieved. 'Now, we should do something to celebrate. What would you like to do?'

I took a big breath, put my finger to my lips, and gazed about the room.

'Anything you like,' he added.

I was still thinking. 'Come along, Bella,' said Mother.

'I know,' I replied. 'Let's go out and buy some new underwear.'

Chapter Two

IN MY RED BLAZER with a buttoned white blouse tucked into the waistband of a pleated navy blue skirt, with my clear eyes, my hair in a long plait down to the middle of my back and a straw hat with a ribbon resting on my knees, I was everything the neat clean schoolgirl ought to be.

My uniform combined the colours of the Union Jack and, despite my Mediterranean inclinations, a sense of triumph touched me when I glimpsed the flag waving from the chapel spire at the Convent of Saint Sebastian the Holy Martyr. I was sure we were going to be happy together.

We had driven for an hour through the Kent countryside to the coast. The convent stood on grass-trimmed chalk cliffs, a yellow brick building laced with ivy and protected behind high walls that made me wonder if they were designed to keep people out or the girls in. Why we were forced to dress in uniform I had no idea, it was so 20th century, but the nuns had their habits, and it was thought that students were more obedient and learned more in traditional dress.

We passed through the open gates and crunched over the gravel drive below tall trees that were shedding their golden leaves along the way. It was the end of September, the smell of change drifting in from the sea as I stepped from the car. Mother marched off to the Bursar's office and the nun waiting at the entrance with her hands gripped behind her bustled down the steps with an intense expression and guided us to the dorms. 'Sister Theresa, geography,' she said in introduction and leaned forward to gain traction like a duck racing across the surface of a pond.

She led the way as we circled the building beneath an arched colonnade. Girls in the same red jackets gazed at me as I passed with a mixture of interest and hostility. I was late starting at the school because I had been in Italy for a memorial service and then stayed on with my grandparents at La Montepietra, their lovely old palazzo. Mother had returned home early to be comforted by Mr Daviditz.

Although Sister Theresa was small and cumbersome, she moved at a furious pace and Mr Daviditz became pink and breathless as he followed with my bags. We entered the building and climbed a narrow flight of stairs to a sunny room that smelled of deodorant and looked out over the sea. There were four beds, four large cupboards, a table with chairs and a general air of neatness of which I approved. On the walls were posters from *Pirates of the Caribbean: Dead Man's Chest*, there was Brad Pitt with rippling muscles and Dallas McTee looking awfully common in an animal print bra and not much else. Next to the dorm there was a bathroom and shower, shelves of thick white towels and the lamentable lack of a full-length mirror.

'Here we are,' said Sister Theresa. 'I'll leave you to your goodbyes,' and she was gone.

'It's lovely here,' said Mr Daviditz, glancing at the beds as he dropped the bags.

'Thank you, Mr Daviditz.'

'Simon,' he said.

I stood looking out the window for a moment and turned as he approached for his kiss which I planted, fairy like, one on each side of his mouth, the tip of my tongue darting out to brush his lips. Beads of perspiration broke on his brow and his cheeks grew redder.

He pulled at his moustache and sighed. 'I'm going to miss you,' he said, and I knew it was true. He'd been missing me for a week because I'd been so busy preparing for school there had been no time to sunbathe in the garden in spite of his frequently whispered suggestions that for the sake of my health I should do so. I thought for the sake of his health it was probably better that I didn't.

11

We heard a pair of feet tapping up the stairs and he stood back as Mother entered with a girl I would have thought was a boy if she hadn't been wearing the school uniform. Mother glanced at her watch.

'Bye, Mother,' I said. We touched cheeks and I turned away. 'Bye, Mr Daviditz, thank you,' I said again, shaking his hand this time.

'Just, you know,' said Mother. 'Just work hard.'

'Oh but I will.'

'It's the right atmosphere,' said Mr Daviditz.

The strange girl who looked like a boy stood with her arms folded watching as if this were a play and, as the director, she wasn't entirely satisfied with the performance.

'Goodbye,' she said in a loud deep voice, urging them on their way, and we listened as Mother and Mr Daviditz descended the stairs.

The girl shut the door and leaned against the woodwork, one foot behind her, arms still folded. As I looked more closely it was obvious that she didn't look like a boy at all, except for her hair sticking up in the same silly way as the boys in the village at home. There was a fierce look about her mouth.

'Your stepfather?' she asked.

'How did you guess?'

'Because I know things. I am in charge of this room. You will do everything I say.'

'Everything?'

'Hang your jacket in that cupboard,' she instructed, pointing. I did so and she looked enormously satisfied. 'Do you always do as you're told?'

I hooked my finger in my mouth to think about that. 'Almost never,' I said. 'Unless it's amusing.'

'I suppose it depends on what you call amusing.'

'Indeed.'

'How old are you?' she demanded.

'Eighteen.'

'Same as me. You don't look it,' she said and paused. 'I suppose you failed all your A-levels?'

'No, actually. I was living in Italy. I didn't take any. How

12

about you?'

'Never you mind.' She took a step closer. 'Pull your skirt up, so I can see.'

This was somewhat abrupt, but I was new to Saint Sebastian and assumed this was some sort of initiation. I hesitated for a moment, lowered my eyes, but did as she asked, holding the hem between two fingers. I was wearing really cool white silk knickers that Mr Daviditz had bought when we'd gone shopping one afternoon at Neuhaus & West in Canterbury and Mother was in a different part of the store. He'd been waiting outside the changing room and got all sweaty peering through the narrow gap in the curtains.

'This top is *really* much too small,' I said, and he scurried off to find different colours and designs.

The autumn sun was warming my shoulders through the high window and when I examined my breasts in the mirror I discovered they really had grown bigger since that day in the woodshed.

'Knock. Knock,' he said, and I opened the curtains.

Mr Daviditz gasped and reached for his moustache. I slipped in and out of those teeny tiny triangles of silk and his head kept swivelling back and forth as he gazed at me then turned to glance nervously over his shoulder. After I had tried on each bra and pair of knickers, I took them off and stood there demurely as I handed them to him. We bought lots of sets and he pushed a £20 note into my hand just as Mother appeared looking furious clutching a new oven glove. She gritted her teeth as she dashed across the changing room and closed the curtains.

I liked being looked at and admired. It was fun, even standing there with this new girl with a boy's haircut studying me as if I were quite mad.

'I suppose you're a little princess, are you,' she said, and I didn't reply. 'Are you a lesbian?'

I shook my head. 'No, most certainly not.'

She came closer and placed her hand over my crutch in the careless way of someone who imagines they know the right way to do things when they don't really know at all.

13

'Are you a virgin?'

'Yes,' I replied and she sneered like a real woman of the world.

She started rubbing her hand slowly over the fabric between my legs, backwards and forwards, the movement opening the lips of my vagina.

'What's your name?' she demanded.

'Bella di Millo.'

'Jacqueline Bennett. Call me Jack.'

'Hello, Jack.'

My knickers were wet already and my breath caught instantly in my throat. She slipped her hand in the elastic, a finger slid inside me and I shuddered as if an earthquake had suddenly hit the Kent coast.

She took her hand out and put the wet finger between my lips. 'What's it taste of, fish?' she asked.

I sucked her finger.

'Honey,' I answered.

She looked back at me haughtily. The door opened and Jack dropped my skirt as another girl entered. She had brown hair cut in a page boy and dark green eyes. She looked at me but didn't smile.

'Saskia,' she announced. 'If I'm rude next time I see you it will be my twin.'

'Tara,' Jack explained.

'Tea,' Saskia added and disappeared.

'If you're lucky I'll introduce you to Sister Nuria,' Jack told me and I knew instantly that there was no one else in the world I would rather meet.

We trailed downstairs to the refectory where 200 girls found places at long tables. The nuns were seated on a raised platform, their heads bowed. At the end of the line was an extremely beautiful nun; she was in grey not black and was much younger than the rest. She had pure white skin, dark Madonna eyes and pink lips that trembled as she whispered her prayers. I'm sure they were the most divine lips I had ever seen although I couldn't recall that I'd ever really thought about lips before.

'Sister Nuria,' whispered Jack. 'Our Spanish teacher.'

14

Mother Superior, a matronly behemoth with gigantic breasts pressed like balloons against the folds of her smock, stood and we were silent as she said lots of nasty things I'm sure God wouldn't have liked at all.

'God knows you all, each and every one of you. He is watching you at all times. He knows your thoughts,' she said and stared straight at me. 'Obey God's word or he will cast you into the pit of Hell where demons and vipers will suck and prise the flesh from your lissom young bodies and throw the pieces into the everlasting flames where they will burn forever more. Thank you God for the food we eat. Amen.'

'Amen.'

Amen, I thought. I'd lost my appetite. I stared as the strawberry jam passed along the tables on china saucers and envisioned all that hot flesh in the everlasting flames. It gave me goosebumps. Then I shook my head, thought about my grandfather in Italy, a famous atheist, and concluded that everything Mother Superior had said was just too silly. God, if he had any preferences at all, liked things that were beautiful. Of that I was absolutely certain.

There were crusty chunks of bread, plates of butter and I noticed there were anorexic girls who didn't eat anything and there were little tubby girls who ate everything that was put in front of them, and there were girls like me who just picked at our food and were choosy about what we put in our mouths.

I studied the twins. Saskia and Tara were identical like two dolls straight from the factory and I imagined how excited Mr Daviditz would be when I brought them home during half-term.

After tea, I went straight to the front. The nuns were pushing back their chairs and leaving. I smiled up at Sister Nuria. Now I was close I could see that she was hardly any older than me.

'Hello,' I said.

'Hello,' she answered.

'I'm new today.'

'Well, I am pleased to meet you. I'm Sister Nuria.'

'Isabella di Millo.'

'Isabella.'

I shrugged. 'Just Bella,' I said, and Jack came bustling up

behind me.

Sister Nuria lowered her voice. 'Sometimes I like to pray in the small chapel in the catacombs,' she said. 'Would you like to join me?'

'Oh, yes please.'

She glanced at Jack. 'You can show her, Jacqueline?' Her English was almost perfect and was so pretty and charming on her lips it was better than perfect.

Jack nodded. Sister Nuria lowered her head and followed the other Sisters out of the refectory.

Jack looked terribly put out.

'What's wrong?' I asked.

'Nothing,' she replied, and rushed off so that I had to chase after her.

We hurried along the corridor to the beat of a hundred pairs of leather shoes, the smell of old stone accompanied by the scent of damp schoolgirls. Jack's teeth were clenched tight and I wondered if she had a tattoo. When I took her arm, she pulled away.

'Don't be pushy, or you'll end up on your knees,' she said, turning to me with an evil glint in her eyes: 'Praying.'

'Jacqueline,' I said in my best accent. 'I didn't mean anything.'

She didn't smile and I realised that Jack was going to be hard work.

We were confined for a reflective period to our rooms. Then we had chapel, which was useful for doing manicures and catching up on reading *Cosmopolitan*.

During supper I gazed at Sister Nuria and avoided the food which was truly unmentionable. I couldn't imagine why the chefs in boarding schools didn't watch all those cooking programmes that are always on the television, even if they are boring.

After supper we retired to our rooms to do homework or read the bible or do whatever it is nice girls are thought to do. I unpacked and washed my hair.

At lights out Jack crept into my bed and laid very still beside me. 'We have to wait about ten minutes,' she said, and pulled at my chin. 'Do you like snogging girls?'

'I'm not sure.'

She stuck her mouth over mine and I felt Jack's teeth damaging my lips.

'You're not very good, are you?' she said, and I didn't answer. The truth is I'd spent half my life in Italy with a tutor. Boys – and girls – were a scarce commodity and, quite aside from my education, I had a lot of lost ground to make up.

'I'm doing my best,' I said.

'Princess,' she replied and squeezed my nipple so hard it really hurt.

'Ouch.'

'Don't you like pain?'

'No, I don't think I do.'

'The greater the pain the greater the pleasure,' she said and squeezed my nipple again.

She slipped out of bed, put on her slippers and dressing gown and I followed her from the room. The twins were sleeping like angels. We went downstairs, opened the door and waited in the shadows.

'We're not supposed to leave our rooms,' Jack told me.

'Oh, good,' I whispered.

She ran across the grass quadrangle to the flint wall of the chapel. I waited until she whistled then followed. It was just like being a secret agent. There was a low wooden door at the end of the wall. We entered and descended a flight of stone stairs to the catacombs. The vaulted ceiling was supported by plump pillars and rows of cándles made quivering shadows that moved in ghostly rings. It was like going into a haunted house and I felt the hair rise on the back of my neck.

Sister Nuria was standing at the far end, hands held in prayer, her eyes closed. She was motionless like a statue. She was aware that we had entered but remained still for a few more seconds. She said amen, then opened her big dark eyes. She held out her arms and, when I reached her, she leaned forward and kissed me on the lips. It was gentle, just a peck. Sister

17

Nuria's lips were warm and soft like goose down. They moved over my lips, gently sucking and shifting until they opened and her tongue found its way between my teeth. I pressed back, my tongue wrapping itself in her tongue like they were two little fishes swimming about in a bowl.

Jack was standing to one side, a director again, watching another scene in the play of my life. Sister Nuria smiled at her.

'Thank you, Jacqueline. You should go.'

Jack seemed reluctant to leave but there was something in the Sister's voice that made disobeying impossible.

'Good night,' Jack said, and there was a little grin on her lips as if she were privy to a secret.

Sister Nuria turned and listened as the door closed in its frame. She climbed the stairs and shot the bolt into its hasp with a loud ring that echoed over the flint walls and sent a delicious shiver running up my spine.

As she approached, the candle flames danced and her long shadow slid over the ceiling. I was anxious for a moment, but excited, as if something inside me that had been slumbering like Sylvester in front of the fire was about to be awoken forever. Mr Lawrence slipped briefly into my mind but he slipped away again as Sister Nuria moved closer and I could see my reflection in her eyes.

She held my two hands and leaned back to look at me. She pulled my hair to one side. She studied my neck like a vampire and I thought *Buffy, where are you now when I need you?* She leaned forward and kissed my throat. I felt a tremor pass along my shoulder blades and move down to my fingers like an electric charge.

I am blessed, as Mother complains, with thick wavy hair which Sister Nuria held above my head in a fountain, stray strands toppling about my cheeks. She was studying me like an object on display at the museum. The shadows made by the candlelight were dancing faster and faster like natives in Africa and I thought I heard distant drums, but that was probably the beat of my heart.

Sister Nuria stood away and removed the grey noviciate head-dress they call a wimple, which I think is a silly word. I had expected her to be bald underneath. Instead she had lush dark hair that fell halfway down her back. There were buttons along her shoulder which she unhooked and when her habit fell to her feet I thought she looked so beautiful I wondered if Jack had been right: perhaps I was a lesbian. She was naked, a marble sculpture, every curve softly rounded and perfect. Sister Nuria had large high breasts with tiny pink nipples that I bent to kiss. I heard the breath catch in her throat.

'Bella, Bella, Bella,' she said, and kissed me again, a soft, long kiss that made me feel quite faint.

She pulled the cord tied around my dressing gown and unbuttoned my pyjamas. They fell to the floor and we stood very still, both naked, our breasts just touching. My hand reached for the lush mound of dark hair between her legs as if drawn by some force unknown to me and my fingers slipped straight into the oily wet pool. Our nipples hummed like fuses. My whole body fizzed and sparkled and I thought for a moment I was going to catch fire. She stood back and cupped my breasts in her palms.

'You have the most beautiful breasts, Bella,' she said and smiled. 'They must have been made in heaven.'

I couldn't help thinking this was heaven, the warm September night in the catacombs, standing there naked with Sister Nuria, the candle flames dancing around us. Her hand was stroking my bottom. I was soon wet of course; I was like a tap with a leaky washer, and the liquids gushed out of me as her fingers pressed between my legs.

It was awkward standing there kissing and fingering each other and it was nice when she went down on her knees, eased my legs apart and slipped her tongue between my legs. I'd had Mr Lawrence's fingers inside me in the woodshed and I'd nearly had Mr Daviditz's fingers inside me, and, it didn't really count, but that afternoon Jack had put her fingers in too.

But tongues, I discovered, are something quite different, at least, Sister Nuria's tongue was warm and clever as it licked over my vagina lips and found its way into my fairy cave.

There was a piece of carpet on the stone floor beneath our feet. She pulled me down, and remained on her knees with her head between my legs. She was like a slow machine, her tongue working itself deeper and deeper into my drenched pussy. As I felt myself coming, the tip of her tongue pressed hard against my clitoris and I exploded in spasms that made me shriek.

She drew herself up my body and I sucked my own juices from her swollen lips and I'd been quite right, I did taste of honey.

Sister Nuria laid me flat on the floor like a magician about to do a magic trick, then twisted round in order that now, when her lips returned to search deeper into my vagina, her own glittering sex opened like a dark eye in front of me. I held the cheeks of her bottom, drew her pussy into my mouth and, just as she had taught me, I worked my tongue inside her, slowly at first, then faster and faster. I felt her warm oil like nectar washing over my face and as we started to writhe in orgasm I found her clitoris and kept pushing, harder and harder, the soft lips of her sex opening over my mouth and filling me with her delicate fruit.

Her tongue started collecting the liquid from my pussy and transferring it to my bottom. It felt strange at first, the muscles pushing her tongue back, but gradually my bottom grew to like this strange warm object. It became more demanding and sucked her tongue right up, deep inside me. I didn't know your bottom could be the avenue for such wonderful surprises and gave myself fully to the experience.

Then she came again in fast spurts that shot into my mouth and it tasted warm and bittersweet like cappuccino. Her body shook and trembled, and she didn't shriek as I had done, but hummed like a train slowing its way into a station.

She changed her position and pulled my legs higher in order to get a better angle. Her tongue plunged deeper into my bottom and I trembled and felt myself coming again. It was different this time, a gurgling that moved through all my secret passages and settled like a long quiet sigh. She turned and moved her lips close to my ear.

'Has anyone ever done that before?' she asked and I whispered back.

'No, Sister Nuria, never.'

'Then I am the first?'

'Yes.'

'That means you will always remember me.'

She put her tongue in my ear and gently caressed all the folds of skin. Then she kissed me again on the lips.

'Everyone, Bella, is blessed with one gift,' she whispered.

I thought for a second. 'What's my gift, Sister Nuria?'

'You shouldn't ask. In case it goes away.' I went to speak but she put a finger to my lips. 'Good night, angel,' she said.

We dressed and climbed the steps to the door. The moon was full, the sky filled with stars. Sister Nuria kissed my cheek and I hurried across the grass between flint walls and up the stairs to my room. I opened the curtains and laid in my narrow bed staring into the night, every nerve stretched tight like strings on a musical instrument.

Daddy had chosen my school and would have been pleased that after only one day I knew I was going to be happy there. I closed my eyes and, as I drifted off to sleep, Daddy's face faded into the face of Mr Lawrence.

Chapter Three

I WAS A LITTLE bit cross that Sister Nuria wouldn't tell me *anything* about my gift. I knew it had nothing to do with singing or playing Mozart because she had never heard me try. I knew is wasn't learning about gravity or how much water tips over Victoria Falls, and when I thought about all the things it couldn't be, I came to the conclusion the only thing it could be was sex. Daddy always said it is important to have one real talent and I was relieved it wasn't something tiresome like playing chess or doing the pole vault.

These days I only had to look at Sister Nuria across the refectory to get a damp feeling in my knickers. She must have felt the same and avoided my eyes, especially in Spanish class. I asked her questions like how do you say "you are" and how do you say "beautiful" and then I'd practise: *Tú eres guapa*, and her white skin would turn pink like fresh salmon.

I was waiting for her to invite me back to the catacombs and, when I suggested it during a private moment, she told me she was studying for her final nuns' exams and pleasures of the flesh would have to wait.

Pleasures of the flesh, I thought, that does sound nice, and she kissed me quickly on the lips. The other girls were soon gossiping, rumours spread like head colds and tummy aches, and the jealous ones whispered nasty things that I just ignored.

It was Mr Lawrence who had encouraged my breasts to grow and I'm sure if Mother hadn't disturbed us in the woodshed his fingers would have journeyed like an explorer to all my undiscovered parts. I'd also thought about something else, not that I actually cared, but the way Mother had slapped

Mr Lawrence across the face that day and the way he'd looked boldly back at her, made it clear that there was a lot going on that Mr Daviditz didn't know about. The newlyweds were in the Caribbean and were sending postcards of tropical sunsets, which was most inconsiderate.

I was working hard. I like to do well, and when I wasn't memorising Latin verbs and reading about Dr Livingstone, I spent a lot of time in front of the mirror massaging my breasts, willing them to grow bigger. I had also been doing some research and had reached the conclusion that, like me, the rest of the world had the same fixation. They were *everywhere*. An endless tide of pert rounded breasts rose buoyantly each day from the pages of newspapers and magazines, movie posters, billboards, advertisements for toothpaste and floor cleaner, satellite dishes and sore throat remedies. Breasts were omnipresent. Actresses and models, news presenters and pop stars were wearing less and revealing more, and they all had the same cheeky smiles as if their breasts were little toys or babies or puppies and they expected everyone to admire their playful antics.

Breasts, I read in one magazine, were in fashion, and I thought how silly. Breasts, I was sure, were always in fashion. Mine were perfectly spherical, high and full; everyone said so. But if I put my hands beneath them, they became more *out there*, like the models in magazines, like Dallas McTee in the poster on the wall.

One of the twins, I still got them mixed up, had said I looked just like her and I was most put out. We both have wide mouths with full lips and good teeth, the same delicate features, but that's where the similarities end. She was a blonde; blondes don't wear that well, and I was sure those breasts in the animal print top weren't all hers anyway.

Of course this "push up and plunge" look wasn't exactly natural and breasts liked to be given a little bit of help by the fine wire frames invented by the clever men at the bra factories. There were all sorts of bras; bras with silicone gel and booster pads, the bioform bra which has hard, lightweight cups, there's a bra with three-dimensional support, techno bras with a cobweb mesh, and I couldn't wait to wriggle into the heat-activated bra that "adapts to the bosom".

Bosom!

What a silly word, I thought, and said it over and over again: 'Bosom. Bosom. Bosom.'

There are brassieres in silk and satin and lace, cotton for hot days, and I was dying to try the hands-free bra designed for partygoers with its side pockets for lipstick and keys. I adored underwear and could understand why girls wanted to rip off their clothes and show everyone. I certainly did. With our curves and angles, our jutting bones and soft tender places, we are made to wear nothing, and if you have to wear something, those little tiddly bits of silk and satin like sweetie wrappers were quite enough. And like sweetie wrappers they are easy to take off. Not that I eat sweets mind you.

I sat in Sister Theresa's geography class staring out at the grey English sky thinking about Sister Nuria's tongue snaking into my fairy cave. It was the first time I'd done it, I mean *really* done it, and she was right, I would always remember. You have the gift, Bella, she'd said, and as my knickers began to get moist my thoughts were cruelly interrupted by the rapping sound of bony knuckles against the blackboard.

'Bella di Millo, are you with us?'

'Yes, Sister Theresa.'

'And where exactly are we?'

I put my finger in my mouth. This was a trick question and I didn't like tricks.

'I imagine we are either steaming up the Zambezi or standing with sore feet at the top of Kilimanjaro,' I replied and all the girls laughed.

'Thank you.'

'The longest river and the highest mountain.'

She made a buttoning motion with her fingers and stared at the gold cross in my cleavage.

'Do it up,' she said.

The third button on my blouse had popped open and the girls were hysterical when I gazed down in shock and horror and covered my breasts with my palms.

Not all the girls liked me, but there is a difference between being liked and being popular and popular was what I would rather be. Everyone was getting to know Bella, the girl with the beautiful breasts, and the only thing that was disappointing was that Tara and Saskia, if they had views on this subject, they kept them to themselves.

The convent was always turning off the boiler and it was often freezing in the dorm, but still I bravely walked around topless while the twins giggled over their laptops and never glanced at me at all. Jack said the girls had stunted development and the sex button inside them was sound asleep.

'Then I feel it is my obligation to wake them,' I announced.

'I don't think so.'

I do like a challenge. If the twins were Sleeping Beauties, I was Princess Charming and resolved to give those mystery buttons a jolly good kiss.

'Do you want to bet?' I said.

'How much?'

'I didn't mean money. It's just a phrase,' I explained. 'I meant a friendly bet.'

'No way, Princess.' She rubbed her fingers together like a market trader. 'Five pounds.'

I picked up scraps of knowledge like a magnet with iron filings and remembered that when you are in a negotiation it is best to keep quiet and think for a few minutes before you respond.

'Twenty,' I said.

'Twenty?'

'Or forget it.'

Jack nodded her head slowly up and down. We shook hands, then she leaned over and squeezed my nipples as hard as she could.

'Ouch,' I screamed. 'You're such a bitch.'

'You love it,' she said and left the room.

Jack was trying to ingratiate herself with the American girl Tabby Van Deegan, who was 20, positively an antique, and considered the school beauty. She was pretty in that wilting lilac sort of way, but I was beginning to think that all the adulation came more from the fact that she was "rich in her own right", as Jack liked to say, and invited girls to orgies at her country house. I just adored the word orgy, although I wasn't exactly sure what it meant. Orgy. Orgy. Orgy. It was like the opposite of bosom.

I was nursing my poor breasts. They stung as if they'd been pierced or something, which some of the girls were doing and I thought it was just silly. I dropped my book on the windowsill and checked in the mirror to make sure Jack hadn't done permanent damage. She was becoming a nuisance with all this pinching and at the appropriate time I would get my own back.

The place by the window was always warm and I could sit there for hours. I returned and carried on with my Latin. I was reading about Pliny the Elder and was intrigued to discover that Mother was using a phrase that had come down to us from ancient times.

Pliny had created an antidote for poison which consisted of taking 20 leaves of rue – whatever that is – and grinding them up with two dry nuts, two figs and *a grain of salt*. Somebody by the name of Pompeius (which sounded pompous to me) doubted whether it would really work and now, like Pompeius, when something seems unlikely, Mother just loves saying it should be taken with a grain of salt. Too many cooks spoil the broth. A stitch in time saves nine. An empty vessel makes the most noise. Mother was bursting with wisdom.

I began what I called the Gemini Project the day I got hit with a hockey stick and went to lie down with a bruise on my side. Saskia was excused games because she had a tummy ache. Tara, the sporty twin, was out on the playing fields and I laid on the bed crying until Saskia asked me what was wrong.

'I've got this terrible pain here,' I said. 'Come and see.' I pulled down the top of my shorts.

'What, that little bruise?'

'It's bigger inside.'

'It will go away.'

'Will you just massage it a second?'

'What for?'

'To make it better.'

She hesitated and shrugged. 'If you like.'

She did so and if there wasn't a bruise before there certainly would have been if she hadn't stopped.

'No, no, Saskia, softly, like you're caressing someone, not pummelling them,' I said. 'Pretend I'm your boyfriend.'

'I haven't got a boyfriend.'

'That's even better, then, you can learn.'

I pulled up my hockey shirt, took her hand and moved it slowly down my side, my rib cage, my narrow waist, my hips where the bone stuck out like a handle on one of the old tools in the woodshed. I was lying on my side and shifted to my back. I directed her hand to my hip bone and she stroked it tenderly. I smiled up at her.

'Is that nice?' I asked

'I'm supposed to ask you that.'

'It's nice for me. I want to know if it's nice for you too.'

'*No pas mal*,' she shrugged.

I unfastened my shorts and pulled them down. I was wearing pink silk knickers with lace fronts. 'Just there,' I said. 'Please.'

She moved her hand down towards my groin. The air caught in my throat and I breathed heavily. Someone had scored a goal out on the hockey pitch, there was a loud cheer and I decided they were cheering me in my efforts with Saskia.

'Mmm, you've got healing hands.'

'Shall I stop then?'

'Do you want to?'

'I don't care.'

She kept rubbing her hands over my groin and I manoeuvred myself so that her fingers slipped between my legs. The pink silk was wet and I stared into her eyes like a serpent mesmerising its prey.

'Don't stop,' I said.

'All right.'

I lifted my bottom and pulled my knickers down. I directed her fingers inside me and, when I closed my eyes, I had a vision of Sister Nuria standing naked in the candlelight. I thought about her clever tongue searching inside my pussy and an eruption began to bubble and gurgle inside me.

'Ah, ah, ah.' I was coming already and when I opened my eyes Saskia looked completely startled.

'What are you doing?'

'I'm having an orgasm, Saskia.'

'Well, yes, I gathered that. It's weird.'

'It's wonderful,' I told her. 'It's the most wonderful thing in the world.'

She pulled a funny face. 'My fingers are dripping,' she said, and took a long hard sniff.

'Taste,' I said, and pushed her fingers into her mouth.

'Mmm.'

'Well?' I asked.

'Well what?'

'Does it taste of honey?'

'A bit,' she replied and I was suddenly dying to know what Saskia tasted like, and if Tara would have the same flavour. I mean, they were twins.

I was sitting up. Saskia was kneeling and I slid my hand up her skirt. She stopped sucking my fingers and watched my hand burrowing through the folds of material.

'Someone might come,' she said and I hid my smile. I'd touched her button.

'Everyone's on the field. We've got loads of time.'

'We haven't.'

'We have,' I said forcefully like an order.

Saskia froze like a frightened bunny and I realised that with this sort of thing you have to be strong and demanding. You have to lead, even if you appear to be following. I unzipped her navy blue skirt, pulled her flat on the bed and slid her skirt down her long legs. She was wearing the most hideous pair of knickers I had ever seen, great big maroon things that were recommended by the school and absolutely none of the girls wore.

'Saskia, these are a no-no,' I told her. 'You will never get a boyfriend wearing these.'

I pulled them down and tossed them under the bed. I only like pretty things and these maroon monsters were most upsetting.

'I've never, you know ...'

I pulled off her shirt. She was very boyish with small breasts and between her legs there was a silky coating of hair like a shadow. She had a birthmark shaped like a heart to one side of that sweet little tuft and I bent to kiss it. I wriggled out of my own shirt and leaned over her. She took my breasts in her palms and gently squeezed as if to check they were really all me.

'They're lovely,' she whispered. I leaned over and directed my breasts to her mouth. 'Softly, like you're sucking a dummy,' I instructed. 'First Pinkie and then Perky.'

The names just popped into my head and I sat back straddling her feeling like a mother who has just christened her babies.

Saskia's dark green eyes seemed trusting and nervous as she looked up at me. I flicked her hair from her forehead.

'You're very pretty,' I said.

'Am I?'

'Now you're fishing,' I said, and gave her a little slap.

I took her breast into my mouth and gently sucked the nipple until it popped out and became hard. I did the same with the other. I took her two hands and directed them to her nipples. She squeezed the pink buds between her thumb and first finger and started softly purring like Sylvester, who I missed sometimes. I ran my hands down her skinny sides, eased her legs apart and lifted them at the knees.

Her sex was pale pink like a ribbon. I had read in the books kept out of reach in the library at home that men liked to sleep with virgins and now I knew why. There was something exciting about being an explorer and I could understand why Dr Livingstone wanted to go where no other person had been before. I had plucked Saskia like a flower, bewitched her with my velvet brown eyes and now she was mine.

I bent between her spread thighs and detected the smell of Pears soap as I licked her waiting vagina. The lips opened and turned from pink to purple as they swelled with blood. Saskia made pussy cat noises and lifted her bottom from the bed in order to draw me inside her. I plunged my tongue in and she

29

gave a little scream.

'Oh, Bella. Oh, Bella,' she cried. 'Please, please, please,' and I thought how polite as I tried to decide on her taste. Then it came to me: it was mozzarella with Italian olive oil and, how interesting, I thought, *a grain of salt*.

Another goal was scored, and as another cheer rose from the hockey field it occurred to me how silly it was running around in the mud when you could be tasting a girl on a warm bed with the pale winter sun shivering outside the window.

Saskia took just about forever to get going and my jaw was aching so much by the time she started to orgasm, I slipped my tongue out of her tight little pussy, climbed between her legs and pressed my pubic bone hard into her. She linked her arms around my shoulders and tried to draw me inside, and it dawned on me for the first time that though sex with girls was great, sex with boys was going to be something else altogether.

She came in great swelling waves just like the sea in autumn, her body writhing like a little craft adrift on the ocean and it gave me a sense of power knowing that I could do this and make people so happy.

'Oh my God, oh my God,' she was whispering over and over, and I kept pressing until I came again and our juices washed around together. Saskia pulled my head down and kissed me and it was like kissing Jack that first time, our teeth rubbing together. I pulled my head away.

'I'm going to have to teach you how to kiss,' I said.

'Promise.'

'Cross my heart and hope to die.'

'I love you, Bella,' she whispered, and I put my finger to her lips.

'Don't be silly,' I said. 'It's just fun.'

She looked puzzled for a moment then snuggled herself into my neck. I imagined this was the cigarette stage of making love and decided I should learn how to smoke as soon as possible.

'Bella, you won't tell, will you?'

'Tell?'

'Tara.'

'No, of course not,' I said. 'Not in words, anyway.'

She ran her fingers along the slopes of my breasts to the nipples and followed the line of the curve to my rib cage. Pinkie and Perky, I thought, you are clever girls. They liked being fondled and I wanted Saskia to think of me just as I often thought about Sister Nuria. I was her first. I had pushed the magic button.

At that moment, the door swung open and Jack stood there with shiny cheeks and a towel around her head. Saskia was embarrassed and went to pull away. I slipped my hand between her legs and stroked her firmly, keeping her there on my bed.

'Your first conquest, Bella?' said Jack.

'Mmm, I like that word: conquest.'

'You're predatory,' she said as an insult but I didn't feel insulted at all. 'You should get dressed,' she hissed, 'someone's coming.'

I could hear clunking footsteps on the stairs. I pulled Saskia up and we were just about to enter the bathroom when Tara burst in and saw our bare bottoms vanishing through the door.

'I scored,' I heard her say, and I thought, *so did I*, and the very next moment she barged in.

'Tara, you're covered in mud,' I said. 'Come and take a shower.'

She stood there looking at Saskia, then she looked at me, then she looked back at Saskia, then me again. She finally glanced down at my breasts as if they were suspects demanding thorough investigation.

'What have you been doing?' she demanded.

I didn't say anything. She looked sweet and innocent covered from head to toe in mud. There was mud over her cheeks and matted in her hair, her ears were red from cold and her green eyes had the delicious look of wet grass. I took her two muddy hands and kissed her palms.

'Well done,' I said. 'Did we win?'

'What? Yes ...'

'Oh, goody.'

I leaned forward and rubbed my cheeks against Tara's cheeks, smearing myself in mud. I rubbed the mud from her shirt and coated my breasts, my arms, my shoulders.

'What are you doing?'

She glanced at Saskia but jerked quickly back to my gaze.

'Just playing,' I said.

I pulled her shirt off and she didn't seem to know what was happening. Saskia unzipped her shorts and there below was another pair of those hideous maroon pants.

'These are a no-no,' said Saskia.

I pulled them down and kicked them to one side. She stood there naked and muddy like an Indian brave, the perfect image of her twin, except she didn't have the heart birthmark, and now I'd always know which one was which. I couldn't wait to find out what she tasted like. Sister Nuria was cappuccino. Saskia was mozzarella with olive oil. And I was honey. It wasn't much of a list but there were hundreds of girls and I thought how marvellous it would be to seduce them all.

I unlaced Tara's boots and pulled them off, then her socks. My hands were wet and I made a paste with the mud and covered myself.

'You can help,' I said

Saskia started and Tara joined in, scraping the mud off the boots, working it into a sticky mess and applying it all over my body. I rubbed the mud into my face and hair, between my legs, everywhere. I felt totally wild and started to do a war dance around the bathroom. The twins joined in. Then I turned on the shower. I washed Tara slowly, carefully, over her breasts, the rise of her little round tummy and down between her legs, lingering on the closed cleft and staring into her timid eyes. Saskia washed her back. Then I turned off the taps. Tara stood very still and I ran my tongue down her wet body from her chin to her damp waiting pussy.

'Don't,' she said, and I didn't like that word very much and carried on. It was strange, her teeny slit identical to Saskia's and it was like entering a door and being faced with another door just the same.

I licked her for a long time to get the taste and it was so similar it took an age before I worked out that the delicate tang of mozzarella in Saskia was tarter in her sister, French rather than Italian. Camembert, I decided as her milky warmth oozed into my mouth, and it struck me that if twins were subtly different, every girl in the world would have her own special taste.

I was getting cold but I was dying to try one more thing. I stood the twins close together and licked those identical pussies, transferring their oils from one to the other like an alchemist seeking the elixir of life. I stood, turned them to face each other and eased them forward with one hand flat on each bottom. Their lips met.

'Very softly,' I said. 'Imagine you are kissing a flower,' and it was like looking at a magic mirror as their lips touched.

That night I dreamed I was at an orgy and all the girls at Saint Sebastian's were running around naked having their bottoms spanked by the nuns. It was very vivid and I told Jack all about it on Saturday morning when we made our way to the building society in town so that she could remove £20 from her account and I could put it in mine.

Chapter Four

SEX SHOP.

We were across the street and Jack read the words aloud: 'Sex shop.'

'I didn't know you could buy sex in a shop,' I said and she sneered.

'You don't buy sex, you buy sex aids ...'

'Doooooh,' I said. 'Like everyone doesn't know that.'

'Tabby's got this, like, giant black dildo.'

'How do you know?'

'She brought it to school, that's why. I've seen it.'

I glanced again at the sign and felt light-headed as I imagined things beyond my imagination.

'Let's go in?'

'Tabby goes there all the time.'

'Well, what are we waiting for?'

'She may not like it.'

'Like I care!'

'I care. Tabby's my friend.'

I didn't know if the things Jack was always saying about the American girl were true, but I'd resolved to become acquainted with Tabatha Van Deegan and find out for myself. I could have gone up to her all big eyes and breathless – girls were constantly having crushes on each other – but I was controlling my impatient disposition and waiting for her to come looking for me.

We were outside the post office waiting for Saskia and Tara to catch up. We were allowed out on Saturday afternoon and my mission was to find them proper underwear. They'd been

34

cold and bare below their navy blue skirts since I'd made them search the dorm for all those *gia*normous maroon things. We'd stuffed them in a bag and watched old Mr Gibson, the caretaker, open the boiler door with his tongs and toss them in the fire.

The red and blue flames danced in circles enjoying themselves, I closed my eyes and dedicated those horrid knickers as an offering to my guardian spirit. I had used my gift to awaken the twins and as I stood there staring into the inferno I'd felt an irresistible sense of well-being. I still had plans for the girls but for the moment they were joined at the hip. I suspected there was something narcissistic in this and, when they touched each other, it must have felt like they were touching themselves.

Sister Theresa had called me narcissistic and I spent the entire prep period leafing through the dictionary finding out what it meant exactly when I should have been writing about Sir Henry Morton Stanley discovering Dr Livingstone in 1871. When it comes to the next geography class and I don't have a 500-word essay to hand in it will be Sister Theresa's own fault.

Since that day when she'd told me to button my blouse the dear little nun had joined the rest of the world and become obsessed with breasts; well, my breasts. She was always standing on her tiny toes and staring at them from the front of the class, then she'd walk between the desks to get an aerial view. It was embarrassing. Even for me. The buttons on my blouse would keep popping open, but it was Mother who'd forgotten I was still growing and had bought a size too small.

The newlyweds were back from their honeymoon and we had spoken on the telephone. Mr Daviditz had been sending £10 a week pocket money but it wasn't very much and last time he called I had cooed and cried until he agreed to double it. I planned to give him a treat at half term before entering into fresh negotiations.

I was very happy seeing Jack's £20 added to the bottom line in my building society account. It gave me a sense of security to see my savings grow. Daddy invested everything in totally mad business schemes and sometimes we were rich and sometimes we were poor and I knew which was best.

I glanced back at the sex shop. 'I'm going in,' I said to Jack.

'They'll chuck you out.'

'Let's see?'

'I bet they do.'

'How much?'

'You're so ...' she paused, 'avaricious.'

'No I'm not.' That's the funny thing about debts; people hate to pay them and resent it when they do.

The twins had caught up and wanted to go to the coffee place where there was a pimply boy who stuttered and spilled things when he served girls.

'I'll see you later,' I told them. I patted my flat midriff. The twins had round tums and needed to take care. I glanced at Jack. I knew she wanted to come with me but she was too stubborn to change her mind.

'Anything you want?' I asked her.

'A big black dildo,' she replied, and marched off behind the twins.

The road was busy and I almost got splattered running between the cars, the drivers honking and waving their fists. Everyone's just so impatient. The shop was painted pink with a hand-written sign that looked smart enough from a distance but was crude and amateur when you got close up. In the window there was some tacky see-through lingerie, bras that showed your nipples, some dusty boxes of God knows what, and a mannequin in a nurse's uniform. It was all rather sad but that didn't stop me from wanting to take a closer look inside. Sex shop. The very idea was so English. So weird.

I was wearing my Saturday wardrobe, the brown crushed velvet flares that hung low enough on my hips to show my black thong, a black bra with straps slipping and sliding from my shoulders, and a little pink vest struggling like a defeated army to contain my expanding breasts. It was unseasonably cold those October days on the south coast and I had remained sensibly buttoned to the throat in a floor length camel coat until I was safely beyond the convent gates. I tossed the coat loosely around my shoulders, pumped up Pinkie and Perky, 'Be good,' I said, and marched into the shop.

There was a man who needed a shave sitting on a high stool behind the counter reading a magazine, the naked blonde on the cover horribly similar to Dallas McTee. The man glanced up, but only caught my profile half hidden by my loose hair. I was taller than him in my killer heels.

There were zillions of DVDs and videos with names like *Between My Legs* and *Lesbian Lovers* and *Suck Me Hard* and *Nympho* and *Sixteen*. They all had photographs on the boxes of girls pulling awful distorted faces and I couldn't imagine anyone being in the least bit attracted to them. I studied *Ranch Orgy* because orgy was one of my favourite words, but it was just the same as all the others with these plain desperate girls wearing cowboy hats and leather boots.

I reached for a magazine, flicked through the greasy pages and put it back in the rack. My stomach was churning and I thought I was going to be sick. Girls with scarlet fingernails were bending over with their bums in the air and great ugly hairy men were ramming their things into their bottoms and mouths and vaginas. Yuck. There were girls stretching their legs apart to show the soft pink flesh inside and the photographs made everything look vulgar and sordid when it's the most natural and lovely thing in the world.

There were hundreds of magazines and all of them had the same pictures with barely any difference. Where did all these girls come from? How did the magazines find them? Did they have proper jobs in supermarkets and just do this part time?

The glass shelves contained dildos in plastic and rubber, in green and black and amber, some with ribs on the side, some with buckles and straps, and all of them oddly intriguing. I confronted a chipped plaster mannequin wearing a leather harness covered in studs, and there was a rail of uniforms, a nurse like the one in the window, a teacher, the devil, even a nun, which was just about the only nice thing I'd seen because it made me think of Sister Nuria. Next to the rail of uniforms, a curtain made from coloured strips of plastic led to a shadowy room lit by sickly pink light. I was drawn to the room in the way that your fingers are drawn to touch flames, but the unshaven man must have heard my heart thumping and stopped me before I could enter.

'Can I help you at all?' he asked.

'Just looking,' I said.

I turned with a pose from *Vogue*, one leg angled with my hip jutting aggressively towards him, my entire middle bare and faintly bronzed, the camel coat almost slipping from my shoulders. He did a double take, his blue eyes zipping over my hips and bare waist, my breasts doing their job in their uplift bra, up and down like he was taking an inventory or something.

He glanced back at his magazine then at me again. He was quite old, about 25 or 30. He was trying to look cool by not shaving, but I thought it just looked scruffy. I gave him another pose, hands behind my back, my breasts pushed towards him, and I suddenly had this mad urge to pull up my vest just to show him something pretty and nice and a bit better quality than all those awful pictures in the magazines. It made me giggle.

'Here, how old are you?' he asked.

'Old enough.'

I took the *Lesbian Lovers* DVD and dropped it on the counter. 'I'll take this,' I said. On the cover there were three unattractive girls kissing and squeezing each other's breasts. I thought I'd give it to Sister Nuria as a present because she was always ignoring me lately.

'You will, will you.'

He was staring at my breasts, naturally. They were so out there. I just stood there, sighing, taking deep breaths. He swallowed hard, lit a cigarette and leaned his head back to blow the smoke up at the ceiling.

I pointed at the plastic curtain. 'What's in that room?' I asked.

'Hardcore,' he said.

He took another puff on his cigarette and the smoke drifted out of his nose in two long streamers.

'Mmm, can I have one of those?'

He grinned like he thought I was funny or something and shook the packet at me. 'Here, then bugger off.'

I pouted and popped the cigarette between my lips. He had one of those Zippo lighters all the movie stars have and made a big show of opening the lid and flicking the wheel at the same time. I leaned forward sucking, drew in the smoke and blew it straight out again.

'No, no, no,' he said. 'You have to take it down.'

I tried another drag on the cigarette and handed it back to the man. 'I don't like this very much,' I told him.

He already had his own cigarette in the corner of his mouth, he stuck mine in the other corner and puffed away on both of them at once. 'My imitation of a steamship,' he said and it wasn't very funny but it cheered me up. 'Go on, you'd better go.'

'I'll come back again,' I promised.

'Yeah, when you're old enough.'

'I only look young,' I said. 'And I'm not very good at waiting.'

'What are you good at?'

'Sex,' I said and he fell off his stool and crumpled up in a heap behind the counter.

'Jesus H,' he said as he stood up again. 'You pulling my leg?'

'It's the only thing I like,' I told him. 'Except singing ...'

'I tell you something, darling, you could earn a bloody fortune.'

'Could I?'

He tapped the top of the video case. 'Body like that,' he said, glancing down to give my breasts a more professional examination. He walked around the counter, had a good look at my hips, and stuck the DVD back on the shelf.

I liked the idea of making a fortune. 'How much?' I asked him

He shook his head like he'd never met anyone quite like me before. 'Dunno, about a grand I reckon.'

'A grand what?' I didn't know all that silly slang stuff.

'You're something else. A thousand quid.'

It sounded quite a lot but I knew from when Daddy had to sell his cars because he'd gone broke again that you had to screw up your lips, shake your head and say: 'No, not enough, I'm afraid,' which was what I said.

39

'Well, could be a lot more, of course.'

'What would I have to do?'

'You have to be a film star, don't you, you know ...' and he made a crude thrusting motion with his hips. 'I might be able to set it up.'

I pointed back at the racks of dirty magazines. 'That stuff's horrible,' I said. 'The girls look so common.'

'Well, they are, aren't they?'

I thought it was funny the way he liked to confirm his own questions and gave him one of my best smiles. 'What's your name?' I asked him.

'What do you want to know that for?'

'In case I want to drop something through the door for you.'

He blew a smoke ring and looked me up and down as if he was checking the bodywork before he bought the car. 'Jason,' he said.

I went to the shelves of dildos, took the black one with the buckles and straps and cradled it against my cheek like a doll.

'Now what?'

'Please,' I said.

'What?'

'Please.'

'You want one of them?'

'Please.'

He shook his head in the same slightly disbelieving way then blew another smoke ring. 'Go on then,' he said. 'Then bugger off.'

I wrapped the straps around the dildo and pushed it into the bottom of my coat pocket. I felt pleased with my adventures in the sex shop and I don't know why, but that mad feeling came over me again, I pulled up my pink vest and showed him everything.

The *girls* are getting so brazen I was almost embarrassed as I hurried back across the road to the coffee shop. It was called Greens although Grims would have been a better name, and anyway I didn't like coffee because it gives you lines and sucks the calcium from your bones.

'A glass of water, please,' I said to the pimply boy. He

spilled it, naturally.

'Any-any-any anything else?'

'Good heavens, no,' I said.

Greens was trying to be continental like the cafés in Rome, but the little round tables didn't even have marble tops, the Formica was all chipped and the neon tubes on the ceiling made everyone look ill except me with my perennial tan. Staring down from the walls were ancient film stars in those flower clothes from the 1960s and in the glass display case were bagels, muffins and those cream cakes that all have about a million calories. The pimply boy was busy squeezing one of his pimples.

I sat back sipping my water. Jack had that look people get when they're doing mental arithmetic and, as she was about to leave, I told her if she saw Tabby Van Deegan, Jason sent his love.

'Who?'

'The man in the sex shop.'

'Predator,' she said, and I wandered down to the boutiques with Saskia and Tara.

They tried on frilly bras and lacy knickers. Black underwear on their white skin made them look like those awful girls in the magazines and I reached the conclusion that what suited them best was just plain cotton and I suggested they buy two sets each in white and pink. Pink was my new favourite colour.

'We need more than two,' said Saskia.

'Wait for half term,' I responded, closing the discussion. 'And one more thing, wear the same colours on the same day.'

'Why?'

'It's neater.'

'Is that so important?' asked Tara doubtfully.

Why was it important? I wasn't exactly sure. I just knew it was.

'Absolutely,' I said.

We tried on make-up but, except for a bit of eye-liner and perhaps some blush, too much make-up makes you look cheap. I applied some scarlet red lipstick, pursed my lips together for the mirror and wiped it off again. Yuck. I looked like a porn star. I glanced at my watch. I was getting a bit bored mentoring the twins and wanted to get back to the dorm and take a closer look at the dildo.

'Time to go,' I said. They looked at me, they looked at each other, then shrugged in unison.

The light was fading and women with cigarettes gripped in thin lips were hurrying home in anoraks and trainers with children and plastic bags. Away from the centre, at the end of the High Street, weary men were moving broken things into second-hand shops that all looked as if they were either being rebuilt or pulled down, everything dusty and scratched. Some teenage boys were standing below a fizzing streetlamp waving mobile phones about and spitting through their teeth. There were six or seven of them wearing jogging trousers tucked into their socks and Burberry baseball caps with long peaks bent over their narrow faces so they looked like strange extinct birds.

'Mingers,' one of them said. The others laughed and we walked on with our noses in the air.

The one who had spoken wasn't wearing a cap and had a mop of dirty hair like old bronze and darting, blue rodent eyes. He rode along beside me on his bicycle, his mates following with silly grins and that jerky walk they have.

''Ere, wanna come back to my 'ouse for a party or somink?' he said.

'We can't,' I replied.

'What is it, a prison up there or somink?'

'Something like that.'

'So what's your name then?'

'I'm not telling you.'

'Stuck-up bitch.'

'No, I'm not. I just don't like telling strangers my name.'

'I just don't like telling strangers my name,' he said in imitation and the others all fell about as if this was the funniest thing they'd ever heard.

The boy suddenly shot forward on the bicycle, dragged at the handlebars and rode along on the back wheel showing off. He was actually quite good-looking and I was pleased when he came back again.

'You down the High Street every Saturday?'

'Yes, actually.'

He made scissors with two fingers and pointed the tips at his eyes. 'I'll look out for you then,' he said and rode off on one wheel.

Saskia whispered, 'I think he fancies you.'

'Yuck,' I said loud enough for the rest of the gang to hear as they bobbed away like pigeons.

We rounded the corner and the towers and spires of Saint Sebastian rose up over the crest of the hill. The road turned inland and a narrow track climbed through bare trees to the convent. From the gates you could see the grey outline of the town, the dying sun trapped in the windows of the tower blocks. We were already late for tea and rushed straight into the refectory where I felt so embarrassed in my cut-off vest with Sister Theresa staring daggers at me. I couldn't eat anything and just drank a big glass of milk. I decided it was time to confront the Sister and, after tea, went straight to her room. I knocked three times.

'Come in.'

I entered and stood by the door waiting for her to explain herself.

'You look very pleased with yourself, young lady,' she said and sounded really nasty. I was fingering the cold crucifix around my neck and she took a long look at it as she stood. 'You know what they are for, don't you?'

'What?'

'Come, come, come, you know what I'm talking about, Bella. You are obsessed with your bosom,' she said, and I thought *bosom*, and I thought *me* obsessed.

'I'm not.'

She motioned me to a chair. I sat and she took out a tissue and proceeded to wipe my top lip.

'You've grown a white moustache,' she said. She licked the tissue and worked it into the corners of my lips.

When she was satisfied, she pulled herself awkwardly on to the corner of her desk, her little legs jiggling about just above the floor like the limbs of a string puppet. She stared long and hard at Pinkie and Perky.

'They are for suckling babies,' she said softly, as if this might come as a shock to me. 'You have seen Our Lady with the Infant Jesus.'

'Yes.'

'It is the most natural, joyous thing in the world. It is a miracle. Your bosom is not for showing off. They are not sexual objects.' I looked down at the girls, and boy, were they put out. 'You will start having all sorts of funny feelings and you will start imagining things,' she said. 'You must control these feelings and you really have to cover yourself up.'

I glanced down. 'I don't mean to be silly,' I said. I sniffed and pressed my eyes shut and squeezed out a tear. 'I just like to look pretty.'

She was leaning over. 'You know, something, you remind me of the Madonna painted in the chapel,' she said, and I wasn't sure if Sister Theresa was looking reverently down at the little gold Jesus or reverently down at the golden girls. They were pulsating with my quiet sobs and we enjoyed a few minutes' silence.

The Sister slipped from the desk and landed nimbly on her feet. I stood and moved towards her, babies gently bobbing, and she was just as eager to reach for me as she was eager to keep her vows and the church won. Well almost. She brushed my breasts with the tips of her fingers the way Mother checks for dust after the maid has gone. 'Try to keep yourself covered,' she said and her throat was dry.

'I will.'

She moved her hands away and held them under control behind her back. 'Now, what did you want, Bella?'

'Sister Theresa, I just want to join the choir,' I said and she smiled an acropolis of broken brown teeth at me.

'I'm sure you have a voice like an angel.'

'That's what Daddy used to say.' I paused. 'He's dead now.' I managed another tear and her old eyes became quite misty.

'Come along tomorrow afternoon,' she said, 'we'll see what we can do.'

'Oh, thank you, Sister,' I replied and planted a kiss on her grizzly cheek.

She used the same tissue to mop up my tear and opened the door. 'Thank you,' I said with a little wiggle. She tapped my bottom and I thought, *That's saucy*, as I smiled back over my shoulder and left the room.

'Good night, Bella,' she said, and I hurried along the corridor.

I hadn't intended to join the choir before going to see Sister Theresa, but now it was done, I was looking forward to it. Most of the girls had come to Saint Sebastian during the first year Sixth, but I was a new girl and had yet to join any clubs. So far, I had considered only two activities, photography because it was a good way to keep a secret diary, and fencing because in *The Mask of Zorro* Catherine Zeta-Jones is just so cute when Antonio Banderas cuts the straps to her sexy top, and she looks like me only older.

When I was able to get the bathroom to myself, I took a long hot shower and scrubbed the dildo clean. I gave it a good squeeze. I wondered if a man would feel the same and felt sorry for poor little Sister Theresa because she would never know. I rolled the rubbery head over my breasts, it felt quite nice and my nipples started to get firm. 'You're such naughty girls,' I said, 'showing off to Jason.'

Now that I'd seen all those pictures in the sex shop I knew exactly what men were up to when they pulled out their things. Girls have three openings, the gateways to our innermost secrets, and those big penises like to find their way into all three. I rubbed the rubber dildo down between my breasts, over my flat tummy and into my pubic hair, the head opening my vagina and coming to rest at my bottom. I was sure it was too big to get in there and didn't want to try.

I instinctively slid it into my mouth but it was so big I could only get the top bit in before I started to gag. In the dirty magazines some of the girls had got those giant penises right down their throats and I imagined you would have to have your tonsils out to be able to do that. There were pictures of men shooting their milky semen over girls' faces and into their open mouths and it must have tasted bitter by the look of their distorted expressions. I imagined boys would all have their own special flavour like girls and was dying to find out.

By this time that lovely moist feeling was welling up between my thighs. I slipped the head of the dildo between my legs and pussy is such a clever girl she drew it up inside all by herself. I slowly worked it back and forth. It felt amazing and I wanted to drive it right in but she was just too tiny and tight. I pushed harder but felt a twinge of pain. I had reached a barrier and remembered quite suddenly I was a virgin. I'm not sure how this had happened but it was true. I also knew that it was a valuable commodity not to be squandered. I worked the dildo in and out thinking about being a virgin and thinking about Sister Nuria and the honey rolled over my thighs and I felt warm and tired and happy I was going to join the choir.

I'd almost forgotten about the straps and buckles on the dildo and it reminded me of a pony harness as I tried to work out what to do with them. When I finally held the base of the dildo against my pubic bone it fitted perfectly and everything fell into place. The two straps with buckles went between my legs and met the other two around my waist. I buckled up, let go and the dildo bounced up and down, my very own penis. I wondered if this was what Sister Theresa had been talking about and I was having my first sexual fantasy.

I dried myself on a big white towel, put on loads of anti-aging cream, sprayed perfume in the air and let it rain over me. I kept the dildo on under my pyjamas and went to bed to read about Stanley's travels in the Congo and I couldn't help wondering how people washed and went to the bathroom when they were exploring unknown places. I looked at the clock. I was planning to get up early and write that essay for geography.

The twins were asleep, dreaming of each other, and I glanced up at Dallas McTee on the wall. She did have quite a good voice, I suppose, and she was earning zillions with her new CD, but she was just breasts and pouty lips and I wondered what it was that made so many people think she was special.

I was still studying the poster when Jack arrived back late from one of her secret missions.

'Tabby's angry with you,' she hissed.

'Don't make so much noise, you'll wake the twins.'

'She wants to see you.'

'Well, tell her it will be my pleasure.'

'I don't think so.'

I looked sad and Jack looked pleased with herself. 'Jack, we're always bickering, come and give me a kiss,' I said.

'What?'

'Please.'

'Princess.'

We had been told by Friar Dunstan, our Latin teacher, that when Cleopatra was presented to the court in Rome she was rolled in a carpet and unrolled at Caesar's feet. I had reached the conclusion that I had been Cleopatra that night when Jack took me to the catacombs and had been avoiding her clumsy advances ever since. I pulled her down on the bed.

'I'm going to show you the best snog ever,' I said, and pressed my lips gently against hers. Jack still wasn't very good at kissing but I did my best to teach her. I ran my hand up her skirt and over her bottom and she liked that. 'Do you want to jump in?'

'You predator.'

'Please.'

I unbuttoned my pyjama top and, naturally, she did her favourite trick squeezing my nipples until it hurt.

'Ouch,' I said. 'You're such a barbarian.'

She stepped out of her clothes while I kicked my pyjama bottoms to the foot of the bed. I turned to one side so I could keep the dildo as a surprise.

She stood above me, naked under her punk haircut, as boyish as the twins.

'You should get a tattoo,' I said.

I turned off the bedside lamp and she slid between the sheets. The rubber thing was jumping about excitedly and I had to hold it still. Before Jack could climb on top, I held her shoulders down and kissed her lips, her throat, one breast, then the other. Her head was thrown back, eyes closed, and I sewed a long row of kisses down over her stomach until her legs opened for my little pink tongue. I made her wet and guided the head of

47

the dildo into her open cleft. I worked it slowly back and forth as if it were my fingers until I reached the barricade. Jack pretended to be a great woman of the world but I had a feeling I was breaking virgin soil. I kept up the momentum without hurry, in and out like an oily machine.

As she began to come, her legs lifted around my back. This was the moment. I started going faster and faster and, as she gasped to a climax, I broke through her maidenhead and filled her with the rubber cock. She heaved from the unexpected pain and I could sense by the way she wriggled below me that she wanted me to stop and she wanted me to carry on, and these two longings were equally strong and were fighting a battle inside her.

I kept going, evenly but forcefully in and out. Jack went through the pain barrier, relaxed and her orgasm was long and breathless like she was running the marathon. I kissed her mouth and she squeezed her thighs tight, holding me inside her. She was breathless and in the dim light, penetrating the uncurtained window, I could see two crystal tears slide down her cheeks.

'What have you done, Bella?'

'Only what you asked.'

She wasn't sure what I meant. 'What?' she said.

'You wanted a big black dildo.'

I rolled off her onto my back, the false penis glimmering above my stomach in the half light. Jack looked down as if she couldn't believe her eyes.

'You broke me in,' she whispered and I gasped as if it were a surprise. I ran my tongue over my lips trying to work out her taste.

Jack couldn't take her eyes away from the dildo. I placed my hands on the back of her head and pushed her down across my tummy. 'Cherry,' I said, and she drew it into her mouth, the faint trace of blood mixed with her own creamy juices, the base revolving in a circular motion, and it occurred to me that I had taken my first proper virgin and that thought brought me to the best and biggest O in my short career.

Chapter Five

WOULD YOU BELIEVE IT: I have perfect pitch. Mother was always saying that my voice was too nasal, too Mediterranean, but it turns out that I'm a contralto, which is *so* rare for a girl of my age I was practically unique. My voice had been added to the choir and, twice a week, I was having solo lessons with Sister Theresa.

She had been right about the Madonna, she did look like me. The candlelight lit her dark eyes and, as I stared across the chapel, it was like seeing the ghost of myself projected on the wall. The winter sun glimmered behind the stained glass windows and put a dull polish on the wooden pews that through the years must have numbed the bottoms of numberless girls who had sat through the morning sermon studying the carved features of Saint Sebastian. Arrows pierce his heart and, according to Sister Theresa, his ecstatic look arises from his martyrdom, although I'm sure I wasn't the first to see something far more romantic in that intense expression. The girls adored the statue because the saint is young and handsome, and I imagined that when God handed the Commandments to Moses and banned all craven images, what he actually meant was he didn't want to gaze down and behold anyone unattractive.

I had been making a fresh effort to believe in the Gospels, but like Father Christmas it's just so silly. How can a virgin have a baby? And what did Joseph have to say about this? And if God could send his only Son to raise Lazarus from the dead and feed the multitudes with a few fishes and loaves of bread, how come the little children in Africa are always starving? And if he sent his Son 2000 years ago, why doesn't he send him again now when we have the world wide web? Christianity doesn't make sense and Islam is just as bad, all that hollering and throwing yourself in the dust five times a day. The women aren't supposed to wear white shoes and that's ridiculous. If you're wearing a white skirt and white top, white shoes just go. The Jews have all sorts of daft ideas like circumcision, whatever that means, and not eating shellfish and sausages. As if God cares.

Sister Theresa stepped away from the organ and approached, her little hands fluttering about until they settled, one on my stomach and the other at the base of my spine.

'From here, dear girl, the diaphragm.'

I took a deep breath, stared up at the statue of Saint Sebastian and enjoyed this hour away from Jack. She had been mooning about like I was her girlfriend or something and I'd told her until my throat was sore that I'm not a lesbian. She had climbed into my bed the night after I'd broken her cherry, a phrase I'd learned from one of those American teen films, and I thought it was just so clever because Jack tasted of cherry, and anyway, I just couldn't summon up the energy to do it again. If you keep repeating the same things life just gets boring.

Sister Theresa thought she had a convert to the nunhood, or whatever, and nattered on about focusing on *important* things, and I felt like telling her I was focusing on important things because things that were important to me *were* important. The girls had come to the convent finishing school to work on their A-levels because they all wanted to get into Cambridge and read the news on television. But apart from schoolwork, nothing seemed of any great interest to anyone except sex, music, boys, girls, of course, reading their stars and smoking, which was vile and I was glad I had tried it because I would never try it again.

'Deep breaths, Bella.'

God rest you merry gentlemen
Let nothing you dismay
For Jesus Christ our Saviour
Was born upon this day

To save us from Satan's power
When we were gone astray
O tidings of comfort and joy
Comfort and joy
O tidings of comfort and joy

It was hardly Britney or Dallas McTee but, when you hit the right notes, the acoustics made it sound really great.

I puffed out my chest, she gave my bottom a friendly slap and I got an A star for my essay about Stanley finding Dr Livingstone.

The chapel bell chimed four and I had to hurry. It had occurred to me as I was admiring Saint Sebastian in ecstasy that in the same way that I had grown bored with Jack after I broke her cherry, perhaps Sister Nuria had become bored by me after our night in the catacombs. I couldn't imagine such a thing happening but wanted to make sure.

I crossed from the chapel to the main building. The convent was ancient, the crumbling yellow stones giving the building a certain grandeur that made learning Latin seem right and proper. It was going to be of no use to us during the rest of our lives except as a mark of being educated at the type of school that produced voices that made the news when read on the BBC trusted the world over. I climbed three flights of stairs and found Sister Nuria in her room studying. She asked about my singing and I told her I wasn't awfully good but was doing my best.

'I don't think singing's my gift,' I said, and looked shyly over my shoulder.

'You know what your gift is,' she said and added, 'Now, was there something special?'

There wasn't, and I quickly made something up. 'What's the Rubicon?' I asked.

Friar Dunstan had made it all very exciting when he explained it to us but you only remember things when you are told them twice. Sister Nuria put her fingers to her cheek and I watched her lips as she explained that the Rubicon was the river on the far frontier of the Roman Empire. After Caesar had

51

chased his enemies to the river bank, he gazed out at the forbidding torrent. He gathered his cohorts and told them that they were still able to turn back, but once they crossed the rickety bridge all further progress would be through force of arms and by dint of sword.

'Once you cross the Rubicon there is no going back,' she added. 'You have made an irrevocable decision with far-reaching consequences.'

'And you must stick to it?'

She nodded. 'Yes, you must.'

I decided to make that my motto. Once I make a decision, I shall stick to it.

I was quiet for a moment. 'You know, you haven't been very nice to me lately,' I told her and her pretty eyes became cloudy. 'After that night you never wanted to see me again.'

'Bella, I did, I did. I wanted to see you all the time and I've been praying and asking for guidance,' she explained. 'To have desires and fulfil them is an act of indulgence. To have those same desires and to deny yourself is good for the soul.'

'Course it's not. God doesn't work like that.'

'God,' she said, 'is more complex than we understand, more complex than we *can* understand.'

'Perhaps it's not complex at all.'

'To give in to your desires, Bella, is to be tempted by the devil.'

'Than I shall become the devil and tempt you,' I joked and the devil costume I'd seen in the sex shop popped into my mind.

I had leaned forward and she pressed her soft lips against mine. 'You have the most kissable lips,' she whispered. 'I'm going to miss them.'

It didn't occur to me at the time to wonder what she meant by that and, anyway, I suddenly had a plan and needed to put it into operation. I'd made a decision and I was sticking to it.

I slept like a virgin and next morning Jack joined me in the shower. I gave her a long languorous kiss.

'What are you doing?'

'I've been horrid to you lately,' I said.

'That's because you're a bitch.'

I rubbed my eyes like I was crying and it made her laugh. Jack wanted to hate me but couldn't. I was in her memory like an old photo in an album and always would be. I sponged her back and gave her a snogging lesson. She was getting better and started to get carried away.

'Naughty,' I said, and smacked her bottom in the same way as Sister Theresa had smacked me at choir practice, but a lot harder. 'Stand still,' I said in my most commanding voice and she obeyed instantly. 'Now, bend over, Miss Bennett. She paused for just a fraction, then did so. 'Don't move,' I added, and brought my hand down as hard as I could across the proffered cheeks of her wet bottom.

'Ouch,' she yelled.

'Stay still.'

And she did. Whack. I smacked her again and again, the sound echoing over the tiled walls, whack, whack, whack, until her bottom bloomed like a pink flower and my hand really stung.

She stood up straight, rubbing her bottom. 'What's that for?' she said.

'That's for being good. Just wait until you're naughty.'

I stepped out of the shower and wrapped myself in a towel before Jack could twizzle my nipples. Spanking was fun, at least for the spanker, and I wondered if it was fun for the spankee as well. Time, as they say, would tell!

I slipped one of the miniature pots of honey into my blazer at breakfast and in class all morning I concentrated on my work. We had double Latin after lunch and Friar Dunstan was one teacher who was either bashful or bad mannered and made a point of never glancing in my direction. I waited for him at the door and whispered in his large hairy ear.

'Father, can I go to the lavatory, I've got my ...'

'Yes, yes, yes,' he said and beetled his way into class.

I went as fast as I could without running along the corridor and down to the basement where Mr Gibson was stoking the boiler. I edged by without being seen, scurried up the steps and out to the smelly place where they kept the dustbins at the back of the school. This was the danger zone. Mother Superior's office in the tower looked out over the sea and, like the giant raven, she would often be standing at her window surveying the world below.

This was the first time I had broken the strict rule about leaving the grounds without permission. My heart was pounding in my chest and I had to take about a hundred deep breaths to calm down. Beyond the expanse of grass was a flint wall, the arched wooden gate having spars like a ladder across its surface. I took one more deep breath, said a quick prayer, just in case, and ran for it. I scrambled up the gate, held on to the top of the lintel, and dropped down on the other side, almost twisting my ankle.

I was free and it was exhilarating with the smell of the sea and the waves breaking against the cliffs out on the point where the lighthouse stood pointing at the heavens. The iron staircase outside the convent led down to the beach and, from there, it wasn't far to the steps that zigzagged up to the promenade. I ran as fast as I could and was out of breath by the time I reached the High Street. The sex shop was open and I breathed a sigh of relief.

There were three or four men browsing through the dirty magazines, and another was just going in the room with the pink lights as I entered. Jason still needed a shave and was wearing a sleeveless T-shirt that said FCUK on it. There were Chinese characters tattooed on his arm like graffiti and I didn't know what it said or why he would mark himself in this way.

'What the bloody hell are you doing here?'

'Don't blaspheme,' I said.

'I mean it, I've got customers. Go on, bugger off.'

I pointed at the devil suit. 'I just wanted one of them.'

'You what?'

He pulled me to one side. 'It's £60, you know.'

'I don't care.' There was a flight of stairs behind the counter and he nodded towards them. 'Get up there a minute, we'll see what we can do.'

Above the sex shop there was one large room with lots of unmatching chairs facing a glass wall and I assumed it was where the dirty old men watched those awful videos. Jason appeared with a white box. 'Do they watch films in here?' I asked him.

'Nah, they watch the real fing,' he answered. He gave me the box and hit the switch on the wall beside the door. A light came on behind the glass and I could see a little stage with a brass pole in the centre and a red chair, the back shaped like a heart.

'Girls do shows, don't they? Come and have a looksie,' he said.

We went through a narrow door to the stage and I realised it was one-way glass like they have in gangster films. From the stage, the wall was a misty mirror and you couldn't see out, but the people on the other side could see in. Hanging from the ceiling was a long cord Jason pulled, the light went out and it was like being in an aquarium.

'Right, you got £60 now, have you?' he said, rubbing his thumb and fingers together.

'I'll pay next time.'

'No, can't have that, darling,' he replied and snatched the box back again.

'Don't you trust me?'

'It's not a question of trust, is it. The boss comes in, sees the suit ain't there, checks the till and where am I? Up shit creek.'

I felt defeated for a moment and if I looked sad it was completely genuine. 'Please,' I said.

'Look, I'm, sorry darling. I already gave you the dildo.'

'Can't you lend me the money?'

'Don't have it, do I?' He shook his head thoughtfully. 'I'll tell you something, you look bloody young in that uniform.'

I felt so put out I almost burst into tears. I turned and saw my reflection in the glass wall with slumped shoulders and a bent back. It was so unlike me I bit my lip and shook myself until I had a brainwave. I crossed the stage and smiled back at Jason as I switched on the light.

'Now what?'

I switched the light off again. 'What did you say this room was for?' I asked.

He was about to reply but checked himself. 'Hang on a minute ...'

I switched the light on again. 'Jason?'

'If you mean what I think you mean, the answer's no.'

I just knew the answer was yes. 'Jason, you said I would be great making one of those films,' I reminded him. 'Now you can see what I can do.'

'The answer's no.'

'How many men are there downstairs, four or five? Ask them for £20 each,' I suggested. 'You'll make a profit.'

That seemed to appeal to his sense of manhood and he lit a cigarette to think about it. 'But you don't know what to do, do you?'

'I've seen *The Sopranos* like a million times. Do you have any music?'

'I've got a radio.'

I came close and ran my fingers over the letters on his T-shirt. FCUK. It was so Jason. 'Come on, it'll be fun.'

'I don't know.'

'*Fortes fortuna juvat.*'

'What's that when it's at home?'

'Fortune favours the brave.'

He looked astonished. 'Jesus H, that's what it says here,' and he pointed at the Chinese letters running like beetles up his arm. I eased the white box away from his grasp.

'What do you want that thing for anyway?'

I touched the tip of my nose. 'I'll go and get ready,' I said, and a look of doubt crossed his thin face.

'What if they won't cough up?'

'Tell them I'm a schoolgirl,' I said and he went running downstairs.

Now I was alone, I had a panic attack. But there was no way out. I had set my heart on that devil costume. I had crossed the Rubicon. I took deep breaths and gave myself another good shake. At the side of the stage, there was a table behind a narrow screen. I opened the white box and could hear my heart beating as I peeled back the tissue paper. It grew deathly quiet. My heart had stopped. The face of the devil was staring up at me, a black rubber mask with red-ringed slits for eyes and two curling horns. In the shop among all the junk it looked cheap and nasty, but now it seemed oddly real and sent shivers down my spine. The mask nestled in a pool of coiling straps and, below it, there was a short-handled whip with leather thongs. I put them to one side and lifted out a pair of black plastic shorts with a zip that ran down the front, under the crutch and up the back. There were metal rings on the sides that looped into a weird top covered with soft rubber spikes. There was a black cape that could have been made from a bin-liner and a set of instructions that looked so complicated I put everything back in the box to think about later.

The heart chair was turned with its back to the audience and I only had to study it for a few seconds to work out that, when you straddled the chair, you could actually be starkers and no one could see a thing. I was doing the choreography in my head. I turned the chair to face the right way and placed it under the light cord.

Jason reappeared that moment and turned off the light. 'When I turn the light on,' he clicked his fingers and winked, 'break a leg.'

Every station on the radio was playing those rap songs where gangsters are complaining about the price of drugs and killing bitches. I found some flamenco which I liked, but it came to an end, and I had to settle for one of the pop shows and hope for the best. As it happens, I am one of those people who rarely sweats, no matter how hot it is. *Now* I was sweating like a wrestler. Beads of perspiration had erupted on my brow, my armpits were like a total lake, even my back felt damp. I gave Pinkie and Perky a little squeeze. 'Come on, girls, this is your big day,' I said. I buttoned my blazer, checked my knickers: pink, thank God, and brushed the creases from my navy blue skirt. My hair was in a long plait and I popped my straw hat in place. I sat in the dark facing the glass, knees together, legs splayed out, my feet hooked behind the front chair legs, my shoulders sagging like I was dead bored. Jason poked his head through the door.

'Two minutes,' he said, 'and what's your name, I don't even know?'

'Honey.'

'Nice one.' He went to go and looked serious as he glanced back again. 'Don't let me down,' he said.

I heard his voice muffled through the thick glass and the light came on. It was show time. The radio was playing a dreary ballad I didn't recognise and, to the lazy beat, I rubbed my palm over my leg. Just one hand, slowly, evenly, up and down, my long fingers circling my thigh, climbing up and up. It didn't take much to make my pussy start leaking and, before I got carried away, I rose to my feet, span the chair on one leg and let it come to rest facing backwards below the light cord.

I tossed my hat behind the flap and loosened the band holding my plait. I shook my head and my hair cascaded about my cheeks and shoulders. The music was so slow I was moving without rhythm. I remembered Jason's last words: don't let me down, and I thought what a cheek, while I'm doing all the work, he's taking the money and getting a free show. I unbuttoned my blazer, turned and let it fall to the floor. Now my blouse, slowly from the top, unhooking buttons one at a time, doing my best to make it erotic and failing I was sure.

The music came to an end and the DJ in one of those inane, chirpy voices they all have started going on about cones on the M2. Then over his voice I heard the opening chords to *Body*, the Dallas McTee song, and I started to go with the beat.

You want my body

I pulled my blouse out of my skirt, jiggled my shoulders until it fell away and the babies were free to show off in their little pink bra.

I know you want my body

I sat on the chair and rolled down my socks. There is absolutely nothing in the world more unsexy than those knee socks and thick leather shoes and they were best discarded as quickly as possible.

You want my body

I unzipped my skirt and stepped away as it fell in a blue

puddle to the floor. I turned my back, shoulders sliding up and down, legs tight together, my skinny body coiling like a serpent. I turned again, right hand between my legs, left hand massaging my breast. I raised my right hand to my other breast and pussy thrust herself forward like she was wearing her dildo and I gasped for breath as I remembered that night with Jack writhing and panting below me.

Everybody wants my body

It felt weird dancing in front of a blank sheet of glass. I knew I looked cute in my pink undies and I felt as if I were alone in an empty world. I was Honey and I could do anything. The brass pole was gleaming and I twirled round and round until my body was as hot as fire. I rubbed pussy against the pole, going down almost to my knees and up again so that the metal lay flat against my stomach. I held Pinkie and Perky in my two palms. They were such good girls, so into it.

If you're a guy or a gal,
Or a man in jail

There weren't many words to this song, just a good beat that made dancing easy and natural. I felt the music pulsing through me, directing my arms and legs. I'm Tuesday's child, full of grace, and with all the ballet lessons I'd done as a little girl, I knew how to flow like the river and grow tall like a tree. I hooked my ankle behind the pole, gripped on with my arm and propelled myself just like I'd seen on TV, round and round, faster and faster.

When you see me on the silver screen
And in your wet dreams

My hips were gyrating and my body was electric. The song was fading out and I almost wanted it to go on and on. I unhooked my pink bra, hid the girls with my palms and slowly released them. My nipples were as hard as boiled sweets and felt like they were alive. I squeezed them and winced like I was riding the big wave of an orgasm.

You want my body
I know you want my body
You want my body
Everybody wants my body

I was tempted to take off my panties but I was feeling angry that all I was getting for my performance was a costume worth a measly £60.

You want my body
You want my body

I whispered the words and it was like a chant. I was under a spell and couldn't resist temptation no matter how hard I tried.

You want my body
You want my body

Dallas McTee's murmurs grew fainter. I turned my back, fluttered my long black eyelashes over my shoulder and gazed big-eyed at the glass wall as I slowly, slowly eased my pink panties over my hips, down over my bottom and let them fall to the floor. I was naked and feeling fabulous. I reached up, turned to give the audience a fleeting full-frontal and pulled the light cord as I straddled the chair.

Wow, was that fun!

The DJ was getting excited about something but his voice seemed far away. I was tingling and breathless and I sat there in the dark with my legs spread and pussy oozing a creamy wet goo over the metal seat. I dipped my finger automatically in the pool and was running the balm over my dry lips when Jason turned on the light from outside.

He stepped into the room. '*Fan*tastic. What a star,' he said.

'How much did you get?'

He seemed stumped for a moment and held out his palms as if to show they were empty. 'What do you mean?'

I stood, hands on hips, and he didn't know where to look.

'How much?'

'£60.'

I stamped my foot. 'You mustn't lie to me.'

'Well ...'

I wasn't wearing a stitch but I was still playing Honey and I don't know why, but I felt a sense of power. Even naked, or because I was naked, I was in control and Jason looked nervously away from my body and into my eyes.

'How much?' I demanded

'£100.'

'Then that's £40 profit. You can keep £20.'

I held out my open palm. He hesitated, but drew the money out of his back pocket and handed over £20. I pulled on my knickers and stuck the note inside.

'Listen,' he said, 'next time, I can get a big crowd.'

'If there is a next time.'

As I hooked into my bra he studied me in that professional way he has, shaking his head like I was a crossword clue he couldn't understand at all. I finished dressing, put my hat on and tucked the white box under my arm. Jason lit a cigarette and looked like a fish as he blew a smoke ring and then blew another that went through the centre of the first. I just knew he'd spent hours practising.

'You're a right tasty bit of stuff, I tell you that, Honey,' he said. 'See, thing is, at your age, you can do what you like. You're the master of your own destiny.'

I wasn't sure what he meant but I would think about it later. Now all that was on my mind were the words to Dallas McTee's song. It was so simple I was sure I could write a song that was better.

A man was standing outside the shop pretending to look in the window and I knew he'd been in the audience. I was like a star leaving the stage door, but it was still irritating that someone was there, lying in wait.

'Christian Thomas,' he said with a little bow. 'I just wanted to say how much I enjoyed your performance. You are really rather extraordinary.'

61

My hostility melted. Mr Thomas had startling blue eyes like an Apostle and unruly dark hair that he kept pushing away from his brow. He was casually dressed in that smart way with a green Barbour jacket, he had a nice accent and old-fashioned manners like Daddy. He gave me a card and pointed vaguely in the direction of the lighthouse.

'I have the flint cottage out at the point,' he said. 'If I can ever be of any service, it would be an honour.'

As I glanced down at the address, I noticed the time. 'As it happens, you could do me a service right now. I have to go to the chemist and then rush back to school,' I said.

'My carriage awaits,' he replied and I laughed as he did that thing like Sir Walter Raleigh, tipping forward and bending one knee.

I followed him around the corner and got into the back of a dark green Jaguar with thick leather seats, lots of polished wood and that safe, comfy feeling you only get in old cars.

'You can ride up front, you know.'

'It pays to be cautious, Mr Thomas.'

'Very sensible,' he said as he indicated and pulled into the High Street.

I left the white box with the devil costume on the back seat and hurried through the automatic doors into the chemist. I bought a bottle of baby oil and four boxes of tampons. I asked for two bags which the silly girl gave me in such an uncivil way it was as if she had to pay for them herself.

'Thank you so much. Do have a lovely weekend.'

'It's only Wednesday,' she rasped and by the sound of her voice I knew she was already a smoker.

Mr Thomas had turned the car around and was standing there with the front door open. He had taken off his jacket and was wearing an Aran sweater, brown cords and shiny brown brogues. I shook a warning finger at him as I got in. I put the white box in one of the bags, placed the tampon boxes in the other and then put the two bags together.

'Saint Sebastian?'

'Please.'

'Violation has no elegance,' he said in a serious way. 'Sex is the greatest of all gifts and must be nurtured and cherished, studied and explored,' and his hand drifted away from the gear change and started to explore my knee.

'Mr Thomas.'

'Sex turns on the light,' he said without taking his hand away.

'A girl has to be careful.'

'It's all right, you're perfectly safe. I'm a writer.'

'Then I would have thought the very opposite would apply.'

He smiled and changed the subject. 'How's school?'

It was a stupid question and people always asked it. 'It's the ideal place to get an education.'

'You already seem so,' he hesitated for a second, 'wise,' and his hand started to wander leisurely like a tortoise down my thigh. It was quite nice and I thought I would see how far he would go before we reached the convent. 'It's rare to come face to face with perfection. I'd love to paint you.'

'I thought you were a writer?'

'We shouldn't limit ourselves,' he replied and his hand paused in its journey. 'We should try *everything*.'

'Everything?'

'At least once. I write to live. Everything else I do for fun and that,' he added, 'is the secret of life.'

'I like secrets.'

'Me too. But they are more of a pleasure shared than kept.'

I thought about that. It was relaxing in the big leather seat, my legs open, his hand caressing my thigh. 'So soft. Like cream,' he whispered. 'What I'd like to do is dress you in food. And eat you all up.'

The convent reared into view, the towers and spires dark silhouettes against the winter blue. 'You should drop me at the side of the building.'

'Of course.' He glanced away from the road and his eyes were bright like flakes of sky as he looked at me. 'You're wet.'

'It's my hormones,' I replied, and he smiled.

He stretched his fingers over the crutch of my knickers and the sound of rustling paper reminded me of the money, my share of the profits. I locked my thighs to prevent further

63

examination and removed the damp £20 note, which I folded into my pocket.

His fingers did that Yellow Pages walk back down my thigh and he drew my hand across to his lap. 'Here,' he said. 'Before you leave me.'

My hand moved firmly over Mr Thomas's trousers and as I pressed down he lurched forward.

'There.' I pointed. I could see the gate.

I slipped a finger inside my knickers, made it wet and rubbed my fingertip over his lips.

'Thank you for the lift.'

He reached for his coat and the way he pulled out his wallet reminded me of that day when Mr Daviditz watched me modelling underwear and then pushed £20 in my hand. Mr Thomas did the same.

'For the one in your pocket,' he said like he was James Bond, and I thought it was daft but it made no difference to me. I made the swap, stepped out of the car and only glanced back when he called.

'Remember, if you haven't tried, you haven't lived,' he said. He mimed dialling the telephone. 'Don't forget.'

I hurried through the gate and crunched my way up the gravel below the bare trees. I was looking distressed, which wasn't easy because I was feeling quite the opposite. Sister Theresa was standing on the steps not knowing whether to be worried or furious.

'Where have you been, Bella?'

'I had an emergency.'

'Don't you know the rules?'

I sniffled, opened the bag and she peered in at the boxes of tampons. 'It was like a massacre,' I said and burst into tears.

'Come, come, come.' She put her arms around me and I sobbed into her bosom. 'You know, you should have gone to Matron, she keeps them in the san.'

'Nobody told me.'

'Come, now. Everything's all right. We won't tell anyone.'

The choir was waiting and all those malevolent little faces glared at me as we entered the chapel. I was rehearsing my solo, the rest of the girls confined to singing the middle verses in accompaniment, while I sang the first and last on my own. I stored my bag safely in the choir stalls. Sister Theresa bent over the organ and I sang like an angel as I stared up at Saint Sebastian in his cute little toga.

After the usual disgusting meal in the refectory, which I didn't eat, I was wandering along the corridor when a sharp finger poked me in the back.

It was Tabatha Van Deegan and she invited me for some Machiavellian reason to have tea in her room.

We crossed the quad and entered another building, winding our way along a corridor with a high vaulted ceiling and water-stained walls studded with arched windows and canvases of gloomy Apostles with the same blue eyes as Mr Thomas.

We climbed a flight of stairs and entered a single room done up like an English house in the country with pretty chintzes, plump sofas and hunting prints. This was Miss Deegan's reward for having failed her A-levels – twice: her own room.

The tea things had already been prepared and, within minutes, I was sitting there balancing a steaming cup and saucer in my hands. Tabatha settled like a long pale shadow into the corner of the sofa and I thought Tabatha was a silly name. Tabby was even worse. Except for cats, of course.

'Now, what's this I hear about you seducing all the girls in your dorm?' she said and I almost spilled my tea.

'Well it's only three, and two of them are twins.'

I noticed for the first time, and not because I'm obsessed or anything, that Tabatha had small breasts. In fact, when she folded her arms to prop them up, she didn't actually have any breasts at all. This was probably what gave her thin lips that pinched sombre look.

'It's lovely tea,' I told her.

'Darjeeling,' she said. 'You should always drink Darjeeling after supper.'

'You know so many things ...'

'One thing I do know, is that seducing girls is one thing. Visiting the sex shop is quite another. You'll give the school a bad reputation.'

'O dear!' I said.

'And another thing, Jason isn't all that he seems ...'

'He was quite nice to me.'

'Men are always nice to girls with their tits on show. Take my advice, don't be too ...' She searched for the word.

'Precocious?'

'Cocky,' she corrected. She shook her head from side to side and her hair remained immobile. 'Men,' she added, 'are bastards.'

I lowered my eyes.

We were learning in history how the British had crossed the globe slaughtering natives by their thousand to bring them afternoon tea. I felt, sitting there with this American from Texas, that I was being colonised and my English blood came bubbling hotly back to the surface and reddened my cheeks.

I stood up. 'Thank you very much,' I said. 'Delicious tea.'

She sighed and looked like a pair of scissors as she unfolded herself from the sofa. 'Be careful, dear girl, you are new and you don't want to make too many ... faux pas,' she said.

I wandered back to my dorm irritated that I'd had to drink all that awful smoky tea. I decided Tabatha Van Deegan was best avoided and would never have guessed in a million years that she was the key to my destiny.

Had she known, perhaps things would have been different.

I spent the evening lying on my tummy, legs kicking like windmill sails, my Latin notes all over the bed. Caesar's motto was *Veni, vidi, vici,* not merely because he won all his battles but because he did so with extraordinary speed.

I came, I saw, I conquered.

I liked that.

Saskia and Tara sat at their laptops all night looking up porn sites on the internet and when they went to bed, I took one of my long hot showers. I stepped into a towel, remembered to dry between my toes, and doused myself with baby oil. I even put it in my hair to try and slick it flat. The twins dropped off to sleep like bottles dropping off a wall. Jack was out on one of her late night rambles and I wanted to get dressed before she returned and caught me.

The white box was sitting enticingly on the sink. I opened the lid and the devil face staring up made me quiver in anticipation. I was so glad I hadn't used it in the sex shop. I put on the plastic shorts, then the funny top with the rubber spikes and looped the straps through the rings like it indicated in the diagram. I tied my hair back with a band and pulled on the mask. It covered the back of my head and the top half of my face. The eye-slits were narrow, the line of the slant curling into two short horns. I stood back with the whip and gave my reflection a thorough examination.

Wow!

Before, I didn't understand why people bought uniforms in the sex shop. Now I knew. You could become a different person. Be an actor. Be anyone. I was Honey again. Or was I Bella? It didn't matter. This was fun. I took off the mask and placed it in my schoolbag with the cape, the whip, the baby oil and a pair of high, pointed shoes that were just so *it*.

I took the dildo out of its hiding place in the cupboard and lowered the shorts to put it on. It wobbled about and I held it still with one hand and used the tip of my finger to cover the surface with honey from the little pot I'd dropped in my blazer pocket at breakfast. I dropped the empty pot in the bin, raised the zip on the shorts half way and the dildo was sticky and warm lying flat against my tummy. I put on my dressing gown and felt like the devil's disciple as I stole into the dark corridor. I climbed two flights of stairs and hurried bare foot to Sister Nuria's room at the corner of the building.

Taking deep breaths, I paused for about ten seconds, slipped on the cape and shoes, and tucked my hair under the mask. I put my dressing gown in the bag, twisted the whip in a loop and slipped the baby oil into the side of the shorts. My heart was pounding as I knocked.

'Is somebody there?'

'The devil,' I said deeply from my diaphragm and knocked again.

Sister Nuria looked nervously through a crack in the door

67

and I forced my way in. I dropped the bag and stood with my arms wide, holding the cape like I was Batwoman. I was taller than her in the big spiky shoes and her mouth dropped open as she looked up into my red-rimmed eyes.

'*Dios mio.*'

I flicked the whip and the roar of its tongue slapping the air made her wince. I leaned down and pressed my mouth hard against her lips and she was nervous for a moment but then responded, pressing back as if she wanted the kiss to last forever. I pulled away.

Sister Nuria was wearing the ugliest grey night-dress I had ever seen. I got a firm grip of the neck and ripped it down the front, the shrieking sound of tearing fabric making her whole body tremble. I kept dragging at the material until she was naked. I removed the cape from around my shoulders, then lowered the zip on my shorts.

When she saw the black penis in the half light of her room she stood back as if it were something alive with an evil intent of its own. I stepped forward, took her cheeks in my palms and kissed her again. I pressed the dildo into her belly and she shuddered. It was big and firm and soothing and she started pressing back. I eased her head down and she seemed startled when her eyes neared the dildo.

'*Por favor, Bella ...*'

I touched the back of her head and it was as if she had lost her will and wanted me to take control, to lead her where I wanted to go because she wanted to be there with me in that unknown place. She leaned forward, touching the dildo to her lips. She ran her tongue along its length and back again, then took the head into her mouth. She paused and looked so young and pretty as she gazed up at me.

'*Miel,*' she mumbled, and I rocked back and forth on my heels, drilling deeper and deeper into her throat.

I tried to imagine what it was like for a man being sucked like this and I was suddenly envious that I would never really know.

When I'd tried the dildo, I couldn't get much of it in my mouth. Not so Sister Nuria. She was truly gifted and the entire shaft slid slowly but firmly in like a sword being pushed into its scabbard. The movement made me wet and that feeling of power that had come to me when I stood starkers before Jason was fizzing through my body.

Sister Nuria was gagging as the last little bit of dildo vanished between her lips and behaved as if it was an act of contrition for her to swallow it all. She had never known a man, and I knew that in those dark distant nights when she lay awake contemplating the Holy Trinity, I would slip into her mind like I was at this moment.

I pulled her up by the elbows and drew her onto the bed. I lowered my mouth to the thick copse of her pubic hair and her pussy opened like a sea anemone. She held on to the devil horns, pulling my tongue inside her, releasing the tang of cappuccino.

Mmm. There is nothing like the taste of girls.

She knew what was going to happen next and waited like a diver at the top of the highest diving board, imagining the upward swing, the flight into the void. I eased her legs apart and fed the dildo inside her in one hard thrust that made her yell in agony, and unlike Jack, who had wriggled in protest, she raised her thighs and wanted that pain because she wanted to sacrifice her prize before she returned to Spain to take her vows.

This was her last chance to know all that she was giving up forever and it seemed just so perfect that she was making this pact with the devil, even if it was only me in disguise.

The pain passed. She started to moan with pleasure and I realised they are linked. Pain could be pleasure and all pleasure would become pain, and I thought this was probably profound and I should write it down.

Sister Nuria had her arms around me and was pulling me deeper inside her as if something were lost and we had to keep delving ever further to find it. Her orgasm swept through her and, while she was still throbbing in ecstasy, I withdrew the dildo and rolled her onto her stomach. I removed the baby oil from my shorts. It was warm and I spread it over her back, through the crease of her perfectly round cheeks and into her bottom.

'*No, no, no, por favor,*' she whispered.

I placed my hand on the two tiny dimples at the small of her narrow back and she made no attempt to struggle. I took a breath, dipped the head of the dildo into her dark little hole and eased it up inside her.

She began murmuring prayers in Spanish and I kept thrusting from my hips, pushing and pushing until the entire column of rubber was buried and I knew from the magazines that this was the one thing men wanted to do, to take a woman in her three openings, and I thought, wow, I've had another virgin. And a nun this time. *Veni, vidi, vici.*

You are *so* bad, Bella, and I started to come from deep inside, from a place I didn't know and wanted to explore like an adventurer in Africa. My climax was so long it was like a journey up an endless river to a gorgeous warm place and that place was Sister Nuria. She stopped praying and gasped and I suddenly remembered it was half-term tomorrow and I was dying to go home and see all my things just how I'd left them.

Chapter Six

SASKIA AND TARA WERE sitting in the back of the car. Mother's scent was overpowering in the confined space and I was feeling irritable because Mr Daviditz hadn't taken the day off to meet us.

Radio 3 was playing one of those obscure German operas nobody likes and Mother was making a sort of *cza, cza, cza* noise as she cleared the mist from the inside of the windscreen with tentative sweeps of her gloved hand.

We turned the corner by the stables where I'd learned to ride and when I got my first glimpse of the smoke suspended over the chimney pots at Ickham Manor my mind filled with a rush of different memories.

As we were approaching the drive, a white van was pulling out and I caught a flash of Mr Lawrence's dark eyes. I turned to Mother with a little gasp and noticed the nerve twitching in her neck. We exchanged looks without saying anything and my foul mood had lifted by the time the car stopped.

Everything was just how I remembered, the panels of coloured glass in the wide porch, the two big olive jars waiting for spring when they would be planted with geraniums. It was a thrill returning home and I felt like an explorer staring out from the prow of a ship as I took in the familiar paintings on the walls, the stiff chair with its fading crest from a forgotten family, the hall table with carved feet and unopened letters leaning against the mirror above. At the crook of the stairs stood the slender palm whose only pleasure was slapping your face as you passed.

Mother led the way upstairs, heels tapping, Saskia and Tara

loaded down with cases and bags.

'I don't know why you've brought so much, it's only a few days,' Mother was saying, and I realised why I had grown so fond of the twins. They rarely smiled but seemed to find everything faintly amusing. They joined hands, glanced at each other, then glanced back with glazed expressions.

We left them to unpack. Mother was about to say something but changed her mind and I watched her head descend through the arching prism of palm fronds. Since the honeymoon in the Caribbean her hair had turned a shade lighter, from honey to buttercup.

I went to my room and let everything settle on my senses. The apple tree was bare and the robin perched on the high branches could have been posing for a Christmas card. The flower beds had the look of freshly dug graves and my thoughts went back to the funeral when everything was green and daffodils were erupting across the churchyard. I had tried to feel grief that day as the people gathered with lowered eyes but was more aware of how well I looked in my little black dress and the hat with a veil Mother had said was ridiculous, although by the way Mr Daviditz was gaping at me across the coffin I'm sure that was only a personal opinion.

After shedding my tears I realised I was crying for me, not Daddy. He had lived his life and would never have wanted to grow old and grumpy. Cancer suited him. He liked action. Within weeks of being diagnosed he had gone, and what I missed was that there was absolutely no one I really looked up to or admired. My Italian grandparents lived in Rome and I didn't know when I would see them again. Mother's parents were still in Yorkshire. Their accent put her on edge.

There was a picture of Daddy on the dressing table riding an elephant and dressed for polo. He was terribly handsome with a tanned face and the look in his mahogany eyes was the same look Mr Lawrence had when he saw me from his white van. As I hugged the frame to my chest my attention strayed to the woodshed at the bottom of the garden.

I took off my uniform, dropped it on the bed and was standing there starkers peering into the closet when you-know-who came wandering in. Like a film star, I covered my breasts with one arm and covered pussy with my hand.

'I'm cross with you,' I said.

Mr Daviditz dropped his eyes and stared at my abandoned knickers. 'What have I done?' He was too shocked to move.

'You didn't come to collect us.'

'I have to work.'

'But it's half-term.'

I tossed my head like a pony and stood sullenly with lips in an angry pout. A lock of hair kept falling in my eye and no matter how many times I tucked it behind my ear it wiggled its way out again.

'You can't imagine how happy I am to see you,' he said.

'Like this, you mean?' I said, and he went bright red.

'Bella, *bella* as ever ...'

'Do we have a video camera?'

'... a what? A video camera? Not as far as I know.'

'I've decided to become a film director,' I said and he smiled in that indulgent way people show teenagers. 'And I need a camera because I'm joining the Photography Club.'

'We'll have to see what we can do. Christmas is coming ...'

'Will you show me how it works and everything?'

'I daresay ...'

'You can take a film of me if you want,' I said and his neck turned from pink to crimson as I crossed the room and stood close with my fingers linked behind my back. 'I'm sure if you do it it'll be sexy.' I pushed out my bottom lip in a thoughtful pose. 'Don't you just love that word? It's so ...' I stared into his eyes.

'Sexy?' he said, and I planted kisses on either side of his lips.

Our bodies were pressed together and that August afternoon when he'd held my bare bottom in his hands slipped into my mind and I wondered if the same memory came to him when he snuggled up each night beside Mother. I blinked, fluttering my eyelashes, moistened my parted lips and it took amazing self-restraint for him not to take me in his arms and kiss me properly. I pulled on a white dress without any underwear.

'Come,' I said, and he followed me to the guest room.

The twins were busy on the internet.

'Mr Daviditz,' I said from the doorway. 'Saskia and Tara Scott-Wallace.'

'Simon,' he insisted. He looked at Saskia, then Tara, then back again, shaking his head as if he were seeing double.

They glanced up and spoke together. 'How do you do?'

'Very well, thank you. And your good selves?'

They looked at each other, then back at Mr Daviditz with an amused cast in their matching green eyes.

'Did you say good elves?' Tara asked.

'No, no, good selves,' he said.

'Yes we are,' said Saskia.

'What?' He was confused.

'Good elves,' said Tara.

'What ...'

'Thank you for inviting us,' added Saskia.

Brilliant!

I'd been racking my brain trying to think up something extraordinary for when I made my film and now it all fell into place.

Saskia and Tara had changed into tight jeans and T-shirts. They looked deliciously French with their gamine hair and ripe to start smoking. Mr Daviditz gave them a leisurely once-over, a polite moment passed, and the girls looked back at their laptops. I sent Mr Daviditz off to change and returned to my room to start writing.

I was working on my film script and had finished nearly 12 pages when *the voice* gushed up the stairwell.

'Dinner.'

It was, of course, an ordeal, and when it was over, Mother disappeared, sniffy about something. Mr Daviditz searched without success for the Scrabble and returned triumphantly with Monopoly. He grabbed the racing car, I took the top hat and what the twins chose I have no idea because I wasn't there long enough to remember. Mr Daviditz shot off with a double six and in three laps of the board had landed mysteriously on Trafalgar Square, The Strand and Fleet Street.

He was busy erecting terraces of green houses before we'd even caught our breath. I played recklessly. I watched my money mounting on the piles set out before Mr Daviditz and escaped, bankrupt, for the music room where I sat at the piano and breathed a sigh of relief.

I had started writing songs in my notebook and had discovered it wasn't going to be as easy as I had thought. I had two titles, *The Taste of Girls* and *Come To Me*, and just a few lyrics.

> *Sugar and Spice and all things nice*
> *That's the taste of girls*

That's as far as I'd got with the first. The second borrowed the tune from *Once In Royal David's City*, and I was trying to make it more operatic.

> *You come to me like the devil in disguise*
> *You come to me with secrets in your eyes*
> *Come to me. Come to me*

The next verse was like the opposite of awesome, whatever that is.

> *You come to me like the touch of money*
> *You come to me like the taste of honey*
> *Come to me. Come to me*

I quite liked the last verse and three verses were enough.

> *Come back to me, you just can't see*
> *You're the only one, the one for me*
> *Come to me. Come to me*

I closed my eyes and imagined wild drums and thrashing guitars, violins and cellos sweeping in on the last line, *Come to me. Come to me*. It was a sad line but sexy, and I visualised myself in front of thousands of people all clapping and crying as I went down on my knees at the front of the stage, the babies looking just so cute for my fans.

> *Come to me. Come to me. You just can't see.*
> *You're the only one, the one for me.*
> *Come to me.*

It was working. Simple chords: C, D, A minor, E minor and G. Then repeat.

There was a presence behind me and I stopped singing. I swivelled round on the piano stool and found Mother standing in the doorway holding my tutor card, which I had left on the pillow in her bedroom.

'I'm glad to see all those piano lessons didn't go to waste.' I smiled and she fanned her cheeks. 'You've settled in I can see.' I straightened my skirt and watched as she sat in the big leather chair with the button missing on the back. 'Really, well done.'

'Thank you.'

Mother had those half-moon glasses on a chain as if to say I don't really need glasses, just half glasses. She cleaned the lenses and went through the report picking out the nasty bits like Sister Bridget saying, 'Bella only pays lip service to discipline,' and Mother Superior warning that 'Bella's good mind is overshadowed by her shallow interests,' and I thought that was so unfair. 'So, well done,' Mother added. 'I'm proud of you.' She placed the tutor-card on the rounded arm of the chair and it toppled like a dying kite to the floor.

'I just want to do my best for you,' I said.

'And for Simon.' I didn't know what she meant at first, then she added. 'He's paying the fees, you know.'

'Oh.'

'Do try and call him by his name, all this Mr Daviditz business is so ... unnecessary.'

'I am trying.'

'He's a good man. He can never replace Daddy, I know that. But,' she sighed, 'We have to make the most of what's in front of us. Do try.'

We sat there with nothing more to say. Mother retrieved the

tutor-card from the floor and as she was leaving the room she turned back. 'That dress, isn't it a bit small?' she remarked.

'I just keep growing,' I replied.

'I don't know how, you don't eat anything.'

She ran her hands instinctively over her hips. Mother was concerned with my not eating because not eating was exactly what she would have liked to have been doing herself.

I swivelled back to the piano but the urge had gone and I hummed *Once In Royal David's City* as I wandered through the library, running my fingers over the surfaces, up the staircase, marking every corner of the house with my presence. There had once been a trust to pay for my schooling. That must have disappeared while Daddy was trying to revive his fortune breeding polo ponies and I was relieved that he had created an offshore trust to purchase Ickham Manor.

The building had begun life in Tudor times as an inn. Most of the interior had been remodelled but the attic was original and covered the entire house. I tiptoed up the squeaky stairs and behind the low door at the top I entered my secret hideaway.

Mr Daviditz may be paying the bills, I thought, but he's living under my roof. Moonlight washed through the dimpled glass in the dormer windows and the vaulted ceiling was supported by beams made from the masts of sailing ships that had run on to the rocks around the Kent coast.

The set was perfect.

I made banana on toast and gobbled it down, which you should *never* do, swallowed my vitamins with a glass of water, raced upstairs and cleaned my teeth with the electric toothbrush.

I removed the anti-wrinkle Q10 Plus night crème, a quick shower, hair wash and 30 seconds under an icy power spray to make the skin tingle before smoothing in Q10 Plus day crème with added co-enzyme R, gently over my face, under the chin where Mother was beginning to sag, down my long neck and across the collar bones.

Natural-looking hair is always best but to ensure hair is glossy and subtly tousled the natural look needs patience, rubbing shampoo evenly through every strand and washing out the last trace of soap before applying conditioner. Forget gels and sticky sprays, they're killers; towel dry, then use the dryer for body.

Hair is everything.

When you look good, you feel self-confident. My eyes are big and brown, the whites as pure as Snow White. I used a Flash Crazy eye pencil and hummed to myself as I applied a dash of Peepshow eye-shadow.

I had been thinking a lot about lips lately and had come to the conclusion they are just *so* important. I brush mine with a baby toothbrush before adding lipbalm. I use a lipliner the same shade of pink as my lips, tracing the line just outside the curves and filling in the gaps using the edge of the pencil. I don't need to create fuller lips but, hey: why not?

I use a lip-brush and gently paint on Max Factor with hydra-vitamins, starting at the centre of my mouth and working towards the corners. Blot the colour lightly with tissue, mmm, absorbing any excess oil, then add a light dusting of invisible face powder to set the colour. Finally, a second coat of lippy, smack my lips together and a pouty smile for the mirror. Mmm.

Come to me. Come to me

Next, body cream.

This *has* to be Giorgio Armani's Mania. It's absolutely gorgeous, turns skin to silk and the fragrance makes perfume unnecessary. A little splodge in one hand, warm it in my palms, then slowly, evenly over my arms, breasts, out to the tips and under the swell, mmm, so pretty, rib cage, hip bones, another splodge for the back, over the rocky roller coaster of my spine, one leg, then the other, up over the hill of my round bottom, between the cheeks, back over my hips and down across the line of my pubic hair.

Stand straight, ankles together, knees together, shoulders back, stomach in, inspect the babies, kiss my fingertip and plant that kiss on my little pink nipples. I checked under my arms for hair. Clean as a whistle.

It was almost a shame to have to get dressed and I envied people who lived on those South Sea Islands as I moved out of the bathroom to the bedroom and faced the age-old problem:

what to choose from a wardrobe that starts going out of date almost before you get home and take the stuff you've just bought out of the bags.

Undies?

I peered in the drawer, hooked my finger in my mouth and made a decision: white. I was feeling virginal, bikini briefs and a push-up bra to give the babies some support. Stand back to check. Mmm, delicious. I still can't believe designers make these teeny snippets of perfection *not* to be seen. I chose a black wool skirt and a white cashmere rollneck that clings to your shape and reveals a whisper of flesh when you stretch in any direction, soft fabrics that make you all feely touchy.

Accessorise with a Prada bag and flat shoes. I didn't want to be tall today, something that inspired a moment's doubt when I hurried downstairs with my coat over my shoulders and out to the waiting car.

The twins were *très chic* in white jackets with big furry hoods, red clutch bags, red micro-short pencil skirts, black socks above the knee and spiked pointy red ankle boots. They had long slender legs and the tomboy look Daddy liked. Even Mr Daviditz was dazzled and was dashing about like a chauffeur, opening one door and glancing up at the drawn curtains at the bedroom window as he rushed round to open the other.

'Madame,' said Mr Daviditz and closed the door behind me.

Mr Daviditz was wearing a chalk-striped suit, a blue-striped shirt and a royal blue tie with a narrow diagonal stripe.

'You have to buy a new tie, Mr Daviditz ...'

'Simon ...'

'Too many stripes.'

'What?' He fired the engine and accelerated out of the drive.

I used my fingers for the list. 'The suit, the tie, the shirt.' I glanced down. 'Oh my God, the socks. You need a contrast or it looks silly.'

'Are you sure?'

I glanced back over the seat. 'Stripes?' I said.

'Contrast,' they replied in deadly earnest.

He licked the tip of his finger, curled his moustache and

concentrated on the narrow road that led to Canterbury. We had masses of shopping to do; there's never enough time at school, and Mr Daviditz planned to leave the car as he did each day at the station and catch the train to Victoria.

'We have to get millions of things,' Saskia said suddenly, and Tara added, 'Especially after you made us throw everything away.'

I shuddered and turned to Mr Daviditz. 'Well, I had to. They were wearing those gigantic school bloomers,' I told him. 'Can you imagine anything so ugly?'

'No, I don't suppose I can.'

'See,' I said, glancing over my shoulder, then back again at Mr Daviditz. 'Why don't you come shopping with us? You've got such good taste.'

'Except when it comes to ties.'

'Not ties, stripes. I'll choose a new one.'

'I'd love to but, you know how it is.'

'No, I don't.'

'Work, my dear girl.'

'You're just an old meany. What do you have to do that's so important?'

'I've got clients.'

'And that's more important than helping the twins buy new knickers?'

The colour slid up his neck. 'Bella, I'm seeing a property for an American client this afternoon. Somebody *very* important.'

'I don't care.'

He sighed and pulled at his moustache. I folded my arms and listened to the soothing sound of the tyres rolling over the asphalt, the small villages slipping by as we passed through low hills clad in orchards of empty fruit trees. The cathedral towers grew more prominent in the distance and as the car crested the hill Canterbury appeared, the mediaeval centre where Chaucer had written his stories now surrounded by a maze of little grey houses with red roofs and a car outside every door. We have become so ... dull, I thought, so colourless. Just imagine life in the time of Chaucer, all the gin and revelry.

'You don't want me tagging along,' he said, reviving the

conversation. 'You'll have more fun on your own.'

'No we won't.'

He was shaking his head doubtfully. 'Look, we can go shopping again tomorrow. It's Saturday.'

We pulled into the station car park and I slammed the door as I got out. The twins joined me, and we marched smartly towards the gate. I heard the automatic locks snapping into place and didn't look back. We were just about to exit when he called.

'Bella. Bella! Wait!'

He came towards us, a mobile phone glued to his ear. He clicked it off, threw up his hands and I watched his chubby face settle into a reluctant smile. 'How could I say no?' he said.

The twins instinctively took his arms on either side and we made our way through the old fortified walls into town. In the high street, I noticed the men in suits took just as much notice of the twins with their eight-mile legs in those micro-short skirts as they did of me buttoned up in my overcoat. Saskia and Tara had only recently grown aware of the devastating effect they had on men and were making the most of it.

Neuhaus & West opened as we reached the door.

Underwear.

It was on everyone's mind, and I stood back hanging on to Mr Daviditz's arm like a proud parent as the girls slipped in and out of new knickers and bras in pastel shades, and the assistant, a middle-aged woman with a shadow over her top lip and a tape measure around her neck, watched as if she really didn't know what to think.

Mr Daviditz's eyes were bright with the illicit thrill of peeking through the gaps in the changing room curtains and the twins, little tarts that they are, catwalked half naked like supermodels. There was soon a pile of matching bits and pieces and Mr Daviditz turned to me as if he had watched the movie trailers and was ready for the main feature.

'What do you need?'

'A partygoer's bra,' I replied.

'What?'

I dumped my coat over his arm and took the assistant off to

help me look.

'Your father?' she asked brightly.

'Stepfather,' I said.

'Ah.'

I drew back my shoulders and stood straight. 'Can you measure me?' I asked and the woman did so, holding the measure in her fingertips. Her eyes ran over my chest.

'34 B, Miss,' she said.

'Can you measure my waist and hips? Just in case.'

She did so and by the obsessive way she avoided touching me I guessed she was probably a lesbian.

'22, 32,' she said and I was pleased because I like things being symmetric.

She found the partygoer's set and I grabbed things from La Perla, Agent Provocateur, Triumph, Yves Saint Laurent, something raunchy in black, and I wasn't even looking properly because Mr Daviditz was catching the 11.05 and I didn't have much time. I strode back to the changing room and he looked like a Christmas tree as the girls draped his arms in baubles of silk, satin and lace. They went off to the hat department and we arranged to meet at the main door in an hour.

The woman with the hairy lip was hovering sourly like Mother's musk but it didn't make any difference to me. I left the curtain open, slipped out of my roll neck, unzipped my skirt and folded it on the bench. In the long mirror I could see Mr Daviditz standing like a guard over the changing room entrance and knew by the look in his eyes that I had no need to be jealous of Saskia and Tara. I took off my knickers and bra and spun round to inspect my reflection from the back. I ran my hands down my sides, over my hips. I just loved having no clothes on. I couldn't help it.

I slipped in and out of the darling little sets of undies, not that it mattered, I needed them all. Mr Daviditz had taken a step closer and was panting like Mr Lawrence's black Labrador. He gave an enthusiastic nod for the white Triumph that promises super curves, the pale pink, still my favourite colour, something purple, because I didn't have anything purple, scarlet for inflaming the passions. I'd gone off black because it can look

82

tarty, but it was sexy too and thought I should give it another chance.

'What do you think?'

'Oh, yes.'

The partygoer's bra I saved until last. It came with a loose pair of boxer shorts with a wide band of elastic at the waist and was so foxy I thought if the girls are going out dancing at raves dressed like this it was little wonder they're all getting pregnant at 14.

'Well?'

'Lovely. Just lovely.' His throat was dry.

I turned to unhook the back. It was stuck.

'Could you?'

He glanced over his shoulder. The assistant was serving someone and he hurried into the cubicle, dumped the things he was holding and closed the curtain behind him. He fiddled about with the fastener and the bra fell to the floor. I turned and stared up into his eyes. My lips were glossy and looked their best after all the effort I'd made.

'Bella, I ...'

His voice cracked. I had gone up on my toes, my head at an angle and he lowered his face as if a magnet was drawing his lips over mine. His damp hands slid over my back as he pulled me into an embrace. His lips were rough and the moustache made it feel like kissing a girl between her legs but not as nice.

His hand started sliding over my side and clutching for my breast. He squeezed away. My eyes were open and my arms hung loosely like I was a rag doll. His free hand was over my bottom and he was pulling me closer. I could feel his penis swelling against my belly. He kept kissing my lips and massaging my breast. His right hand drifted round the band of my dancing shorts, his fingers slipped inside the elastic, moved over my hip and down on a diagonal towards my dry little pussy. He stopped suddenly, gasping, and pulled away. My eyes were wide, my mouth had dropped open. I was staring back in shock.

'Oh my God, Bella, I'm sorry,' he said and coughed. 'I got carried away.'

I shyly removed the shorts and started to dress as he moved backwards through the curtain. I noticed in the mirror the assistant with her hands on her hips, her head shaking beneath her bun of grey hair, and I wondered why people get so upset over things that have nothing at all to do with them. I mean, we hadn't just bombed Iraq or something.

Mr Daviditz's credit card was snapped through the machine. I stood behind him looking at his red neck. The assistant's thin lips were pressed so tightly together I knew she was dying to say something. I stared at her until she turned away and began wrapping the new sets of underwear in thick folds of tissue. It filled one big white bag with Neuhaus & West in a spray of pink letters.

Mr Daviditz turned towards me. His lips were trembling.

'Tie first, then the electrical department.'

He took his glasses out of his pocket and frowned as he slipped them on. 'Electrical department?'

'The camera, silly,' I said.

'But, Bella ...'

'You promised.'

I felt a tear jerk into my eye and roll down my cheek.

'Bella, I ...' he began. 'I'm so sorry. I shouldn't have.'

''Specially as you're a solicitor.'

He took a deep breath, the blood seeped up his neck and over his cheeks. He had kissed my lips, he had taken my breast in his hand, and I'm sure if I could have looked inside his head I would have seen two conflicting thoughts, how marvellous it had been and how dangerous, and how the danger had made it even more marvellous. Mr Daviditz's brow was damp and his hands were shaky as we moved towards the stairs. He stopped again.

'You won't ...'

I sniffled. 'Tie first,' I suggested.

He nodded and followed me to the men's department where I found a pale gold tie decorated with red and blue books by Hugo Boss. He carefully folded the old stripy tie in his pocket and I watched him tying a knot in the new one.

He chose another credit card from the long file lined up in

his wallet and we went down to the ground floor where I settled on a modest Samsung VDP77 digital camcorder with the optical zoom, image stabiliser and an LCD screen so you can see what you're filming. I knew I was going to need a tripod and the young Asian boy who was so knowledgeable about all those things persuaded us to take a solid one because the microlites have a tendency to tremble. He was looking at Mr Daviditz's hands as he mentioned this. The camera came with two films and we took two more, just in case.

'What kind of mobile do you have?'

Mr Daviditz pulled out his iPhone for me to examine. Mine was at least six months old and I was bored with the colour. Pink underwear is one thing. A pink phone is just, like, so immature.

'You can hook into email, record your own personal ringtone – you can even find out what's showing at the cinema,' he bragged.

'That's not a lot of good if you're at boarding school,' I replied. 'We should get the same, then I can call you and it won't cost very much.'

'Bella, you are so wicked.' He thought about what he'd said and shrugged it off. 'Come on then, why not?'

The Asian boy reached for the appropriate box and I was amazed how one sweaty palm on my breast had released all this pent-up generosity. Mr Daviditz signed all sorts of forms to put the machine on his bill and paid with yet another different credit card. He probably did tricky things with tax.

We made our way towards the main entrance. Mr Daviditz stopped just before we reached the doors.

'You know I absolutely adore you, Bella,' he said.

'Do you?'

'I'll do anything for you.'

'Really?'

'Truly.'

'Well, there was something, just a little thing. It's really hard to survive on my weekly allowance. There are so many things I have to get, books and things, music. It's a disaster.'

'How much do you need?'

'I don't know, it's so hard. 40,' I suggested.

'£40?' His voice went up.

'That's not too much is it, Simon?'

A shudder went through him as if he'd just been shot by a sniper. 'You called me Simon.'

'Well, I just thought, now we have a secret and everything.'

'Thank you, thank you, thank you,' he whispered, looking up, as if to God. 'I've been waiting for you to call me Simon for I don't know how long.'

'Since the funeral,' I said.

Chapter Seven

I SPENT THE AFTERNOON studying the Samsung manual and that night, when the olds went off to some irksome dinner party, I took all the equipment upstairs to the attic. I found two glass ashtrays the same shade of green as the twins' eyes and hauled them up in a bag with my props. I thought Saskia and Tara had looked so cute in their micro-skirts and red boots I told them to dress the same way with the new Tommy Hilfiger sweaters they'd bought in Canterbury.

I set the camera on the tripod, placed two chairs so that they fit on the outer edge of the frame and asked the girls to sit. I placed the ashtrays on matching side tables and stopped them from lighting up until we were ready. They sat and shrugged impatiently.

'We,' I told them, 'are going to make an erotic film.'

Their heads didn't move, but Saskia's eyes went left, Tara's eyes went right, and I guessed they were telepathically in tune.

'What do we have to do?'

I unfolded the script and, as I went through the scenes, they zapped it all into their memory hard drives. I glanced up from time to time and it occurred to me that now I knew them better, the twins had stopped being just twins and were individuals. Apart from using opposite hands for everything, they had their own mannerisms and habits, as well as different smells. Saskia was always rubbing her stomach and complaining of a tummy ache. Tara liked to scratch the end of her nose when she was thinking and was doing just that as I came to the end and dropped the script on the floor behind the camera.

'And we can get paid?' asked Tara sceptically.

'As long as the demo's good.'

She glanced at Saskia, who was rubbing her tummy, of course.

'Do you have any vodka?'

'Vodka?'

I ran downstairs and found the bottle of Absolut Mother hides in the freezer. I collected two glasses and the girls drank three shots apiece before they were ready. They refilled the glasses, lit their Gauloises and set the two ashtrays at the same angle on the side tables. I put on *Body*, the Dallas McTee song, and was really irritated that I hadn't found time to finish my own songs and record them.

'Take one. Camera's rolling.'

I grinned. They were my best friends and I was lucky because I didn't have one best friend. I had two.

'And ... action.'

Saskia held her cigarette in her right hand. Tara's was gripped at the same languid angle with her left. They had opposite legs crossed and, communicating in their own special way, straightened their legs and dropped their heads to one side. I watched through the camera lens and it looked fantastic.

They stood and turned towards each other as if they were studying their own reflection. They took off their red berets, threw them out of frame, then removed the sweaters, dropping them to one side, Saskia always using her right hand, Tara the left. It was cosmic. They slid out of the skirts, reached for their cigarettes and in matching sheer pink panties and push-up bras studied each other as if studying a mirror.

They returned the cigarettes to the ashtrays. Their hands went inside their knickers and the same intense expressions crossed their pixie faces. The knickers were abandoned and they moved slowly together. When they kissed, I felt so tingly and damp I thought it was just as good watching sex as having sex yourself. I checked the camera and zoomed in, narrowing the frame. I took off my clothes. It was too early but the central heating was going full blast and it was always so hot in the attic.

Saskia and Tara knew each other's bodies like they knew

their own and looked completely natural as each set of hands caressed the other's back and sides. They were so cute in their little red boots. Up until then, the mirror image idea had worked perfectly and I really hoped it would come as a surprise when it changed. They started jiggling about, then they fell on the floor and just wriggled like two eels in a tank.

It was sexy and arousing. I felt warm dribbles run down my legs as I took out the devil mask and unrolled the dildo from the old cardigan I'd brought it home in. I didn't bother with the rest of the costume. It was silly to hide my best features. I strapped myself into the rubber cock and tucked my hair under the mask. The twins were moaning, their long thin arms and legs moving rhythmically.

I started *Body* back at the beginning and moved into the centre of the frame behind the twins. With one jerk of my hips the dildo began to sway like the head of a serpent.

Saskia and Tara turned, gazing up as if they were devil worshippers and I was Satan. They moved closer, drawn by a supernatural force, and just as I'd written in the script, both began to lick the dildo, their eyes focusing on the slits in the mask. I felt in touch with something dark and compelling and my whole body was one vibrant erogenous zone by the time the track came to an end.

As I moved backwards out of shot, the girls fell about laughing. I had what I needed for the demo and was tempted to use the dildo just for fun, just to add two more virgins to my score, but I did have other plans and if you don't keep to your plans everything goes to pieces.

I took the dildo off, patted them both over the heads with it, and we carried on fooling about. I mean, there's so much three girls can do with tongues and noses and fingers. It was super, Tara going into my pussy and Saskia kissing me upside down. Her tongue circled my lips then ran over my chin, she licked my breasts and kept going, over my rib cage, into my belly button and I caught a glimpse of her heart-shaped birthmark as her pretty pink sex opened over my mouth.

Saskia's tongue found a tiny space beside Tara's tongue and I felt them both wiggling and sliding up inside me like two fencing swords fighting a duel for my pussy. I'm not sure who won and it didn't matter. My spine curved in a bow. As one of the twins kept pushing her face into pussy, the other little tongue slid up my bottom and I was suddenly worried about the 16th-century attic my climax was so deafening I thought it might take the roof off.

Saskia and Tara were tucked up and looked so sweet, twins in their twin beds, and I was still awake when I heard the car crunching over the drive. All the permutations of our threesome were running like a DVD through my mind and I just adored being young and having so much fun. It must be horrid to be old and wrinkly and baggy and I suddenly understood why the girls were committing slow suicide smoking and drinking.

I heard footsteps on the stairs and was surprised when Mother opened my door and barged into the room. I'd left the bedside lamp on because I liked the patterns it made on the ceiling.

'I saw the light,' she said and dropped into the armchair.

She studied me in the lamplight. I had gone to bed glowing, hair mussed, lips swollen, cheeks flushed with colour and sex. Mother was tired with red eyes. At parties she drank too much and returned home not exactly sure who she was supposed to be, her accent ranging from the clipped military tones of Mrs Ormsby at the stables to the drawn out consonants of her mum and dad in Ilkley Moor.

Mother was turning the two gold bracelets on her wrist like she was unlocking a safe. She wasn't good at hiding her feelings. Everything was clear by the muscle throbbing in her neck, the impatient way her lips twitched. I wondered if on the drive home Mr Daviditz had confessed all.

'There's something I've been meaning to tell you, but it never seems to be the right time,' she began and took a breath. 'Your father,' she added and paused again. 'Your father was a bloody fool.'

'Mummy!'

'Those bloody horses ... Bloody things. He lost everything,' she persisted. 'He lost more than everything.'

She was shaking her head and the tic was almost bursting through the skin. Her eyes had come to rest on the photograph of Daddy on the chest of drawers. 'When your father went and ...' she paused, 'went and died,' she said, controlling herself, 'he owed nearly £500,000.' She spoke slowly so that the words registered. She stared into my eyes. 'The value of this house.'

'My house.'

'*This* house,' she repeated and I felt my heart drumming inside my chest. Lines were forming under my night crème. There was a long silence.

'Ickham Manor,' I said.

'Simon bought it.'

I didn't believe her at first. 'But it's my house. It's in trust.'

'I have power of attorney,' she said. 'Your father borrowed against the house. Simon paid the debts. It would have been taken away by the bank otherwise.'

'But you didn't ask me. It's my house.'

'It was *our* security.'

My throat had gone dry. Tears prickled behind my eyes. I thought I had been clever letting Simon Daviditz run his damp hands over me, while all the time he was plotting to steal my future.

'But it was mine,' I said.

'Welcome to the real world.'

'You stole my house.' I was screaming. I couldn't help it.

'Oh, fuck off, you little bitch,' she replied, and immediately regretted it. She breathed noisily through her nose. 'I didn't mean that.'

'Get out.'

'Don't tell me what to do.' She smiled. 'In my own house.' I didn't know what she meant. She pushed herself out of the chair, her gold bracelets rattling as she moved closer to the bed. 'I'm a married woman. What's his is mine.'

She stood, looked down at me for a moment, then left the room. Salty tears ran down my cheeks and into my mouth. I glanced at Daddy's photograph before switching off the lamp. I was exhausted and sleep claimed me like a monster coming out of a pit.

During the night the planets had realigned and I was aware in a muddled way as I opened my eyes that I was entering a new world. There was just enough light seeping through the grey winter dawn for me to find my dressing gown. I pulled it on and thought of nothing but my footsteps on the grass as I crossed the garden.

The sound of the van must have awoken me and when I entered the woodshed Mr Lawrence was leaning against the bench rolling a cigarette. Jake was sitting to one side, his eyes glossy, his pink tongue lolling from his mouth. The paraffin stove made the air warm and heavy.

Mr Lawrence nodded and didn't speak. He lit the cigarette and I could see my shadow crossing the wall as I moved towards him. The dog was panting and it felt as if our breathing were synchronised, the air going swiftly in and out of my chest. Mr Lawrence looked me up and down, studying me as if I were one of the cuttings he had planted back in August. His dark eyes stared into my eyes as he pulled at the cord tied in a bow around my waist. It fell and it uncoiled at my feet. The dressing gown fell from my shoulders. He gestured towards the buttons on my pyjamas and, as my fingers went to work, it felt as if someone else was undoing them.

My pyjama jacket slipped to the floor and Mr Lawrence spent a long time smoking and considering my breasts. He balanced the cigarette on the silver tin. He licked his fingertips and gently ran them in circles around my nipples. He didn't pinch, he just kept turning in slow circles until they began to prickle and then he did squeeze, rolling them softly and expertly the way he rolled his cigarettes. My eyelids felt heavy and I sucked in breath. Jake was gazing up at me with those big glassy dog eyes, his tongue moving in and out of his wide mouth.

The sensation in my breasts was hypnotic. A slow calm flowed through me. It was like a drug. I was in a trance. Mr Lawrence gave a tug on my pyjama bottoms and I wriggled out of them. He leaned back and gazed at me like a judge at a flower show, my bronzed shapely limbs, my tiny waist, the neat triangle of pubic hair. He put his finger between my legs. He didn't push it in, but moved it lightly in a beckoning motion back and forth until pussy leaked a few drops of dew on his fingertip. He took his hand away, rubbed his finger and thumb together as if checking the sap from a plant, then held his fingers to his nose.

Jake's panting had grown louder. Mr Lawrence leaned over to pat his head. Then he turned, took a firm grip on the back of my hair and bent me over the bench. My mind was blank except for a vague vision of Jack bent over in the shower at school. I gritted my teeth.

Then, unexpectedly, Mr Lawrence smacked my bottom.

Hard, really hard.

He brought his big hand down on my soft flesh and swatted my cute little backside like you would swat a fly. It stung, it really stung, and I would have screamed but before I could, his hand came down again. My bottom was on fire. I started sniffling and dribbling. I was uncomfortable and something else, something really weird. I slid my legs further apart to get my balance and pushed my bottom up defiantly.

Down it came again, his hand like a giant clanger against a cymbal and the sound of flesh striking flesh rang out like the church bells in the village. Three big hard wallops and then another, a fourth, harder still, his hand like a sheet of fire burning my poor little pink cheeks.

The breath caught in my throat. Dribbles were running down my thighs. I could smell my arousal and he hit me again, harder, even harder. I gritted my teeth, pushed my bum up and it felt right somehow. I was being punished. I wasn't sure for what exactly, but I needed this. I needed to get my bottom tanned so that I could get my head straight.

And again.

Number six. So hard it wasn't even painful, it was almost a pleasure. My bottom was aflame. I stood up and faced him. I was panting like the dog. My body was damp with sweat and fear and something else, something that I would only understand much later.

Mr Lawrence was unzipping his trousers. He bent his legs, gave a little jerk, and when he pulled out his penis I shuddered. It was huge, bigger than the dildo, the blue veins throbbing on the side, the pink head staring up at me. He took me by the hair again and his long cock grazed my swollen lips as he forced me to my knees.

The memory of Sister Nuria gazing up at me with her teeth locked around the dildo was so vivid it was as if it was linked to this moment, that everything that night when I had felt a sense of power was to lead to my being naked on the floor feeling lost and afraid. The fumes from the paraffin stove were overpowering. I thought about Simon Daviditz whizzing around the Monopoly board buying all the houses and now Ickham Manor was his.

Mr Lawrence thrust forward. My lips parted. The head of his cock filled my mouth and I felt the strength leave my body as he drilled it in further. I had tried with little success to do this with the dildo. Then I remembered how Sister Nuria had just willed herself to take it all and I did the same. Mr Lawrence didn't stop until the entire thing had reached deep into my throat.

He kept his hand on the back of my neck, I clung to his legs and he eased my head back and forth, on and on, deeper and deeper, stretching the soft walls of my throat, and I thought about Mother coming to my room with her red eyes and jangling bracelets.

Tears flowed over my cheeks. Mr Lawrence was jerking faster and faster. My head was spinning. I thought I was going to black out. Then he groaned and stopped. I tasted a speck of his semen and he withdrew, holding his cock like the garden hose, and he sprayed me with his come, an unending stream of sticky goo that covered my face and wet my hair and dripped down my chin.

'Agh, agh, agh,' he gasped like he was in pain and the Labrador came to its feet, its big silly eyes staring at me as if it didn't know what to do.

My mouth was still open and Mr Lawrence slipped his cock back between my lips as if the last few seeds were a poison that needed to be drawn out. I sucked as hard as I could. Finally he pulled it out, bent his knees and tossed his giant penis into his underpants like a small animal being put back into a cage.

He turned, took his tobacco from the tin and continued to study me as he rolled a cigarette. His semen was running down my face. In my mouth was the taste of sour yoghurt that would stay there for many days. Jake took a step closer, his nose registering the strange scent. A glob of sperm dropped glistening to my chest and the dog sniffed at it.

Mr Lawrence smiled. 'Here now. Good boy,' he said, and stroked the dog's head.

My breasts were pale and cold in the dim light. My knees hurt from the rough floor. The sperm was drying, tightening on my face. Mr Lawrence lit his cigarette.

'You're your mother's daughter, all right,' he said, watching as I stood and dressed in the way that you might watch a monkey in the zoo.

I was, as Mother liked to say, a show-off. I had been a show-off when I did ballet. I was a show-off when I sang or played piano. Being watched had never bothered me. I liked being watched, and it was this small vanity that impelled me to strip off my clothes in changing rooms, on the stage above the sex shop, before Mr Lawrence's dark eyes in the woodshed.

I hurried on bare feet back across the lawn and sat down to write a letter to my grandparents, the first time I'd written for ages. I told them that ever since Daddy had died I kept stopping to ask myself if I would ever be happy again. As I gazed from the window, I could see my footprints frozen in the frost as if a part of me was preserved there like a memory.

Mr Lawrence had become mixed up in my thoughts with something I had been trying to recapture when I should have known that when something has gone it has gone forever. My mind had been a blank sheet when I entered the woodshed that morning. Anything could have happened and I left with nothing worse than a sticky face, a sore bottom and my virginity intact, not that it seemed that important any more.

Mr Daviditz drove the twins and me back to school on Sunday. The taste of sour yoghurt clung to my mouth and my bottom was still stinging. My stepfather kept asking why I was so quiet, and I kept wanting to tell him: the gardener sprayed my face in spunk, my arse is as pink as a baboon's – and you've stolen my house. Other than that, everything's just purr-fect.

It would have been easy to hate Simon Daviditz but that would have given him too much importance. I needed him to pay my school fees. I needed an ally.

The worst thing of all was pretending to be my little sexy self, when that person had gone. The buttons on my blouse stayed fully buttoned and Sister Theresa stopped patting my bottom. I was always on time for choir practice and, when I wasn't doing prep, I went to the music room to play the piano. I was writing songs, but with a lack of enthusiasm that came from the pressures of schoolwork. I needed straight As in all exams if I was going to get into Cambridge and read the news on the BBC.

During the weekend exeat, the twins had been dragged off to a country house to watch Henry shooting, and I went into town alone. It was all very festive with fairy lights strung across the High Street although I didn't have that feeling of excitement you usually get when Christmas is coming.

I was on my way back loaded with new things when I ran into the boy with the bronze hair. He was standing outside the second-hand shops counting his money.

'Oi, it's you,' he said and pointed. I stopped and dropped my bags.

'Well, what about it?'

'Whatcha doing?'

'Nothing. Buying stuff.'

'Anyfin' you need, just tell me. I'll nick it for you. Sell it half price.'

I gasped. 'You mean steal things?'

He was sort of shrugging and dancing and moving his arms like a nervous insect. His blue eyes were clear and he was almost as skinny as me with his baggy jeans slipping down over his hips.

'What's your name?' I asked him.

'Troy, innit.'

'Bella.'

'You all have those funny names up at that school.'

'I suppose we do.'

'I suppose we do,' he repeated, making fun and I smiled. 'Wanna come up to Greens or sommink?'

I looked at my watch. 'I can't, I've got to get back to school. It's tea time.'

I retrieved my shopping bags. Troy grabbed his bike and walked along with me towards the convent.

'Just be late,' he said.

'You can't do that.'

'My school you do what you like.'

'What about your education?'

His face went out of shape. 'You're havin' a laugh, antcha?'

'It's important.'

'They don't teach you nuffin'. Anyway, I know what I'm ganna do,' he said and we stopped for this announcement. He pushed his chin forward and sniffed. 'Going to start a group and that. I'm getting all the gear.'

'Really?'

'Yeah, I got a guitar, amps, everything. Even got a name,' and he threw out his chin again. 'Fast,' he said, and cycled off doing wheelies all the way to the convent gate.

'Fast?' I asked him when I caught up.

'Yeah, good innit?'

I nodded. He was cute with his blue eyes and now it was time for me to go he seemed embarrassed as if there was something more he wanted to say or do and wasn't sure what or how. I liked this. I had no idea why. I had no interest in the townies for one thing and, for another, Troy was almost certainly younger than me, just as Simon Daviditz was younger than Mother, and the last thing I had in mind was to follow in *her* footsteps. I thought for a moment about kissing him, to see his reaction, but other girls were making their way towards the gate and the moment passed.

'See you around then,' he said, and shot off on his bike.

At tea there were scones with jam which I ate with a glass of milk and I couldn't stop thinking about the way Troy had waved as he rode off. He liked me and that wave was meant to say that yes, I like you, but I'm not going to make a big deal out of it by coming back.

It was getting late. I hurried along the empty corridors and across the quad to chapel. There was one more rehearsal before the Christmas carol service and, as I stared up at Saint Sebastian, it was just so weird because he was identical to Troy.

Troy was still on my mind when I dug through the cupboard in the dorm and took the dildo with me into the shower. I covered it in baby oil and spent like an hour copping off. Tension had been building up inside me and it came flooding out with my rich sticky honey. I was tempted to break myself in but that would have been a waste and I held back from going the extra inch. Poor Pinkie and Perky had been awfully neglected. They may even have shrunk. I gave them a massage and promised never to ignore them ever again.

Chapter Eight

HUNDREDS OF PEOPLE CAME up to congratulate me on my singing and I heard Mr Daviditz telling one set of admiring parents that *he* was my father.

There was tea and biscuits and I finally got to meet Mrs Scott-Wallace.

'Bella. This is Nena,' said Saskia.

She took my hand and stared over my shoulder as if something far more interesting were going on across the room.

'I've heard so much about you,' I said.

'Not all good I hope,' she replied. 'Do excuse me,' and she wandered off towards Alastair Bloom, who owned an airline and was the father of a suicidal girl on Ritalin named Daisy.

The twins' mother was tall and terribly beautiful in Fendi shoes with the longest most lethal points I had ever seen. Her grey Chanel jacket with the velvet collar was cut to reveal what's normally concealed at a convent school and I assumed the display was to rejoice the season of plenty. Mrs Scott-Wallace shook hands with Alastair Bloom. They slid away from his circle and went to stand where the silvery light pressing through the tall arched windows gave them an aura like the saints on the corridor walls.

My dear mother took one look at Mrs Scott-Wallace and placed the chocolate biscuit she had just been at pains selecting back on the plate. She had lost a few pounds but still went on about how thin I was on the journey home and Mr Daviditz said he was going to 'feed me up', as if I were the goose being prepared for Christmas lunch. The man was a walking cliché.

I sat back in the big leather seat with the armrest down and stared out at the frozen landscape. Whether I liked it or not, I was tied to them, both of them. I never mentioned that night when Mother had come drunkenly to my room to announce that the house was no longer mine and when Ickham Manor came into view the pleasure that moment always stirred was as dead as Daddy in his grave.

The car slipped into the drive and sighed as it came to a stop. There was a wreath on the door, in memory of what I wasn't sure. Mother dropped her keys on the hall table and flicked through the mail.

'I can't stand people who send cards so late. You have to go straight out and send one back to them,' she said. I was halfway up the stairs. 'Here,' she called.

She was dangling an envelope in her fingertips and I hurried back down to get it. I gazed at Nonno's elegant script, the smudges of ink made by raindrops, the red, white and green Italian stamp so cleverly the colours of Christmas. It was a real letter, written by hand and it made my heart flutter like a bird against my ribcage.

I ran back upstairs, threw myself on the bed and studied the envelope. I pressed the blue paper to my nose and could smell an early morning in the piazza, old ladies with lilac perfume, the rolling dusty hills of Rome. I could picture Nonno sitting in the square sipping coffee and waiting for Nonna to come out of church.

The letter was written on unlined paper.

'My dear Isabella,' it begun and Nonno in his quaint, old-fashioned English explained how he and Nonna were very happy. The very happy was underlined. They had sold La Montepietra, the old palazzo that had been in the family since the Renaissance, paid off the debts and they were "very happy" living in the little gardener's cottage. And so it went on, one long heartbreaking litany of disaster.

At lunchtime on Christmas Eve, they had invited some of their dreadful friends and Simon was anxious to impress the Big Player he had inveigled into some property deal. I was shocked to discover that Mr Lawrence was included, something that would not have happened when Daddy was alive. It is not a question of snobbishness, it's just that there are ways of doing things; you can't learn it, and Mother just adored getting everything wrong.

I felt nervous at first, but was determined to show Mr Lawrence that what had happened meant just the same to me as it did to him, which was nothing. I spent like *hours* getting ready and knew I looked super in fitted white trousers, pink shoes with heels that made me tower over Mother and a skinny pink sweater that showed Pinkie and Perky were back. I closed the bathroom door and stared at Dallas McTee.

'Well?' I asked and she just kept smiling down her cleavage.

Mr Lawrence appeared with his turnip-shaped wife Sheila and pimply son Luke.

'Are you going to be a gardener when you leave school?' I asked him.

'Nah. Gonna be a footballer, an' at,' he mumbled.

'Wicked.'

I turned to Mr Lawrence and looked straight in his eyes. 'How are the cuttings?' I asked.

'Coming along nicely.' He paused. 'How's school?'

'It's another learning experience,' I replied, and was sure he wouldn't get it.

Esperanza, the new maid, was passing a tray with schooners of sherry. He took one and held it towards me as if in a toast. It was hard to believe this man had folded me over his work bench to smack my bottom and shot his creamy semen over my startled face. It was so decadent, so degrading. Yet, when the little scene came back into my mind I remembered the oily juices leaking from my pussy and it gave me a sense of living completely in the moment. My bottom had stung for days and when the pink stain faded I almost missed it.

I watched the light in the men's eyes come on as I approached and introduced myself and I watched it go out as I slid away like the memory of other times. I avoided Mr Daviditz senior with his watery eyes and the same reddish moustache that his son had sheared off, skirted Mrs Ormsby with her polished brogues and the perfume of mucking out, and made my way towards the log fire where Simon was dancing attendance on Zach Kessler with his granite jaw and wavy grey hair. He dwarfed everyone in the room and my hand looked like a white flower as it entered his palm.

'We didn't get a chance to say hello,' I said. 'Bella di Millo.'

'My daughter,' Simon explained, and I rolled my eyes.

'Yeah, how do you do,' said Mr Kessler. He was looking appreciatively at my breasts.

'You must be the Big Player,' I said, and Simon's cheeks coloured.

'That's what they say.'

'I'm going to do business studies at university.'

'Yeah, well, when you're ready, don't do any business in this country,' he advised. 'Too much red tape.'

He was looking at Simon who shrugged apologetically. 'This is England. These things take time.'

I was intrigued. 'What takes time?' I took Zach Kessler's arm. 'You can tell me. I'm Italian.'

'Nah, you wouldn't understand.'

'I'm a *very* quick learner.'

His steely blue eyes swept over me. 'I bet you are.'

'So, come on, tell me.'

As he turned back to Simon, Zach Kessler took out the largest cigar I'd ever seen. 'You explain, you're the attorney,' he said. He bit the end off the cigar and dropped it among the vol-au-vent scraps.

'Zach is buying a high-rise in Battersea,' Simon began and I watched Mr Kessler holding a match to the cigar, drawing the flame over the end. 'It used to belong to what's called a housing trust and the people pay inappropriate rents. The trust went bankrupt and Zach bought the freehold.'

I squeezed his arm. 'Well done,' I said, and he slid his arm around my waist.

'Go on,' he said to Simon. 'I'm dying to hear the rest.'

'Zach's company is going to turn the flats into luxury residences and sell them at their true value.'

'What's wrong with that?' I asked.

'Nothing's wrong with it. It's market forces,' Mr Kessler

said. 'People living there have to move somewhere appropriate.'

'The people are being offered the chance to buy the properties, naturally,' added Simon.

'And he's kicking his heels, churning his fees.' He took the cigar out of his mouth and leaned down. 'That's lawyers. Can't do without them. Can't kill them and get away with it.' He paused. 'Except maybe in Tennessee.'

Mr Kessler turned to let out an enormous cloud of smoke that filled the room and made me feel quite dizzy. He squeezed my hip bone and it was meant to be gentle but an electric charge zipped down my leg and made me weak at the knees.

'Are you really a billionaire?' I asked.

'Yeah, but only in dollars.'

'Then if you gave me a half million you wouldn't really miss it.'

'Only on principle,' he said. 'In this life, no one will do anything for you, unless it's good for them. That's the way it is. In the end, there's just you. You're on your own.'

I stood there looking up at Zach Kessler and the way he looked back it felt as if I had been let in on a secret. I also realised something else. He was the first man I'd ever been actually attracted to, I mean, in *that* sense, and he must have picked up on my confused thoughts. I retrieved his cigar as if I were going to take a puff and pushed it back into his mouth.

'When you're in business give me a call.'

'I intend to,' I said.

Mother kept a careful eye on me all over Christmas and it wasn't until New Year's Eve that she went alone into Canterbury to have her hair done. It was then that Simon Daviditz sprung his surprise and I, in turn, sprung mine.

He tapped on my door and entered with his hands hiding something behind his back. He was wearing his naughty boy look and play clothes, a polo shirt and blue jeans that had grown too tight.

'Look what I found,' he said. 'Father Christmas left it in the wrong place.'

103

He gave me a parcel wrapped in shiny gold paper.

'For me?' I put my arms around his neck to kiss the corners of his mouth.

'Open it.'

I got all breathless with excitement as if I didn't know what I was going to find and made a big show of slowly peeling back the paper. Inside there was a gold box and inside the box was the smallest set of bra and panties in the history of the world.

'*Du Paris*,' he mumbled with that French accent people have when they can't speak French.

'They're just *so* pretty.'

We stood there for like *an hour* with Dallas McTee staring at me over his shoulder.

'Do you want me to ...'

He nodded vigorously. I smiled, and kept smiling. I remembered the words of Zach Kessler as if they were written in indelible ink in the back of my mind and the heavy, brittle feeling in my chest didn't seem quite so bad.

I pointed up at the ceiling. 'Upstairs,' I said. 'Ten minutes,' and when he finally got it he backed out of my room with his teeth shining.

In the bathroom I undressed, plaited my hair and washed my face. I was pale as ivory as if my Italian skin was slowly turning English. The new undies weighed no more than butterfly wings and were spun from fine golden thread like the filigree on goblets in royal palaces. After he'd had my breasts and bottom in his palms, Simon Daviditz knew what size to buy.

I put on the black dress I'd worn at Daddy's funeral, my hat with the veil and white trainers. If it's wrong, it's right. Everything I needed was already waiting in the attic, except the camera, which I took with me. I attached it to the tripod I'd placed behind the low beams in the corner and focused on the pathway of light stretching between the dormer windows. I filmed myself for a couple of seconds and rushed back to check. Then I put on *I'm A Bitch*.

I'm a bitch and I like it

104

I'm a bitch and I like it
I'm a bitch and I like it

I was standing in the light path when he entered. He came towards me.

'Take a hike. On your bike. I'll do *anything* you like,' I whispered, singing softly, changing the words.

He was standing so close I could feel the heat of his body through the thin fabric of the dress. I turned slowly and gave the camera eye a tragic look. I dropped my head and the veil toppled over my eyes. I remained motionless as his fingers fumbled at the zip running down the back of the dress. He lowered it slowly, enjoying the moment, like it was his turn to unwrap a last-minute gift. The dress fell from my shoulders. He took a step back to study me in the golden underwear. He ran his thumbs over my hip bones like a sculptor seeking the figure inside the block of stone.

'You are the most beautiful thing I've ever seen, Bella,' he said and raised the veil on my hat.

I dropped my head to one side. *Thing*, I thought. A piece of bric-à-brac you might pick up at a flea market, and I remembered the way he had inspected me at Daddy's funeral. Dallas McTee was still singing away and I didn't have that much time.

'Take your shirt off,' I whispered.

His eyes were glassy and glazed. He was unsure what miracles were in store. As his shirt hit the floor, it occurred to me that Mr Daviditz was crossing the Rubicon.

'Jeans,' I murmured.

As he lowered the zip it was like a Christmas balloon was hidden there, his tummy welling out over his big white pants. It took him so long to get his legs out of his jeans I had to slip away and start the music over again.

I'm a bitch and I like it
I'm a bitch and I like it
I'm a bitch and I like it

I hate to admit it, but I was getting to like it. The beat was great and I had to refrain from dancing around the attic. I stood close to Mr Daviditz in his white pants and finally he did what he'd been planning to do. He turned me round, I looked sulky and terrified at the camera, and he removed my top. He turned me back to face him, Pinkie and Perky in his two palms.

'May I?'

He dropped his head down to my pink nipples, taking them one after the other and sucking at them like a newborn baby. While all this slurping was going on, he began to roll down those little golden knickers, slowly, as if I wouldn't notice, or it would turn me on. I didn't know. Or care. I was thinking about Zach Kessler and I was thinking about Mr Lawrence, and I'm not sure why, but I leaned over the arm of the long leather sofa below the dormer window and presented the gift of my white bottom highlighted for the camera by the winter sunlight. Mr Daviditz wasn't at first sure what this meant.

'Ah, Bella, Bella.'

'I've been naughty,' I whispered, and finally he got the message.

'And what do we do with naughty girls?' he asked

'We punish them,' I replied.

This was not something that Mr Daviditz had ever imagined but I had a feeling that once a girl's bottom is in the air the natural instinct is to give it a good hard smack and that's what he did, well, not that hard, it was quite soft actually. I wriggled and sighed with contentment and the next one was a bit harder, the sting as the blood fled from the surface of the skin reminding me that for the first time that Christmas break I felt alive.

I didn't move. I pushed my bottom up and Mr Daviditz was less cautious in his approach, slapping me over and over again, drumming my bottom as if he were beating dust from a carpet, slap, slap, slap, slap, coating the surface until it felt as if I was sitting on a bonfire. This was my second smacking but it was different to the first. My thighs weren't wet and my pussy was as dry as grave dust.

I stood and turned towards him. He pushed his face at me

and as I felt the touch of his lips my tummy churned. It was just too *yuck*, too intimate. Kissing was something you do for fun with people you like and I moved my mouth away. He was fiddling about in his pants until he found his bent little penis and set it free. He curled my fingers around the thing and I remained motionless as if unsure what to do. He put his hand over mine and showed me how to slide the loose skin in gentle forceful strokes up and down the shaft.

He was panting like old Jake as I got the hang of it. I edged slowly round, changing the angle, showing the camera a mystified look, my long fingers moving to the rhythm, up and down, up and down.

A squeal escaped from me as a plump finger started to burrow its way into my pubic hair and almost immediately his body was jerking forward in rapid, uncontrolled spasms. I thought about Mr Lawrence, the way he had slid his big cock back down my throat after he'd sprayed my face and it didn't matter. It didn't matter at all. Simon Daviditz pressed himself against me and I felt his hot come sliding wetly down my thigh. For all the pushing and poking between my legs, I was still dry.

The track was coming to an end.

'Was that a car pulling up?' I whispered.

He became still for a moment, then gathered his clothes and hurried to the door. He stopped and glanced back with a sheepish grin as if we had unfinished business and I thought, how right, we do.

I sat on the floor in the bridge of light, naked except for my white trainers, and cried and cried until the video tape came to an end.

Chapter Nine

I WAS FIVE FEET eight inches tall and weighed 100 pounds, which was just so, like, totally symmetric. The New Year had begun and, as I stood under the hot shower, it felt such a relief to be back with the girls. They were my family now.

Saskia and Tara had totally changed. Like Dallas McTee they seemed older, cooler, more chic, more *everything*. During the holidays they had gone to Spain where they had pulled two boys from Henry's school named Xavier and Sergio, who were related to General Franco. They, too, were twins, and being identical the *Mademoiselles* Scott-Wallace didn't know which one they'd done it with and as they'd done it twice they were counting it as two hits rather than one.

A shadow entered the shower. Two hands covered my eyes.

'Happy birthday to you. Squashed tomatoes and stew.'

Saskia twisted me round and a little tongue wormed into my mouth. She was dead thin and her breasts were swelling up nicely after doing it twice. I loved the feel of her long hand stroking my bottom. We sucked face, as Americans say, for like ages, and I remembered Simon Daviditz trying to stick his mouth all over me.

'*He* tried to kiss me,' I said.

'Vile.'

'I had to toss him off.' She pulled away and stared into my eyes. I grinned. 'For the camera,' I added.

'Brilliant.'

We kissed some more. 'I finished editing our video. It's absolutely amazing,' I told her.

'Good. We need the money.'

'What for?'

'I don't know. I just *know* we need it,' she replied.

'We're living in desperate times,' I said, and it sounded like a song title.

'Henry was blown out that you didn't come to Spain,' Saskia went on. 'In the chapel there's an old bed for smoking heroin with curtains and stuff. That's where he was going to do you.'

I was quiet for a moment. 'What's it like?'

She shrugged and pulled a face. 'It sucks,' she said. 'You know, lots of grunting and groaning, and it's over in like ten seconds.' She pushed her pubic bone against mine. 'Bang. Bang. Bang. Bang. Groan. Groan. Groan.'

I soaped my fingers and slid them into her. She did the same to me and we slid over each other singing: *I'm a bitch and I like it.*

We kissed properly again. Her fingers moved inside me. I rolled my hips and felt warm spasms whipping my insides to cream. As I started to come, Saskia went down on her knees, filled me with her tongue and it was just *awesome*.

On Saturday I went straight to the building society. I had £262 in my account and added £180 from my birthday money. Just £442 between me and starvation and I had to get new lipstick, body cream, face wash, eye-liner and that whitening toothpaste that comes in tiny tubes and costs a fortune. The smaller the boxes the more they charged and I wondered if anyone else had realised that.

Jason was pleased to see me. He said I looked older and I told him I was.

'I've just had another birthday, as it happens.'

I took off my coat because it was so hot in the sex shop and Jason stroked his designer stubble while he gave me a radical body search. I was wearing blue jeans, which are always sexy, a wide strappy belt and a white crossover top with the lace from a pink bra trimming the deep v of the neckline.

'You know somink, Honey, we have to get another of them dance sessions going,' he said and lit up professionally with his Zippo. 'Could be a ton in it for you.'

'Tonne of what?'

'Hundred quid, darling. What do they teach you at that school of yourn?'

From my bag I took out a plain brown envelope with the DVD and my script with the unfilmed extra scene. I had printed it out in the IT room at school.

'Is this what I fink it is?'

'Just a demo,' I replied. I had pixelated the twins' faces and thought pixelated was such a cool word for the twins. My own face was hidden by the devil mask, although anyone who knew my body would know it was me.

Jason dropped the envelope in the drawer.

'Do you know Christian Thomas?' I asked, changing the subject. He blew a couple of smoke rings and shook his head. 'Sort of good-looking with lots of wavy dark hair.'

'Don't ring no whatsits.'

'He drives an old Jaguar.'

'Oh, yeah, the la-di-da one. Why, what's he after?'

'He's not after anything. I just wondered what he bought?'

'Uniforms, whips, chains.'

'Gruesome.'

'Wouldn't know, darling, not my cup of tea,' said Jason and I thought, how sweet, he works in the sex shop and doesn't know what goes on in the big bad world outside.

He promised to pass on the DVD to his *contact* and wrote down my mobile number. I buttoned my coat, clamped on my headphones and ran through the drizzle to Greens where the twins were dressed as chess pieces, one in white, one in black, chain-smoking with the local chavs.

Troy was at another table talking to the fat girl with spots who worked in the kitchen at school and, if looks could kill, I'd be in the cemetery beside Daddy. I totally blanked Troy, but when I sat down he sloped up with his funny little dance and pointed at me.

'Oi, I know you.'

'No you don't,' I replied.

'Bella, right?' He sat down and put his arm around my shoulders.

'Do you mind?'

'Do you mind?' he repeated and the chavs behind us fell about as if he were the funniest man alive.

'This is Troy,' I said, introducing him to the twins.

They did their party trick, looking at each other, then looking back and speaking at the same time.

'How do you do.'

'Very well, I'm sure,' said Troy, trying to imitate them.

'Excuse me,' I said, removing Troy's arm as if it were a dead branch. '*Hasta la vista*,' I said to the twins, and made my way back out into the street.

Troy was on a skateboard and soon caught up. 'Where you going?'

'Nowhere.'

He jarred the back of the board with one foot, leapt up on the pavement and swirled round in front of me.

'You wanna see my guitar and that?' His blue eyes were sparkling.

'Not particularly.'

He shot off, jumped the board back down onto the street and almost got killed by a granny driving an orange sports car and I thought: grannies in sports cars, what is the world coming to? She was waving her fist and let out a trail of rainbow smoke as she swerved. He kept going, chasing after the car, did the kicking trick and tumbled in a heap on the pavement. I ran to catch up.

'You're going to kill yourself one of these days.'

'Live fast. Die young,' he said and I thought that was so brill.

I pulled him up. 'Can you play anything then?' I asked and he walked along rubbing his shoulder.

''Course I can,' he said. 'I know loik, *all* the chords.'

I looked at my watch, a little Cartier, another mystery surprise I'd found under my pillow at Christmas. 'I can't be long,' I told him.

'Fuckin' prison,' he said.

He scooted along beside me. The shops became more tumbledown. The off-licence had the appearance of a cage and the man inside bending over the counter looked like a Neanderthal. Where the street curved along the coast, we turned the other way into a maze of half-demolished houses with slits where windows had been. Smoke from abandoned fires curled into the cold air. I pulled up my coat collar and covered my ears. Fat pigeons were stamping about in the wet gutters among cars without wheels and small children carrying sticks.

'Great 'ere, innit?'

'Home is just somewhere to get away from,' I said because I'd read it once in *Cosmo*.

We passed through metal doors covered with dents into one of the grey blocks. Troy punched the lift buttons. 'Fucked,' he said, and I followed him up six flights of concrete stairs. We reached a pale blue door with three huge locks that were only for show because we walked straight in.

The narrow hallway was made even narrower by the boxes piled along each wall, cases of long life milk, breakfast cereal in coffin-sized packets, plastic sacks of oven chips. The living room was crowded with black armchairs with orange cushions on a sea of orange carpet and a girl about my age with sallow skin pitted with zits turned from watching the largest television I had ever seen.

'What?' she said.

'Fuck off,' said Troy. He left the skateboard behind the sofa. I smiled at the girl and followed him along the hall to his bedroom.

'Who's that?' I asked him.

'No one.'

Like the hall, Troy's room was heaped from floor to ceiling like a bombed museum with clothes, smelly shoes, a Gameboy, a TV stacked with DVDs and obscure gadgets. There was a red guitar on the unmade bed.

Troy plugged the guitar into an amp, hit the strings and my heart sank.

'Is it in tune?' I asked.

'Near enough.'

'Do you have a tuning fork?'

'A what?

'It doesn't matter.'

He strummed away at something. He had all the actions and his voice wasn't bad. He just needed about a million years' practice.

Under a T-shirt with Eminem on it was a keyboard. It was connected to the same amp and when his solo came to an end I tentatively picked out the latest version of *Come To Me*. I closed my eyes.

> *You come to me, the devil in disguise*
> *You come to me, secrets in your eyes*
> *Come to me. Come to me*
> *You come to me, I feel the touch of money*
> *You come to me, you're the taste of honey*
> *Come to me. Come to me*

I had worked out an instrumental break called the middle-eight, then let myself go on the last verse. I adored having an audience and my deep contralto swelled out and filled the small room.

> *Come back to me, you just can't see*
> *You're the only one, the one for me*
> *Come to me. Come come come, come to me*
> *Come to me. Come come come, come to me*

I opened my eyes and saw the spotty girl gaping at me through the door. An older, thinner version of the girl was standing there in dangly earrings with her arms folded leaning against the frame. She took the cigarette from her mouth.

'See, that's the way to do it, innit.'

She was nodding like a wise woman at Troy and he looked like he was going to kill someone. He turned to me.

'Fucking slag,' he said.

The spotty thing was grinning.

'You can fuck off as well,' Troy screamed. 'Go on, get out.'

He leapt up and chased the girl from the doorway. The woman just took another puff on her cigarette and shook her head.

'Hello, I'm Bella ...' I said and stopped before I added my surname.

'You are, are you?'

'Me mother,' said Troy.

'Where 'djoo learn to play loik that?' she asked.

'I had lessons.'

'See,' Troy spat at his mother. 'Now, if you don't mind. This is my room.'

She wandered off and he closed the door. He threw himself on the bed looking beautiful and despondent, and I felt so guilty because I'd made him feel silly.

'I'm sorry,' I said.

'What for?'

'I don't know.'

He turned away and I felt ... I wasn't sure how I felt; they were feelings I'd never had before. I stroked his bronze hair. It was soft like a girl's and he liked it. He turned and looked vulnerable with his frightened blue eyes.

'It's not fair,' he said.

'Troy, nothing's fair. There's just you. You're on your own.'

'Yeah, you're not.'

'Aren't I?'

That made him think and while he was thinking I leaned over and pressed my lips against his. It was awkward but nice, like when you learn to ski. He started pushing at me with his teeth and making stupid noises. I let my coat fall on the floor among the rubble and swung my legs over him, pinning him to the bed. I held him down with the flat of my hand.

'Slowly,' I said, and leaned down towards him, my hair spilling around his narrow face.

I held his head still and kissed the corners of his mouth. I ran my little pink tongue over his smooth cheeks, then his lips, the inside of his gums.

'Softly.'

His teeth opened. Our tongues met and swirled together. I loosened my crossover top and when I pulled it from my shoulders he gazed my breasts in their lacy bra as if his eyes were about to go pop. I unhooked my bra and he sucked my

114

nipples, rolling them around his tongue as they swelled, and a delicious feeling ran through me.

I stroked his hair and felt him growing hard through my tight jeans. Pussy was getting wet and I wanted to take off the rest of my clothes and draw his tongue up inside me. I wanted to suck him and just thinking about it made me all warm and goosepimply. I pulled his T-shirt over his head and kissed his neck and chest. I kept going, down to his belly-button. I undid his belt and his jeans just sprang open.

I was just sliding my long fingers into his boxers when my mobile played *Come To Me*. It was only on Saturday that I could leave it turned on and I didn't want to miss a call.

'Honey.'

I thought for a moment it was a wrong number then remembered that was my stage name.

'Yes.'

'It's Christian Thomas.'

'Where did you get my number from?'

'From Jason ...'

'Then that's a lucky coincidence. Do you know a music teacher?'

'Oddly enough, I do. My next-door neighbour teaches piano and guitar.'

'That's what they call serendipity,' I said and Christian Thomas laughed.

'Come over, you have the address.'

'We'll be there in,' I glanced at my watch, '20 minutes. I don't have long.'

'You're always rushing.'

'*Tempus Fugit*.'

Troy was stroking the toggles down my back and it was nice. I had the mobile in one hand and his warm hard cock in the other. I clicked off and helped him ease down his jeans and boxers.

He looked at me looking at him. His cock was so pretty and slid smoothly into my mouth as if it had been made to measure. I licked the little groove at the top, flicking it with my tongue, then swallowed it down to the base, up and down, slowly, smoothly like you're playing tennis. I kept my eyes open so I could watch him. He had his hands lightly on my shoulders, his eyes closed and after about two seconds a painful look crossed his features as he started to come, and he just kept coming and coming, and it was just so beautiful.

My mouth was like totally full and I kissed him slowly and let his hot creamy sperm run through my teeth into his mouth.

'Marzipan,' I whispered.

He was shaking all over, his little hips thrusting up at me. I slipped it back in my mouth to suck out every drop, and I thought I'm *really* good at this and it's all due to Mr Lawrence.

I glanced at my watch. Time really *does* fly. Then looked sternly down at his little pink soldier. 'There, is that better?' I asked, and tucked it back in his boxers. 'We have about five minutes to get to the harbour.'

Troy unearthed a bicycle from among the plastic furniture in the living room. The girl with zits hexed me with a mean look and I thought one day I'd teach her about skin care and then she wouldn't be so nasty.

I followed Troy down the concrete stairs with the bike on his shoulder. I sat on the saddle, my legs sticking out, and he pedalled like a demon through the traffic and I thought live fast, die young. The wind propelled us along the sea front. We aquaplaned over the damp cobbles by the harbour and fell off right in front of the flint cottages below the lighthouse.

'The Myth of Adolescent Invulnerability,' said Christian Thomas. He was outside cleaning salt spray from an elaborate door knocker in the shape of an Indian goddess.

I stood and dusted myself down. 'What are you doing?'

'She needs a lot of attention,' he replied, and made a big show rubbing the yellow cloth between the shiny brass knockers on the knocker.

Troy had untangled himself from his bike and was looking at his trainers as if for damage. 'This is Troy,' I said. 'He needs guitar lessons.'

'Hello, Christian Thomas,' said Christian Thomas. He stuck out his hand and the way Troy looked at that moment I thought he was going to hit him.

Finally he shook hands. 'Troy,' he announced, his voice an octave lower than normal, and carried on inspecting his feet.

'Now, what have you two been up to?' asked Mr Thomas, pinning me with one of his long hard stares, and I knew he knew exactly what we'd been up to. My inflamed lips and the smell of marzipan were a dead giveaway.

I pointed to my nose and he laughed.

'Come,' he said. 'It isn't far.'

He knocked at the next cottage and an old man with a moustache and greasy tie opened the door and I thought, *wow*, is he having a bad hair decade. He looked like Beethoven only madder.

'Vladimir, a musician anxious for instruction,' said Mr Thomas, glancing briefly at Troy. 'This is Mr Gropius.'

'Hello,' said Troy and I thought, mmm, he's a fast learner.

'How do you do,' said Mr Gropius. 'Do come in.'

The cottages had that magical quality of appearing small from the outside and growing bigger as you entered. The wind roared across the grey sea, the waves pounded the rocks, but in the living room with its leaded glass windows and wooden beams it was completely silent.

'So, what do you want to play?' asked Mr Gropius. He had an accent that was hard to place.

'You know, hip-hop.'

'Excellent. And the instrument?'

'A Stratocaster.'

'Very good,' said Mr Gropius as if we were talking about a Stradivarius. He opened a tall cupboard and hanging inside the back of the door was an electric guitar. 'Now, it's £40 an hour ...'

'40 quid?!'

We were all quiet for a moment. Money always does that.

'It's worth it, Troy,' I said reassuringly.

'Yeah, but I ain't got it, have I.'

I glanced at Christian Thomas. 'Lend me £40. I'll give it back to you.'

He had a little grin as he slipped the two £20 notes from his wallet. I gave them to Troy. 'Here.'

Troy's mouth dropped open. 'What if I don't pay you back?'

'Then you get £40 once and lose a friend forever.'

He weighed this up before handing the money on.

Mr Gropius folded the money into a brass box on the mantel beside an old photograph of several women in long white dresses and large hats and two men with tail suits and picturesque moustaches.

'Sit. Sit,' he said to Troy. He did so and Mr Gropius placed the guitar in the classical position across in his two arms.

'Do you have a pen?' I asked. I looked at my watch. 'Never mind,' I glanced at Troy. 'Give your phone number to Mr Thomas, he can text it to me.'

He just nodded and Mr Thomas followed me out. The wind was cold and the air smelled of fish and chips. We walked along the harbour wall and came to a stop at the main road. Christian Thomas was staring like he'd never seen me before.

'You look positively ...'

'Gorgeous?' I suggested.

'Well, yes, that, of course. But I was thinking how much you reminded me of a fruit salad.'

Chapter Ten

WHEN DALLAS MCTEE CAME to do a gig in Canterbury I almost wet myself I was so excited. Of course, I had to sneak out of school, the first time I'd done that at night, and luckily I had an accomplice with a green Jaguar to help me.

Christian Thomas was waiting on the promenade. I climbed into the back and he fired the big engine. I took off my uniform and folded it into the backpack with my shoes and socks. I was wearing my little gold undies, probably the sexiest set of undies in the world if you've got the figure for it. I put on a red sarong, a pair of Kurt Geiger gold strappies with towering heels and a red leather jacket I'd swapped for the silly clothes Mother had bought me for Christmas. I climbed over the seats and used the mirror to check my make-up. I was wearing heart sunglasses and lowered them to study my companion.

He turned to examine my outfit and before we ended up in a ditch I turned his head back to the road. He jiggled the mirror into the right position and my stomach lurched as he put his foot down. He produced a camera from the glove compartment. 'Do you know how it works?'

'It's a camera, isn't it?'

'It was an absolute *bitch* to get two tickets. I told them you were a photographer, it would be quite a scoop if we could get a decent photograph,' he said. 'And there's this.' He dangled a red lace with a plastic card printed with the words Dallas McTee *The Bitch Tour* and PRESS in big letters.

I put it round my neck but it interfered with the line of my top. I shortened it into a choker and I was pleased the red lace went with my jacket and sarong. Christian glanced down at my legs. They were pale in the green light from the dashboard and it reminded me that I really did have to do some research into that bronzing oil.

'No,' I said, and he kept his hands on the wheel all the way to the reserved parking behind The Marlowe. The cathedral towers rose up in the distance. There were crowds everywhere and I felt mediaeval as I strode into the press entrance with my gold heels clicking.

All the seats had been taken out and girls dressed in their best in Calvin Klein's and little else were pushing through the entrance doors at the back of the theatre. We were lucky to have a great view but I did wonder what it would be like to be at the front with the fans. There was music I didn't recognise but it had a good beat that made you want to get up and dance. I slung the red leather jacket over the back of a chair. It was hot and my body was tingling as if I was fully awake for the first time.

At the back of the press area was a bar and the journalists were fighting to get their hands on the free drinks. I was strutting around taking pictures and some of the photographers gave up the struggle and started taking pictures of me.

Christian returned from the bar and I acted as if I wasn't very pleased when he led me away like I was his personal property but it was nice to feel protected.

'Never trust the press,' he whispered.

'We are the press,' I reminded him.

'Exactly.'

He'd got me a coke and I was so happy I just drank it.

Some message passed telepathically among the crowd and, at exactly eight o'clock, everyone raised their arms above their heads and started clapping, softly at first, and slowly growing louder, a constant boom, boom like a giant heart beating.

The lights grew dim and suddenly it was black with just a few prickles of light. The noise was mesmerizing and gave me the feeling that we were taking part in something decidedly pagan, all those girls with damp bodies chanting Dallas, Dallas, Dallas, and I suddenly knew what it must be like to be at an orgy. I was writhing like a fish in dark water and giggled as I closed my eyes and imagined all those hands reaching for me.

A single spotlight lit the centre of the stage and a scruffy man with straggly hair came out through the gap in the curtains looking completely lost. He tapped the microphone to make sure it was working. He coughed. Then he sniffed.

Then he said: 'Ladies and gentlemen, please welcome the fabulous, the enduring, the sensational, the greatest performer in the world ...'

The curtains opened. Spotlights criss-crossed the hall like there was a war and the music exploded from speakers the size of little bungalows.

'... Dallas McTee ...'

She was standing with her back to the audience at the top of a flight of steps in a long black cape with a hood. The girls at the front surged forward into the black ring of security guards. They were screaming, the guitars were rocking and the lights span into bangles of red and blue as she turned and descended the stairs.

Her face was hidden by a gold mask she held on a stick. She stopped at the front of the stage and two men appeared from the flaps, one peeled back the cape and I thought: Oh, my God, that's not fair: she was wearing a gold top and a little gold sarong. The other man took the mask and she started singing Body, her first big hit.

Christian's arm stole around my waist to my hip bone. 'Better hips,' he whispered.

'I don't need reassuring,' I hissed and let him keep his hand there just for fun.

I was feeling great standing there with less on than Dallas. The crowd was growing hysterical as she raced around with her dancers and I was thinking that this must be the absolutely best thing in the world, singing your songs under the bright lights with thousands of people chanting your name. *Bella*, *Bella*, *Bella* and I wondered what made Dallas what she was; what made me me?

The show went on for two hours and Christian's fingers reached halfway down my knickers before I stopped him going any further. Dallas sang one slow number playing her acoustic guitar and I thought, wow, some of the girls at school play

121

better than that. Then she went through the songs on her last CD, which I knew by heart.

When it was over, the flashing lights span into darkness and the audience started chanting '*I'm A Bitch, I'm A Bitch*' over and over again. I thought the floor was going to give way when they began stamping their feet and when Dallas came back on stage wearing this gorgeous silver top and the smallest thong in the world, I had a feeling that it had been planned that way, that nothing was left to chance. She sang *I'm A Bitch* and everyone joined in.

'See you later,' I said to Christian and before he could stop me I made my way out of the press box, downstairs and along the corridor to the area backstage. There were various people loafing about looking self-important and, as I turned the corner, my way was barred by a bouncer with a big belly in his black T-shirt and a leather waistcoat that was just so passé. He took a long draw on his cigarette. I threw my shoulders back and pointed at my choker.

'Press,' I said.

'If you insist,' he replied, and pressed Pinkie like he was pressing a bell.

'Do you mind?'

'Not at all.'

'I'd like to pass.'

He crushed his fag beneath his heel and pointed at the pass hanging around his neck on a blue cord. It said ACCESS ALL AREAS.

'Please.'

'Can't be done, darling.'

'Please. Please. Please. It's really important.'

'No pass: no pass.'

He had folded his arms, his legs were wide apart and he was assessing me with a sort of sceptical curiosity.

'There's always a way,' I suggested. I lowered my sunglasses and gazed at him over the two red hearts.

He puffed out his cheeks. 'You know something, I just love this job,' he said.

He slipped his finger under my PRESS choker and drew me

along the corridor into an empty dressing room. I could hear the crowd still roaring for more in the auditorium but as the door closed the voices grew muffled and far away. He pointed at the tattoo on his right arm: it was that Rolling Stones tongue. It was blue and beginning to fade. Then he pointed to the little bird on his left arm.

'You know what that is?'

'A bird?'

'A swallow,' he said and unzipped his fly. He pointed at the two tattoos once more. 'Don't spit. Swallow.'

He thought this was terribly clever and I was wondering what else you would do. He pulled down his jeans and his cock sprang out of his boxers like a hat from a cracker. It wasn't pretty like Troy's or huge like Mr Lawrence's or short and fat like the thing Simon Daviditz had stuck in my hand. The bouncer's was bent like a banana and I nursed it slowly back and forth.

He was leaning against the wall and put his hand on top of my head. I dropped to balance on my haunches and, as I ran my little pink tongue over the tip and down like a feather along the warm skin, he began to gasp out, 'Oh yes, oh yes,' louder and louder like the audience screaming in the distance for Dallas McTee.

I had been feeling dead randy ever since Saskia had barged into the bathroom and now, when I closed my eyes, it was Mr Lawrence who came into my mind. It was strange, but that morning in the woodshed had once been a bad memory and now it was just something I thought of as valuable experience like helping people in Africa dig wells or something.

I wasn't, like, aroused by the bouncer. Sex was just something you use when you want to get what you want. It was easy. The bouncer was soon filling my mouth with his warm sperm. I removed the ACCESS ALL AREAS card from his neck and made my way to the inner sanctums of The Marlowe, the moment forgotten except for the lingering taste in my mouth. Chips, I thought, really fattening, especially after the coke.

At the end of the corridor, masses of people all talking loudly were crowded around the double doors that led to a large room. I squeezed in and for a change no one took any notice of me. All eyes were on Dallas McTee.

She was sitting in a big leather chair all damp and glowing, a tall black man with a shiny head massaging her feet. Everyone was saying, Jeez, that was great, cool, wicked, amazing, all that sort of thing and Dallas was sipping champagne through a long straw from a miniature bottle like you see on aeroplanes. Musicians were draped like discarded clothes over the sofas and rock babes with Celtic rings were massaging their sweaty bodies. There were girls with big bottoms rushing about with clipboards and some older men in jeans and ponytails – managers I assumed – all smoking, and everyone moving around Dallas as if she were the sun at the centre of her own little galaxy. I made my way through the throng and, when I raised my camera, Dallas slapped the black man's bald head and shouted at me.

'Hey, no photographs.'

I almost jumped out of my skin.

She was looking at me.

Dallas was looking at me.

Everyone hushed and, if they did carry on talking, their lips moved without any sound coming out. Dallas was examining me like Mr Daviditz on the day we buried Daddy. She beckoned and I approached slowly as if I were wading through syrup. There were butterflies in my tummy and I just hoped I looked my best. Dallas kept crooking her finger and I kept getting nearer like a moth to the flame and only stopped when I was practically on fire. She was staring at me as if I had a zit or something.

'Get me a Kleenex, Rupert,' she said to the black man with the bald head. He went lumbering off like a giant spider and Dallas pushed my sunglasses up into my hair so she could look into my eyes. I was wearing both passes, and these seemed to be of great interest to her. She took a firm grip on the ACCESS ALL AREAS pass and shook it.

'Have you been interfering with my staff?' she asked and I felt the blood rush up my neck.

'Well, kind of, it's like ...'

Thank heavens she didn't let me finish. She tugged at the pass and as I lowered my head towards her I thought, oh my God, she's going to kiss me. Instead she traced her fingertips over my cheek and then rubbed her thumb and fingers together in a way that reminded me of Mr Lawrence. At that moment, Rupert returned with a Kleenex. Dallas wiped her fingers and gave the Kleenex to me. I wiped my cheek and when I gave the Kleenex back to Rupert, Dallas laughed and that was the signal for everyone to relax and join in.

'That's disgusting,' Rupert said and minced off with the Kleenex held at arm's length.

Dallas sat back in her chair and looked me up and down. 'You're not exactly overdressed, are you,' she said. The girls with big bottoms laughed. I thought it was funny, too, although what struck me as even more amusing was that Dallas McTee had the same voice as Troy and the chavs.

'For a woman, less is always more,' I said, and something else struck me. In the newspapers it said she was 22, but close up Dallas looked really much older, like 25 at least.

'What paper are you from?'

'The local,' I answered. 'It would be a real scoop if I could get a photo.'

'No, no pictures after the show. I'm a wreck,' she said and I had a brilliant idea. I'd noticed the mask Dallas had worn at the beginning of her performance on a table and rushed off to get it.

'You can wear this,' I suggested.

'What, I need it, do I?'

'No, no, of course not. You're beautiful. It's just that you said ...'

'Don't do it if you don't want to, baby,' said one of the men in blue jeans.

'I'm not your baby, Baz. You're my baby. And I do whatever I want.'

She grabbed the mask and posed peering over the top with arched eyebrows as I took a couple of photos. Rupert had returned shaking his hands like he'd just washed them and I gave him the camera.

'Can we have one together? Please,' I said.

''Ere, 'ave you ever met anyone so pushy?' Dallas said to Rupert.

'Only you,' he replied.

'You know the trouble with this business, getting good people,' she said.

Rupert threw back his shoulders. 'You are such a bitch ...'

'... and I like it!'

And I thought, wow, that was so clever it sounded rehearsed.

Rupert had taken control of the photography session and had squeezed me into the leather armchair beside Dallas. He got us peeking out from either side of the mask before standing back and clicking away on the little camera. Dallas retrieved the champagne from the table. When she offered it to me I took a long hard suck on the straw and my head began to swim.

'You are fantastic,' I said. 'I know every one of your songs by heart.'

'Oh, yeah.'

'I play the piano and write songs and I want to be just like you.'

'Then make sure you get good people,' she said, and the way she looked at Rupert it was hard to know what she meant.

'I will. I promise. What else have I got to do?'

'You hear that, what has she got to do?'

'Bring your own Kleenex,' he said and as Dallas rocked about laughing she spilled champagne down my front. She tried to brush it away, which made it worse, but I didn't mind. All the other people had gone back to doing whatever they had been doing and it was hard to believe I had Dallas all to myself. We were pressed together so tightly our skin made sucking noises against the leather chair as she leaned over and licked the damp puddle on my chest. I wriggled and purred and she poured more champagne on me on purpose. It ran over my tummy and made my knickers wet.

'Do you like girls?' she asked me.

''Course,' I said. 'But I think I like boys more.'

'You're something else. What's your name?'

'Bella, I mean Honey. I'm not sure.'

Dallas dropped the straw from the champagne on the floor

126

and offered me the bottle. I shook my head.

'Never say no to champagne,' Rupert said sternly. 'It's the unwritten law.'

Dallas tipped back the bottle like I was a baby. She cradled me in her arms and, as I swallowed it down, I realised that the more you drink the more giggly and silly you feel. Rupert was back on the floor massaging Dallas's feet. He moved his palms up her legs, over her thighs and then across to my thighs and down my legs in a smooth motion that made my skin feel like champagne bubbles. He undid the straps, removed my gold shoes and started pressing his thumbs into my soles. It felt delicious and I wondered if it were true what the girls said about black men.

'He has magic hands,' Dallas whispered.

My eyelids dropped. The chair made a sighing sound and I rose into the air like a feather carried on the wind above the noise into a quiet place where the moon was passing through clouds just outside the windows. Two sets of hands started peeling off my little clothes, stroking my breasts, my bottom, my hips, the curly damp patch of my pubic hair. I loved being the centre of attention and this was Dallas McTee with her warm tongue worming its way between my thighs.

Suddenly I was flying again. Rupert lifted me up and placed me down on a narrow table with my head hanging over one end and my legs stretched out over the other. Dallas plunged deep into pussy and Rupert seemed to have lost his clothes and eased his cock into my open mouth. It felt like porcelain, smooth and perfect, and slid in and out with long, even strokes. It was the first time I'd taken a man in my mouth and a woman in my pussy at the same time and it was just the best ever.

As Rupert started to move faster, I bit gently on the warm flesh and felt long spasms like the warnings before an earthquake shuddering through me. The tremors went on and on. Then he came in fierce spurts and I came at the same time, my little body jerking so much Dallas had to hold my sides to stop me falling off the table.

When the eruption settled, they changed places. Rupert's bubbly come was sparkling in my mouth and Dallas drew it out and licked my cheeks and chin, over my eyes, my ears. Rupert's tongue was as long as his china cock and reached new places that he cleverly massaged, the tip caressing my little button and I started to climax again. It was different this time, longer and slower like I was jumping between two high buildings and I didn't know if I was ever going to reach the other side.

I'm not sure what happened next. I know the mood was broken by a knock on the door and, when it opened, the man standing in the light made me think of Mother when she entered my room at night.

It was Baz. He was holding the long cape Dallas had worn on stage and she stepped obediently into its embrace.

'You sweet like sugarcane, sugarbaby,' Rupert whispered in a Jamaican voice and it sounded strange because he'd been speaking really posh before.

Dallas turned in the doorway as I sat up. She was wearing my sunglasses.

'Gotta go,' she said.

Rupert was dressing. 'Don't look sad, sugar.'

'You didn't tell me what I have to do?'

He pulled on his shirt and leaned against the door jamb.

'Yeah?'

'To be a singer?'

'You want to hit the big time, baby? All you need is that elusive little four-letter word. And it ain't fuck: it's luck. Lots of luck.'

'Is that all?'

'Is that all?' He polished his bald head with his hand. 'That's for starters. You need a shitload of talent, amazing music, good arrangements, a great demo and a sexy little body.' He paused and pointed a finger at me like it was a gun. 'You get lucky, sugarbaby, everyone gonna wanna piece of your ass.'

'Wow.'

He made a peace sign with his long fingers. 'Keep it gangsta,' he said, and I sat cross-legged on the table with the bittersweet taste of champagne in my mouth and the moon was brighter now and my head just kept spinning, and I was wondering how I was going to make a demo.

Christian was leaning against the back of the Jaguar. The night was cold and I shivered in my little damp bra and sarong. He put the red jacket around my shoulders and it felt nice being held. He ran his palm over my hair and I thought this was what it would have been like if Daddy had been alive and he'd been waiting for me.

'Come on, it's warmer inside.'

He opened the door and we were soon rolling through the sleeping streets, the big car purring.

'I was beginning to worry about you,' he said. He was brushing his palm swiftly up and down my leg to make me warm.

'I like that,' I said. 'No one *really* cares.'

'Poor Honey.'

'It's not Honey. It's Bella.'

'What?'

'Isabella di Millo.'

'You're always full of surprises.'

He carried on stroking my leg. I pulled away and gave him the camera. 'I got some fab photos,' I said.

'That's brilliant ...'

'Christian, I have to make a music demo.'

'That shouldn't present a problem.'

'Shall I make you a tape?'

'Absolutely. As soon as possible.'

I drew my legs up into the leather seat feeling content. The skin on my cheeks was stretched tight and I remembered with a little smile that Dallas McTee had started out rubbing sperm off my face and ended up slurping it back on again. I'd had like the best sex *ever* and it was odd that Rupert had said don't be sad because I did feel a bit sad, but that's the same as being melancholic and that's normal for a Capricorn.

The car was blowing out warm air. It had started to rain and I watched the wipers swishing back and forth. The tyres were going bumpety-bump, my head was spinning, and I couldn't recall whether Zach Kessler was still staying at The Dorchester. I must have dropped off to sleep and woke feeling groggy when the car engine was turned off. We were parked across the bay, the convent silhouetted against the black sky.

'We're here,' Christian said.

I scrambled into the back and changed into my school uniform. Christian took the step-ladder I had told him to bring from the boot of the car. There were spars on the convent gate to climb out but I needed a ladder to climb back in again. He locked the car and we followed the torchlight down the zigzag steps. When we reached the beach I couldn't quite believe what I was seeing and gasped as I looked back for an explanation.

'God, the tide's still in,' he said.

'Did you plan this?'

'Honey ... Bella, I resent that.'

'You live by the sea. You know about tides and things.'

'No I don't.'

I stood there, hands on hips, really angry. 'I'll get sent down now, and it's your fault.'

He thought for a moment. 'The tide's already on the turn. In an hour or so the bay will be clear. It will be better then, anyway.'

'No it won't.'

'It's only just gone midnight. The insomniacs will still be reading. Look,' he said and pointed at the light in the tower. 'You won't get caught if you go over the wall later.'

I traipsed back up to the promenade and we drove round the coast to Christian's cottage. I was wide awake now. I had a headache, which I'd never had before, and felt hungry at the same time.

'I'm famished,' I said.

'What would you like?'

'Nothing.'

The cottage was warm and it reminded me how cold it was in the dorm. The living room was lined with shelves full of interesting things I wasn't interested in, there were modern paintings, Indian statues that were just *so* rude and a big soft black velvet sofa where I deposited my blazer. Christian put on music I recognised.

'Bolero,' he said.

'Where are your books?' I asked.

He rushed over and his apostle eyes became shiny blue as he pointed to the narrow row. 'I'm a biographer mainly,' he said proudly. 'And this is for you. My first novel.'

It was called *All Things Considered*.

'What's it about?'

'Everything.'

'If you write about everything it's like writing about nothing,' I said and dropped into the velvet sofa.

I opened the book in the middle and started reading aloud: *There is an inch of wine at the bottom of the bottle. Silence outside the shuttered windows. The night is black like animal fur without stars or vagrant moon.*

While I continued reading he started undoing my blouse. I let him because I was bored and there was a lot of time to kill before the tide went out. He untied my shoelaces, rolled down my socks and stuffed them neatly inside the shoes. He unzipped my navy skirt, pulling it down, and drew my arms from my blouse. The champagne had dried in silver rings on the golden underwear. He gently eased down the little knickers and unhooked the top. He'd seen me without anything on at the sex shop but I knew he'd been dying to take my clothes off himself ever since.

'Christian, I haven't, you know ...'

'You mean you're unplucked,' he said and looked so pleased as he plucked me straight up into his arms I didn't want to say that I hadn't been planning to either.

He carried me upstairs and I was surprised how strong he was. We entered a low room with wood beams and he settled me down at the very centre. 'It's not plucking that you need, my girl, it's discipline.'

'But I haven't been naughty.'

He licked his finger, rubbed it over my cheek and put the finger in his mouth to suck it. 'I would say you have been very naughty indeed.'

As he was speaking, he lifted my left arm above my head and attached my wrist to a strap suspended on a chain from the ceiling. Then he attached my right wrist. I was hanging there, stretched out, my breasts pushed forward, my bottom sticking out all perky and I thought I rather liked this, naked, the centre of attention. My body was glowing.

'Now, we don't want to mark you, but we do want you to know what discipline is, now, don't we?'

I didn't think it was a question, but I nodded.

He went to a drawer and removed what I discovered was a gag, a leather thing with a rubber ball in the middle and two straps that he buckled at the back of my head. 'We don't want to wake my neighbours, Honey.'

I suckled on the rubber ball and shook my head.

'Agh, yes. Bella.'

He went back to the bureau and searched about until he found what he was looking for. He returned with the sort of slipper an old man would wear. It had a rubber sole and when he slapped his palm it sounded loud. Very loud. My little bottom that I was so proud of was going to get some attention and I gripped my teeth into the rubber ball as Mr Thomas circled behind me.

'Just six,' he said.

And the slipper came down across my bum like a branding iron. It wasn't painful. It was agonising. It was like nothing I could imagine. Mr Lawrence had given me a spanking, but that was with his hand. The slipper was something else. Crash. Down it came again, searing my flesh and sending shockwaves up and down my spine. Tears were flooding my eyes. Snot rolled from my nose.

He changed angles and brought the slipper down once more, the sound ricocheting over the low ceiling and I'm sure he must have woken Mr Gropius from his dreams in the cottage next door. I was dancing around on tiptoes, trying to avoid the slap of the slipper and was aware in some peculiar way that by moving my bottom from side to side I was making the target more tempting.

How many was that?

Three.

Three more.

The fourth was harder than the first three. My tummy felt

132

weird all of a sudden and with the pain there was a tingly feeling like diving into a warm swimming pool. I could feel the heat from the beating rising over my back and spreading down my legs.

The fifth came down, crashing on my flesh like a giant door closing, and I realised that I was leaking. Girlie juices were trickling from my pussy and coating my thighs. Then the last one came.

Number six.

He put a lot of effort into it and as the rubber sole on the slipper branded the cheeks of my bottom I sort of exploded in a fit of ecstasy. I was coming. Really coming. The contractions were so long and explosive I thought I was having a baby. My insides had turned to liquid and as I stood there hanging from the chains the most embarrassing thing happened. I wet myself. Golden pee squirted in a long stream from my pussy and formed a puddle around my feet.

Mr Thomas leaned over and kissed my ear. 'You are a miracle,' he said.

He unstrapped me from the chains, lifted me again into his arms and carried me back downstairs to the kitchen where he laid me down on the pine table. He straightened me like I was being measured for a coffin and then raced off.

'Don't move.'

I couldn't speak because I was still wearing the gag and I didn't want to move because I felt as if I were floating. Girl juices were flooding out of me still and my bum hurt. It really hurt. But it was a new pain, a pleasant pain, a delicious pain that made my whole body feel silky and totally alive.

Mr Thomas was away for ages and I laid there thinking this is it, this is what all the girls obsess about. *I'm going to get done*, I said to myself, and remembered the twins when they came back after Christmas and they'd already done it twice.

I had been sort of saving it for Henry, their brother, or Troy even, because they were young and it's natural and doesn't mean anything doing it when you're teenagers. It was just sex. But Mr Thomas was 30. He was a man and I didn't want him to think I was just a kid.

When he came back dressed as a French maid I totally freaked.

He removed the gag and smiled down at me.

'You are clinically weird,' I told him.

'You should always officiate in the appropriate attire,' he explained. 'Do you know who said that?'

'I'm not sure, Napoleon?'

'Salvador Dalí, the greatest painter who ever lived.'

He now started pulling out mangoes and apples, big shiny pears, tins of peaches and plums, bright red strawberries, kiwis that he peeled and sliced and I leaned up on my elbows watching as he carried on chopping, cutting and dicing, the mounds of fruit growing into mountains on the counter.

Finally, he found a spray-can, laid me flat again and ran a long stripe of foamy white cream down my front from my chin to my pubes.

'It tickles,' I said and he was reaching for a *gia*normous bottle of chocolate sauce that belched impolitely as he made spirals over the cream. He ran circles round my boobs and whirls down my legs.

When he turned away I dug into his artwork and sucked cream and chocolate sauce from my finger. I watched over the end of my nose as he started to lay the fruit on my sticky body in patterns like shells in wet sand. As busily as he pushed the slices into place, I picked them out and thought there was something decidedly sexy about fruit as I dropped the pieces in my mouth. It was so bacchanalian.

'Why are you wearing that costume?' I asked.

'I told you, it's always best to wear the right thing.'

The last thing he took out was a banana and bananas are always silly. He jiggled his eyes making one go up and one go down which was just awesome.

'Don't move,' he said and placed the banana *you know where*, wedging it between my legs like a dildo, and a few minutes later I knew just what it was really like to be a fruit salad. Nibbling teeth were climbing their way up my legs. I watched as he took the banana into his mouth and it felt sort of nice as he pushed it backwards and forwards into pussy. My

134

legs arced into the air like they'd lost all sense of gravity.

Oh my God, I'm going to be busted in by a banana, I thought, but I didn't care. He'd promised to help me make a music demo and that's all that mattered.

Cream and chocolate sauce were sliding in and out of all my little places and it felt as if my insides were being whipped to a fruit smoothie. I was gasping for breath when he pulled the banana away, and as he replaced it with his tongue it came to me that the interesting thing about sex is it doesn't matter how many times you do it, it always feels different, it's always fantastic and I liked it better than anything in the world.

Christian Thomas finally slipped out of his maid's clothes and climbed up on the table. We rolled on to our sides, his tongue coiled into my pussy and his penis pushed into my cheek. It wasn't huge or china smooth or like Troy's little pink soldier, but different again, delicate and clever as he swivelled his hips and let it revolve in my mouth, moving between my lips and my teeth, then over my tongue and down to my tonsils. His sperm tasted of mangoes and, as it filled my mouth, I thought I'd probably had enough protein to last a month.

Most of the fruit had fallen on the floor and I wondered who was going to clear it up. He rolled me onto my tummy, pulled my knees up in an arch and pushed his tongue into my bottom. I liked this. It was different and I closed my eyes tight and thought about Sister Nuria. He stretched the cheeks of my bottom and pushed his tongue in as far as it would go. I wanted more and remembered the Sister saying how it was good for the soul when you don't give into your desires. But that was just silly.

'Do it,' I whispered.

He took his tongue out of my bottom and his eyes grew blue like neon as he looked up at me. He put his arm under me for support and pushed the head of his cock into my dark little bottom. He was very slow and gentle, sliding back and forth, and I moved with him, drawing it up deeper inside. I was gripping the end of the table with both hands and pushing my hips up into the shaft and it was beautiful and painful and I thought you need a little bit of pain to remind you how beautiful it is.

I was glad Christian had already come in my mouth because men always seemed to climax so quickly it was probably best to get it over and done with so you can take your time and enjoy it the second time.

My bottom was so tiny and tight it behaved as if this weird thing didn't belong there. But we started to get the rhythm, the waves of pain receded like the tide and I thought if anyone had been shooting a video we would have looked like two parts of a jigsaw glued together. I'd read about anal orgasms in the girlie magazines and knew they were rare and special. You have to relax, let it happen. Pussy wasn't exactly sure what was going on and was fizzing gently, the pressure tickling my clitoris in a way that was new and really nice.

Christian had been moving slowly, gently, in and out, but like the music in the next room, the tempo was building, he was going faster now, pushing harder and the receding pain returned and became so intense it was like he was trying to saw me in two.

I was screaming no, no, no and this made him grip my hip bones more tightly and he rammed into me so brutally I felt totally numb. He roared agh, agh, agh as he started to come and it was like something extraordinary had been completed, like a key had turned in a lock, or a bridge had been thrown over a river, or you'd passed a hundred A-levels.

He jerked forward in a last violent thrust and it felt as if his entire body was disappearing inside me. He came long and hard. I could feel the heat of his sperm. And then I came. I was a geyser erupting. A deluge. I screamed and screamed. I screamed like a siren at sea. I screamed in pain and joy, and I thought whoever it was who made me a girl was just so clever and so wicked to keep this special joy a secret. I wondered if there were other secrets and I intended finding out. We only get one life, I rationalised, and surely the point is to unearth all those yummy secrets.

We collapsed like a broken statue and it was soothing as he slipped out on the tide of his creamy warm come. My knees were killing me and it was a relief lying flat, sticky and sweaty and covered in bits of fruit. I felt his tongue move through my cheeks into all the little crevices and pleats. It really, really hurt but he took a long time licking away the pain and then it felt better. He paused to whisper, 'Now I don't care if I die tomorrow,' and as I drew a stray strawberry into my mouth I thought, what a stupid thing to say.

Chapter Eleven

AT BREAKFAST I HAD my usual banana on toast with Manuka honey and unzipped an extra banana because I just felt like it. I was idly pushing it against my cheek when Saskia caught my eye and spewed milk over Tara's sleeve.

'You klutz,' Tara snapped.

'That will be quite enough,' yelled Sister Bridget.

'Are you going completely bananas?' Saskia hissed.

'*I* nearly got *done* by a banana,' I confessed and the girls looked at each other before turning with wide gaping mouths like they were in a horror movie.

'I drank like a magnum of champagne.'

'Finally,' said Saskia with a sigh.

'*And* I lost my shades.'

They sat there with puzzled expressions. They wanted to know more but didn't want to seem too interested and I didn't really feel like talking about what had happened because what is going to happen is always more interesting.

I couldn't eat the banana after all. My heart was suddenly thumping, my cheeks were on fire. Christian Thomas had been the perfect gentleman and I'd dropped into my little bed during the darkest hour with a tingly weird sensation in my bottom like after you've been to the dentist and the anaesthetic is wearing off.

I had awoken to find a text from Jason telling me to come to the sex shop to meet Mr Glick at two o'clock and told the girls they should be there at half past if they wanted to meet up.

'How shall we dress?'

'Sex it up,' I advised.

I swallowed my vitamins with a litre of water and some echinacea which you need if you're getting a cold and I didn't think I was, but when you don't get much sleep that's when trouble strikes. I grinned and looked along the tables at the girls in their scarlet blazers. I'd been to the *Bitch* concert and no one else in the refectory could say the same.

After breakfast, I slipped into the lavatory and watched as everyone flooded across the quad to hear the Reverend Oombalongo preach at morning chapel. I waited until I heard the first hymn and zoomed off to the music room. I had 30 minutes to tape *I'm A Virgin*, my new song, and said a little prayer as I closed the door behind me.

The tape machine was the dusty old thing Sister Theresa had used to record the Christmas concert. I tested it a couple of times. 'One two. One two,' I said, and played it back. I'd been feeling like a zombie since the morning bell had jerked me from sleep but as I flexed my fingers the vitamins kicked in and a blast of new energy zipped through my little body. 'One, two, three, four ...'

Once In Royal David's City
...
...
Yeah ...
Everyone wants to be a virgin
Everyone wants a virgin
I'm a virgin
No I really am
I'm a virgin
That's just the way I am

The song was only three-and-a-half minutes. The recording was a bit tinny but good enough to play for Christian. I thought about doing a second take but I'd been lucky so far and I didn't want to tempt the devil.

I tiptoed back down the corridor through the bars of light cut through the arched windows and took the shortcut across the grass to chapel; the chips of flint on the stone wall twinkled like stars in the morning sunshine and crocuses were dotting the lawns. I crept into the back of the chapel and Sister Theresa raised her eyebrows and made a smacking motion with her hand against her bottom. Like so saucy.

I sat gazing out the window through my classes. A-levels weren't for me. I was too old for one thing and, for another, I didn't want to read the news or be a model or work on a girl's mag. Once you've had your bottom thoroughly serviced everything slides into place. You know just who you are and what you can achieve. I adored anal sex. And I adored being a virgin. I just loved being me.

As soon as class was over, I changed into satin gloss tights, my lucky pink bra from Yves Saint Laurent and thought *Yves Saint Laurent* was such a cool name, the blue suit I'd got in the sale at Monsoon and Gucci shoes to match the Louis Vuitton shoulder bag. I telephoned for a minicab. It was only a 15-minute walk to the lighthouse but I didn't have a second to spare.

The driver was from one of those Asian countries where Alexander the Great had butchered half the population and drove so slowly I was certain he'd never driven anything faster than a camel before.

'That way. That way,' I kept saying. 'Thank you very much. Thank you very much,' he replied and I gave him an extra 50p because he'd probably got lots of children to feed.

There was a silver Audi outside Christian's cottage. I banged on the knocker about ten times before the door finally opened and Christian just stood there staring at me like I was a Jehovah's Witness.

'Bella ...' His feet were bare and I was wearing a little smile as I dug out the tape. '... I wasn't expecting you.'

'Well, here I am.'

I held the box for him to take.

'What?' He had raised his shoulders and was shaking his head.

'My tape. I told you. You were going to help me make a proper recording.'

'Why don't you leave it?' He stuck his hand out. 'I'll listen to it later.'

'We'll listen right now. I've got a lot to do as it happens.'

'You can't *always* get your own way, you know.'

He was sounding *just* like Mother. Then it made sense.

'Chi-chi,' I heard from inside and a blonde with streaked highlights came to the door.

'Chi-chi!' I said.

'Iona, this is Bella.'

'Is it?' she said, and seemed about as pleased to see me as I was to see her in an Aran sweater and red hipsters. She looked closely at me, then back at *Chi-chi*, then at me again.

She was pretty in that blonde sort of way and I could feel tears prickling behind my eyes. I turned away before I looked like a complete loser, shoved the tape back in my pocket and went straight to the building society to check my account, which usually cheered me up. I had £685.42 and took out the odd £85.42 to make it even.

I called Troy's mobile from outside but there was no signal. I scrolled down the phonebook to Christian Thomas, paused for a millionth of a second and stabbed the DELETE key.

Troy lived at Yuri Gagarin House in Elm Tree Gardens and I assumed there was someone on the council with an ironic sense of humour. There were no elm trees, there were no gardens, and Yuri Gagarin sounded like one of those composers no one has ever heard of.

The tower block rose up like a space rocket and I remembered the cathedral keeping watch over Canterbury as we'd parked at The Marlowe, my gold heels clicking. I'd felt at my best because I'd looked my best and Christian was proud of me. I was sure he liked me just for me. I knew men wanted to take advantage, I'm not stupid, but it wasn't like that. I wasn't pressured into anything. It was just fun.

I'd sucked off the bouncer to get what I'd wanted. He wasn't taking advantage of me. *I* was taking advantage of *him*. It was the same with Dallas and Rupert. It was just amazing sex. I'd let Christian undress me because I'd wanted him to and now he didn't want to hear my tape because some blonde had turned up.

They say revenge is sweet. I'd never really thought about that, but now I did.

The lifts in Yuri Gagarin House were broken still and I trudged up the concrete stairs. I knocked softly as if half hoping no one was there, but the locks turned and Troy looked out from the pale blue door. I followed him down the crowded hall to his bedroom and, when I looked up into his eyes, I was glad he was taller than me.

'Gently,' I said.

He lowered his lips on mine and I realised he was a really great kisser, much better than Saskia. His tongue slid into my mouth and, as we snogged, a really spooky thing happened – tears began falling from my eyes, and they didn't come from the corners but welled up over the brims, great big salty tears that rolled one after the other in a stream over my cheeks and down to my chin.

'You're crying.'

'No I'm not,' I sniffed and pulled his belt again.

He licked away the tears and I just wanted to carry on kissing and sucking his tongue with its taste of fizzy drinks. He started groping under my jacket. I pushed his hand away. He didn't even mind. He just kept pressing his mouth against mine and I kept a grip on his belt.

'How's the guitar?' I asked, coming up for air.

His eyes lit up like he was a little boy.

'Loik amazing,' he said, and reached for the red Stratocaster. He sat on the bed and strummed, singing: 'DD, CC, GG, E minor. DD, CC, GG, E minor.'

'Good.' It was in tune and he was hitting the chords cleanly. 'Are you seeing Mr Gropius?'

'Yeah, and I have to work every afternoon down the grot shop to pay for it.'

'What about school?'

'Rules are for fools.'

I thought he said really amazing things sometimes and sat next to him on the bed. He started kissing me again. His hands wandered up my skirt and under my jacket like he was an octopus and I don't know why but I just didn't feel like it and kept pushing him away.

'Cockteaser,' he said.

'I'm not.'

He forced my hands between his legs and it's impossible to fight with boys because they're stronger. 'Come on,' he said and looked desperate as he shuffled down his cargo pants.

He was wearing boxers with guitars on them and when his willy jumped out it looked like it was made of rubber. I pulled his willy down like a lever as far as it would go and it sprang straight back up again. The head was pink and shiny and warm and I rolled it over my cheeks and it was really great for massaging my swollen eyes. I ran the tip of my tongue in the little hole at the top and flicked it with my nose.

Troy had a sweaty sweet musty smell, different from girls, and I thought it must be really nice to have one of these to play with. He was rolling his skinny hips. I slid his pink willy in my mouth and sucked it like I was a baby sucking a dummy. It was nice like that, not going fast and squeezing hard, just sucking softly and soon my mouth filled with marzipan.

'Fuck,' he groaned.

'Don't swear,' I said, and as I looked up I heard a faint tapping sound and saw Troy's mum standing in the doorway flicking ash on the carpet. She was wearing cut-off denims and had good tits in a cropped yellow vest.

'It's the music girl, is it,' she said, and I just wanted the earth to open up and swallow me I felt so embarrassed. I swallowed the marzipan instead and dabbed at the corners of my swollen lips.

'Come in,' Troy said.

'Bye,' I whispered as we passed his mum.

Troy got his bike out and I squealed with pain my bum hurt so much sitting on the narrow saddle as we rolled down the hill back into town. Troy went off to Greens 'on business', he said and I crossed the road to the sex shop. Jason had dyed his hair yellow and it was plaited in corn rows like he was a famous footballer.

'Hi, Jason, that's funky,' I said.

'Mr Glick's here, Honey,' he whispered like he was talking about the Pope.

It was nearly 2.15 p.m. I climbed the stairs and found Mr Glick sitting in the corner reading the newspaper. He stood nursing his hands.

'Am I late?' I said.

'Stars should always be late,' he replied and I knew he was trying to put me at ease.

We crossed the room to the dirty windows so we could inspect each other in the light. Mr Glick was wearing a shiny dark suit, a black tie, polished shoes that needed a polish and a raincoat.

'Sit, sit,' he said and I sat with my back straight and my legs together, not crossed, like I was a secretary about to take shorthand or whatever they do. I slipped my sunglasses in my bag and watched Mr Glick warming his hands.

'I looked at the film. I looked at it again and, you know, it's not bad.'

'It's just a demo,' I explained.

'And the ... the others?'

'They'll be here.'

He hummed to himself as he thought about that. We had to discuss money and money I realised requires a respectful moment of silence.

'Now in the demo you don't, you know ...'

'That's because it's only a demo.'

'And you're all right about, you know ...' I nodded. 'I have read the script, I watched the demo and I think we can do something, something very ...'

'Pretty?'

'Yes. That's what I would like to do. Three nice girls from a convent school. It's something, yes, pretty.' He paused. 'You are, you know, of age?'

'Oh yes,' I replied. 'So we just have to talk about money, Mr Glick.'

He hunched forward. 'That's not a problem,' he said and I waited while he rubbed his hands together. He readjusted his weight in the chair and lowered his voice. 'I am going to give

144

you £500.'

I pushed the stray curl from my eye. '£500,' I repeated. I stood and straightened my skirt before making my way towards the stairs.

He leapt up. 'What did I say?'

'I'm sorry to have wasted your time,' I told him and bit my lip because I remembered Nonna telling me that never, ever, under any circumstances say that silly little word *sorry*.

He was shaking his arms. 'I meant each, of course. £500 each,' he said. 'I'm taking a big gamble. I've got to hire a nice place,' he glanced around the scruffy room, 'pay a cameraman and a sound man, it doesn't come cheap ...'

'Mr Glick, that's just not fair.'

He shook his fingers and raised his voice and looked shocked. 'Fair? It's fair, my goodness it's so fair. You get £500 ... each, and I will look after everything, especially you girls.'

He paused and, at that second, the door downstairs rattled open and two sets of heels started clip-clopping their way towards us. Saskia and Tara crossed the room unhurriedly like geishas and I almost fainted they looked so awesome.

'Hi,' they said in unison.

They looked at Mr Glick looking at them and must have thought he'd had an attack of lockjaw. The girls were wearing skinny pink mesh tops with *nothing* underneath, the shortest red mini-skirts *ever*, red sling-backs, new Union Jack bags and long red coats. They were smoking Gauloises and made the perfect mirror image, Saskia with her cigarette in her right hand, Tara with hers in the left, their pink nipples playing peekaboo through the mesh tops and I thought *wow*, even their little tits are getting bigger.

'My cohorts,' I said. I turned to the little tarts. 'We haven't finished yet,' I told them and they went and sat in matching chairs crossing unmatching legs and blowing out smoke that spiralled through the dusty light.

'Well, I can make it another hundred pounds,' *pause*. 'Each,' said Mr Glick and as he wiped his brow with a handkerchief I knew I'd got him. I shook my head. I'd spent weeks making calculations.

'If you sell a thousand DVDs at £10 each, that comes to £10,000.'

He showed me his palms. 'And where's my profit on that? It's pennies,' he said.

'Sell a hundred thousand and you'll be a millionaire.'

'In this little shop?'

'You have the weird wide web,' I told him and you could see he was doing the arithmetic.

'There's the room to pay for, the boys with the camera, the cost of the film, the editing. Even the music. You have to pay a lot of money for music.'

'We want four grand,' I said.

The twins recrossed their legs and said nothing.

'£4,000!'

'And I'll supply the music.'

'Impossible.'

I glanced at the girls and he looked in their direction as they trod out their cigarettes below the red sling-backs; Nine West, I was sure, and really smart.

'I can go to two because I like you and that's a lot of money.'

'I don't like to bargain, Mr Glick, it's not my nature,' I said.

'Then you can take it or leave it,' he answered.

We fell silent. We knew we were going to reach a compromise and I had a feeling that by saying 'four' I'd made a mistake. He'd said 'two' and now it was obvious where we were going.

'Four,' I said and stamped my foot.

'Four, my life. What am I going to do? I can go to two-and-a-half and that really is the end of the discussion. It's been nice to meet you and you're a lovely young girl.'

'Flattery and business don't go together,' I said.

'I'm not sure that you're right,' he replied and rubbed his hands together. 'Two-and-a-half, that's my final offer.'

'Three,' I said, and knew by the hurt look in his little eyes that we had a deal.

'£3,000. I've never paid so much. Never.' I put out my hand

for him to shake and he carried on looking sorry for himself. 'I can't eat for a month.'

'Just drink lots of water,' I suggested.

The moment we left the sex shop, I waved to the girls and flew like the wind down the road to the harbour. The silver car outside Christian's cottage was clamped and that, I thought, was what they call divine justice. I went straight to Mr Gropius's cottage and rat-a-tap-tapped on the dolphin knocker. The door opened and he stood on the threshold looking lost.

'I came before with Troy and Mr Thomas,' I said.

'Yes, yes, now I remember. Come in. What can I do for you?'

I didn't have much time and produced my tape. I'd show Christian that nothing was going to stand in my way. 'Do you have a machine, Mr Gropius? I want you to hear something. It's really urgent.'

He trotted off, his mad hair flying, and I was standing by the mantel looking at the picture of the elegant ladies in their long white dresses when he appeared with a ghetto blaster balanced on his shoulder. He swivelled about in a little dance and I thought there was a lot more to Mr Gropius than meets the eye. He placed the machine on the coffee table and plugged it in.

I slid in my demo and pressed play.

When *I'm A Virgin* came to an end, Mr Gropius didn't say anything. He pressed replay and listened again.

'What I need, Mr Gropius, is to have it arranged properly and record it.'

He gave me a quizzical look. 'Come,' he said, and crooked his finger.

We crossed the room to the piano. He lifted the lid and I sat.

'Play,' he said, and I realised he probably didn't believe it was really me.

While I performed my song, Mr Gropius was leaning over me adding little riffs. He was humming along in descant and altering the tune slightly. At first, I thought what a cheek, but I could see that it doesn't matter how good you think something is, it can always be better.

When we came to the end it was like we were playing musical chairs and Mr Gropius literally pushed me out of the way to get to the piano stool. 'Sing, sing,' he commanded, and while I sang, he played, and my song started to sound like totally different. 'Again, please,' he said and threads of his silver hair were flying about as he threw back his head and started beating at the keys.

He stopped and when he turned and stared at me it was nice because he wasn't staring at my boobs or my bum or my legs or anything, but at me the songwriter.

'Ze rol of ze musician is to get to grips vith reality,' he said and his voice was suddenly Russian. 'You must interpret ze vorld in vitch ve live. You have to be honest.'

'I will.'

'Gut rock is like gut Tchaikovsky. Ven somezing iz gut, it iz gut.'

'Is it gut?'

He shook his head. 'Not yet.' He must have noticed my bottom lip quiver. 'Ve can make it gut.'

'Mr Gropius, that's what I want.'

'Music iz verk.' He shrugged his old shoulders. 'For zis, to make it as gut as it can be, you require the orchestra, session musicians, singers. It all costs ...'

'Whatever it is, I'll get it,' I said and I knew the £600 in the building society wasn't going to be enough and wondered if there was any way I could squeeze some money out of Simon Daviditz.

The clock on the mantel chimed the quarter hour which meant I had 15 minutes to get back to school. I didn't have Mr Gropius's phone number and he took forever to find a pencil and write it down.

'I *always* do what I say I'm going to do,' I said, and rushed out the door.

Chapter Twelve

JASON LEFT A MESSAGE that Mr Glick was booking a room at the Grand Hotel and after a reflective period, Simon Daviditz had again started texting in his chirpy irrelevant way and I texted back a matching stream of gobbledegook. *Lvbellaxxx*.

It was lucky I was close to the bathroom and could put my head down the lavatory pan.

Christian Thomas called every day but I had decided never to speak to him again and it was my rule that once I'd made a decision I kept to it. I called my new best friend Mr Gropius and he was *wery* excited.

Every cloud, they say, has a silver lining and I wondered what the opposite was because there was bad news as well. Mr Gropius was involved in various spheres with the orchestra in Canterbury and with the director they had worked out a budget. With some session musicians on guitar, saxophone and drums, a trio of backing singers, a half day for rehearsals and a half day in the studio, the total cost of the recording would come to £3,500 and give me 100 CD pressings.

I was standing in the bathroom and slipped to the floor. 'Three-and-a-half grand,' I said.

'And we have to pay a deposit of £500 immediately.'

We were silent and I listened to his old breath huffing down the phone.

'I'll get a cheque for you on Saturday.'

Again we were quiet.

'You take a big risk.'

I thought about that. 'If you want to be twice as successful you have to be prepared to fail twice as much,' I said. I'd read that somewhere and thought it was totally brilliant. I sighed. 'I'll see you Saturday.'

It was *so* lame life being divided by Saturdays and I had to wait until the following week before I could go to the building society and get a cheque. Mr Gropius was totally shocked and I was totally shocked that he had done so much work on *I'm A Virgin*. It was still basically the same but about a million times better, and now he had changed it so much I had to learn how to play the new version. He was a really great teacher but we couldn't do the recording until after Easter and that was like *forever*.

Outside the wind rocked the boats in the harbour. I glanced at the Indian goddess on Mr Thomas's door and felt a sudden compunction to hammer on the woodwork and tell him just what I thought of him: he calls himself a writer and he is no more than a *plagiarist*.

If you can believe it, Saskia had waltzed into the dorm that morning with a copy of the *Gazette* and on page 15 there were two photos of Dallas McTee, one of her on stage, the other with her peeping out from the gold mask. Along the bottom of the article it read: "Report and pictures by Christian Thomas".

We were going straight from filming to Barcelona and I packed mountains of stuff. Mr Glick sent a minicab to pick us up and, as the car pulled up at the Grand Hotel, I watched a windsurfer zigzagging across the bay and shivered in my camel coat.

Mr Glick was standing at the top of the steps giving his hands a good polish and the manager – a short man with wide shoulders – turned to him in that way men have when they're selling cars. The porter was a pimply boy who collected the bags and piled them in the room beside reception. He kept peering at us over his shoulder with that *I bet you don't know what I know* sort of look that chavs have when they don't know anything.

Saskia and Tara raised their eyelids as if they were removing their clothes and looked vaguely superior waiting for the lift to take us to the top floor. The contraption was one of those antiquated cages with an iron grille you had to close yourself and rose so slowly we were overpowered by the nervous smell wafting from Mr Glick's nylon shirt. We entered the Royal Suite where Queen Victoria used to stay and she *never* paid her bills. That's what Mr Glick said, anyway.

The set was just how I'd described in the script, the chairs at an angle, the tables with glass ashtrays, the bed like a pale green iceberg floating below overhead lights as big as the floodlights around the tennis courts at school. They were so hot they frizzed your hair and black cables bound with silver tape slithered over the floor.

The girls strolled around examining everything with slow sweeps of their chilly green eyes then went to change. I took the envelope Mr Glick drew from his shiny jacket and sat at the table counting the red £50 notes. They were new and smelled of fish, 60 of them and I counted twice to make sure. I pushed the envelope with £3,000 in my coat pocket.

There were two technicians adjusting the camera and light stands. The cameraman was wearing leather trousers, which are so dating, and the other man had the *de rigueur* ponytail with a few strands of hair like cobwebs over his shiny head.

They turned with professional interest as the girls made their entrance in red minis, red heels, red zipper shirts and their red berets. With their eyes obscured by the red masks they'd found in Spain they seemed oddly sinister and sat smoking as Mr Glick bantered on like he was a real director. I left to get ready.

I studied myself as I undressed, wind tossed and frowning in the long mirror. I took the devil mask from the bag and tucked my hair up inside. I removed the dildo from my bag and it had been so long since I'd used it I'd almost forgotten how to strap it on.

My fingers were all thumbs as I did up the buckles and the dildo was bobbing up and down with my sighs. I gave it a rub and, as I looked back in the mirror, I had become a Greek myth, half man, half woman, and I pinched my pink nipples to make them sting. I swung the cape around my shoulders, raised the hood and took the new tape we'd made from my bag.

Mr Glick was waiting outside the door warming his hands when I emerged from the bathroom. 'You ought to buy a new suit, Mr Glick,' I said. 'First impressions in business are very important.'

'Good. Good. You should always learn from the young,' he replied. 'Now, what about that music?'

I was hiding the new tape I'd recorded with Mr Gropius behind my back. 'It will be ready in a few weeks,' I answered.

'You're not going to let me down?'

I gazed around the suite, at the twins waiting with crossed legs, at the film crew nursing the big camera, at the towering lights like creatures from a planet far, far away. I gave Mr Glick the box.

'An early version,' I said, and the doubts fled from his features.

He played it through for a few moments and looked really impressed. He glanced at the girls.

'I'll start the music,' he said. 'When I say "action", just, you know, go with the flow.'

They gave a little jerk of their chins. He rewound the tape and nodded towards the cameraman.

'When you are, Yoram,' Mr Glick said and gave the thumbs up.

The music started.

'And, action.'

The camera turned, the lights were bright and the twins did their party trick, each at opposite angles facing away from the camera, flick flick with the fag ash, the smoke rising as they crossed their legs, dropping their heads, Saskia to the right, Tara to the left, and I was sure they'd been practising they were so natural.

They tossed the berets aside and peeled off the red shirts. They stood, facing each other as if they were standing before a full-length mirror, studying their matching expressions and I knew the telepathy was working because at *exactly* the same moment they wriggled their hips and slid out of their red minis.

They took a step closer, thumbs hooked in the sides of their white knickers. They moved like two beautiful snakes and the little buds of silk fell to the floor. They examined their ghostly second self once more and took another step closer, so close their pussies were touching and, when they kissed, shattering the mirror effect, I could see Mr Glick swallow a lump in his throat.

The camera crew carried on, unfazed, and I suppose they must have filmed millions of girls engaged in lesbian sex if the number of porn sites on the internet is anything to go by.

Saskia unhooked Tara's bra. Tara unhooked Saskia's bra. They held each other's hips and jiggled their nipples together in an impromptu dance, their bodies steaming under the bright lights, the masks totally bacchanalian. Tara slid her tongue between Saskia's lips and their snogging was so sensual, so natural, so pretty, it was more erotic than if they'd had full on sex. They moved towards the bed and, at that moment, Mr Glick totally ruined the mood.

'Cut!' he cried.

I looked at him with daggers in my eyes, but he ignored me and when he spoke to the girls he sounded like someone who has just swum a length under water.

'When you move towards the er ... the bed, you should pause for a moment, then glance at each other, then glance at the bed as if it's, you know, a sudden decision.'

The girls nodded. Mr Glick counted down three beats for the cameraman.

'Action,' he said.

The girls did as they'd been told. They gripped fingers, glanced at each other, raised their perfectly arched eyebrows and fell on the pale green sheets. As they were sucking face, the dildo was growing hot in my sweaty palm and the camera kept turning and the sound man had his mouth open. Mr Glick loosened his tie and the cameraman's face was glued to the eye of the camera.

Mr Glick glanced at me.

I moved to one side, entering the scene backwards. The twins paused, *as if mesmerised*. The CAMERA panned in SLO MO *from their POINT OF VIEW* as I pirouetted like a giant bird, the cape in outspread wings, the dildo leading the way on set. The girls *arched forward and ran their tongues in long strokes across the crinkly black rubber*, and it is amazing how much you can learn in two hours in the library. All knowledge is secreted in the written word and what I had written was becoming real before my eyes.

Last time we'd done this we just fell about laughing but erotic movies are deadly serious. Tara untied the cape and, as it fell to the floor, Saskia drew the dildo towards her. She took it into her mouth and the way she swallowed it down I realised she had been getting some practice. She laid back on the bed and, as I slid between her slim thighs, I thought it was a shame I couldn't see the faces of the men because you know when something's going well by the audience reaction.

Saskia's strong little muscles drew the dildo up inside her while Tara gripped the devil horns and lowered her wet pussy over my mouth.

My skin was electric under the hot lights. Saskia was a wriggling fish slipping and sliding away from me, and every few minutes Mr Glick shouted 'Cut', which was *so* annoying, although at least I knew why we needed two hours to make a short film.

I did Saskia, then I did Tara, and my only regret was that they weren't virgins. Juicy smells filled the room and, as the base of the dildo tickled my magic button, we made wet puddles that stained the pale green sheets.

'That's a wrap,' Mr Glick finally croaked.

The dildo was sticky and slicked in juice when I withdrew it from between Tara's skinny legs. It stood up straight and she flicked it backwards and forwards.

'Dahlink, you're still hard,' she said like a German and we all giggled because sex needs so much concentration you can only relax when it's over.

Saskia removed her red mask and slipped two cigarettes between her lips. Tara lit her Zippo and the technicians avoided their eyes as the girls strolled around the room smoking. I was dying to get out of the dildo. The straps cut deep into your skin and after a while it really hurts. I glanced at Mr Glick as I swung the cape around my shoulders.

'What can I say?' he said. 'You're marvellous. You're wonderful. You won't forget the music?'

'Mr Glick,' I said, and pulled off the devil mask. 'Italians never forget.'

'I was thinking of calling the film *Slappers from Hell*. What do you think?' he now asked.

'I think it's the worst title I've ever heard in my short life. You must call it *I'm A Virgin*,' I told him. 'It's the title of the song.'

'We have to do the editing, the post. There's lots of time.'

'Remember, you should learn from the young,' I said to jog his memory. 'It has to be *I'm A Virgin*.'

'The music will be ready in two weeks?'

'After Easter.'

He held out his hand again and it was like shaking a wet sponge.

I went to the bathroom and turned on the shower. I was about to step in when Tara stopped me. 'Don't,' she said and grinned. 'It's nice being all sticky,' and I thought these girls were really getting ahead of me.

'You're better than boys,' Saskia added and it was such a nice thing to say it made the little knot tighten in my empty tummy.

I felt sick. It seemed like destiny that I had received £3,000 from Mr Glick and that £3,000 was weighing like a tombstone as I slipped into my coat. But I needed it. I really needed it. I had to give Mr Gropius the money to arrange *I'm A Virgin*. There was nothing, absolutely nothing else that I could possibly do.

The twins weren't really concerned with money and if I had told them they would probably have given it to me anyway. But I didn't tell them. I betrayed them and in their unique and subtle way I knew they would get their own back. Cross twins and you're in double trouble.

The Asian taxi driver waiting outside the hotel drove us back to the harbour. I gave the envelope with the money in it to Mr Gropius. He kissed me and I let his old lips wander over my mouth – it's nice to do things for older people – and as the car drove us to Gatwick I don't recall ever having sat in such absolute silence before in my life. We were on our way to

155

Spain.

Finally I was going to meet Henry Scott-Wallace.

The monastery was high in the hills beyond the village and was in darkness by the time we'd negotiated the death ride to get there. It was called San Pi of all things and looked like the sort of place where monks murdered each other and young girls were eaten by wolves. The staff were all sleeping.

We found Henry lying beside a swimming pool looking up at a sky pierced by a million billion stars and so close I thought, if I tried really, really hard, I would be able to reach up and touch them.

'They've made up the opium bed for our guest,' he said and propped himself up on his elbow. He glared at Tara. 'You do have some fags, I'm gasping.'

'You're such a scrounger,' she said, and gave him the carton of 200 Camels she'd bought at the airport.

Henry sprang to his feet. He was wearing a maroon velvet jacket and a sarong with his school tie knotted around his forehead and his hair gelled in points. They all lit up and in a fug of blue smoke we entered the monastery.

'12th century,' said Henry. 'That's what they say.'

We wound our way through narrow corridors to the chapel. It was shaped like a mosque with saints peeling from the walls and naked nymphs on the ceiling. Dry yellow flowers coiled around the chandelier with its unlit candles; they were entwined like cobwebs in loops that hung from the walls and sat braided in crowns on the crumbling statues.

We entered through a low arched door that opened onto three stone steps that were cut from the rock and pitted with holes filled with table tennis balls. Totally surreal.

Saskia carried my bags up the steep stairs that led to the gallery where the opium bed that filled the entire space had the appearance of a Chinese junk with its swags of lace curtains drooping over the four sides. While I unpacked, the twins stood there with the light behind them and their faces were as shadowy as the crumbling saints.

There was a table tennis table in front of the altar and I

156

watched the twins playing and it was like watching spiders spinning a web, their limbs extending in all directions, the ball flying across the net and clacking on the bats as regular as a heartbeat. I was glad they didn't ask me to join in and they were busily amassing points when Mrs Scott-Wallace entered like a bride in a white dress, a white hat with a veil and white Jimmy Choo shoes.

I remembered she had a whole room full of shoes in boxes and I was dying to see them.

Henry put his arm around his mother's slender waist and they pressed their bodies close together like lovers.

'The guest,' he said.

'Ah, yes,' she responded and looked me up and down. 'I'm sure you'll be happy here.'

'Yes, thank you.'

Then she turned to Henry. 'Now, darling, let's go to bed.'

She turned and marched out. Henry followed obediently and I thought, wow, this family is even weirder than my own. The twins were still playing table tennis, the ball like a white moon arcing across the table and back again. Suddenly they stopped.

'I'm dead,' Tara said.

'I'll show you where the bathroom is.'

They led me out through the narrow door and along the corridor to an old-fashioned bathroom with a wonky floor and a single brass tap. The twins didn't kiss me. They didn't say good night. They just left and I felt tears swimming once more into my eyes.

I went back to the chapel. I unpacked the rest of my things and placed them on the shelves in the opium bed, the devil mask, the dildo smelling of smelly girls, my little clothes and creams. I climbed into my pink Terrycloth pyjamas, turned off the light and lay there listening to the wind blowing over the eaves. Moonlight streaked the walls.

The shadows moved tirelessly and then I heard the door open on its antique hinges. Footsteps crossed the tiles. I heard a table tennis ball being patted up and down, up and down, then it fell and tap, tap, tapped into silence. I heard animal noises, yapping and snarling, then Henry lurched like Quasimodo up the stairs to the gallery. 'Phee, phai, phoe, phum I smell the blood of an Ital-ian,' he intoned and pulled back the curtains.

He threw his clothes off and dived across the big bed like he was diving into the swimming pool and it was just hysterical the way he started attacking me like a wild wolf, barking and biting my neck, but the bites were real bites and really hard.

'Henry, stop. That hurts.'

'Grrrr,' he growled and I erupted in a fit of giggles.

He grabbed my pyjamas in his teeth and pulled, shaking his head, pulling me across the bed and ripping off the buttons, and I thought, wow, boys are just awesome. He tore the jacket from my shoulders and pulled the sleeves off, and the way he did it didn't seem quite so funny.

'Henry, don't.'

'There there,' he whispered. 'There there,' and he gently fondled my breasts, running his hands over me in soft caresses like he was stroking a cat and it was nice until he squeezed my nipples and I shrieked in agony.

'You love it,' he said, and started licking and biting them in a way that really, really hurt.

I tried to wriggle away and, as I jerked him forward, he kissed my neck but the kisses became bites again and I just wished it had been Troy in that opium bed because he was gentle and nice and knew when to stop.

As fast as I moved one way, Henry moved the other, and it should have been fun but it wasn't. He kept on making animal noises and did the same thing with my pyjamas bottoms as he had done with the top, shredding the material and ripping it to pieces with his strong teeth. He twisted round and was grinning as he tapped my nose with his hard cock.

'No, Henry. Don't,' I said.

'No,' he repeated and started forcing it into my mouth. 'Here, boy. Here, boy,' he kept saying and as he pushed it between my teeth I bit him as hard as I could.

He fell back. 'You fuhking shit bitch,' he screamed, and slapped me across the face. 'That's what you need.'

The blow was so hard I was dazed for a moment. He was levering my knees apart and as he plunged forward I rolled to one side and just avoided getting pinned to the sheets. He slapped me across the other side of my face and it was just as hard, but I didn't even feel it this time. I got hold of his arm and bit the soft flesh and kept biting until he howled in pain and I slipped to the floor.

I ran screaming down the stairs but he caught up with me by the time I reached the table tennis table. We stood at each end like we were going to play a game and he picked up the bat and whacked the palm of his hand.

'I know what this little slapper needs,' he said and I was still catching my breath.

'Just leave me alone,' I pleaded. 'I haven't done anything to you.'

'I beg your pardon. You said no.'

He ran round the table. I fled the other way, and as we ran in circles we were like reflections of the naked nymphs swirling around the chapel ceiling. I knew he would catch me because boys are always quicker and instead of chasing me, he just separated the table and charged through the middle.

I raced for the stairs leading to the door but he overtook me, charged up and closed the bolt. He slapped his palm with the bat as he walked slowly back down the stairs, his cock pointing at me like a reproachful finger. I looked round but there was nowhere to go, and I was beginning to wonder if it was best to lie on the floor and just get it over and done with.

'Come along, little bitch, come along,' he was saying. 'Come to Henry.'

When he stopped in front of me it was my instinct to turn and run again. He caught up and forced me into one of the arched recesses where a statue of the Virgin was kneeling in the shadows. I remembered the statues without heads lining the drive at La Montepietra, Nonno's mediaeval handwriting, Daddy losing his fortune breeding polo ponies, the past crumbling to dust, the dust vanishing on the wind.

Henry grabbed me, turned me round and slapped my bottom with the table tennis bat over and over again. 'No one says no to Henry. No one says no to Henry. No one says no to Henry,' he kept saying and he hit me every time on the beat. 'No one says no to Henry.'

He dropped the bat and carried on smacking me, using his hand, and I realised that if I was going to be smacked, I preferred hands to bats or slippers. It just feels, I don't know, it just feels nicer, more personal, if that makes sense.

Wallop. Wallop. Wallop.

I spread my legs so that I didn't fall over. I have to admit I was getting wet even though I was angry and the smell of my arousal made him roar like a beast. He pulled my legs viciously apart. He lunged at me, his cock pressing between the cheeks of my bottom, but before he found a way in, I used all my strength and jabbed my elbow up into his eye.

'Bitch. You fuhking bitch.'

I wasn't going to give it away that easily. Not even to Henry Scott-Wallace. He staggered back and I ran, my voice amplifying and echoing over the domed roof so that it sounded like all the little nymphs on the ceiling had joined me and were crying for help.

I reached the top of the steps but he got there a second later. I punched him with both fists but he hit me so hard the blow knocked me back against the door. I pulled the bolt before I slid to the floor and he fell on top of me, his knees around my neck. He was making the sound of a helicopter while he whirled his cock in circles. He kept slapping my nose and cheeks, and he was still doing this when Mrs Scott-Wallace entered with the look of somebody who has been called from a dinner party by the babysitter, her features carved by the light from the candle glimmering in the old-fashioned lamp she carried.

'Henry, please,' she said and he got up, crossed the chapel and climbed the stairs to the opium bed where he dressed and slid his school tie back over his brow. I stood naked, trembling, covered with bruises.

'He's been hitting me with a table tennis bat,' I said and burst into tears.

'Henry, what have you been doing?' she asked without raising her voice and he marched down the stairs looking pained and slightly bored.

'Nothing, really,' he replied.

'He tried to rape me,' I yelled.

'Don't shout, there's a dear,' said Mrs Scott-Wallace and turned to Henry. 'When a girl says no ...'

'She left the door open,' he said.

'That's because I was afraid.'

'There's nothing to be afraid of here,' said his Mama. She looked at me. 'You're still intacto?'

I nodded.

'Then no harm's done.' She glanced around the chapel with its flickering lights and dying saints as if she had just finished decorating and was admiring the result.

I turned around and showed her my bottom. 'Look,' I said, and it was bright red where Henry had hit me.

'Henry, don't do it again,' she said and he looked surly.

'Absolutely,' he answered. He rewrapped his sarong and stalked off up the stairs back into the monastery.

'Don't mind Henry, he's just high spirited.'

'He ripped my pyjamas off with his teeth,' I told her.

'His teeth,' she repeated and looked as if she was filing this away as she reached for my hand. 'Now, we'd better find you some more night clothes.'

We wandered along the dark corridors to a pine cupboard where she found a long white nightdress. The candle glow stretched our shadows over the walls and followed like two assassins as we made our way back to the chapel. We stood at the top of the stairs.

'Are you going to be all right?' she asked.

'I'm not sure.'

She cupped my cheeks in her hands. 'I should stay,' she added and slipped the bolt on the chapel door. 'Boys can be so beastly.'

We walked down the stairs, between the two halves of the table tennis table, and up the stairs to the opium bed.

'Now,' she said. 'Let me have a look at that poor little bottom.'

Chapter Thirteen

WHEN YOU GET BACK from Spain, you buy a book about Salvador Dalí and he said every great fortune begins with a great theft and all success starts in scandal. He was right.

Luck is the view from the top of a mountain. First, you've got to climb the mountain.

One day, I would explain all that to Rupert de la Rue, the black man with the shiny bald head, and in the meantime I was furious that Salvador Dalí had called his autobiography *My Secret Life* because it is such a cool title.

Mother was so excited I was coming home she had made an appointment with the pedicurist in Canterbury.

The brother-in-law of Mr Fat Choy, who owned the restaurant in our village famed, according to Simon Daviditz, for storing dead Alsatians in the deep freeze in the cellar, was waiting at the airport with a cardboard sign with Bella misspelled; if you can believe it, it said Vespa, and I thought it's just as well I know who I am.

Mr Fat Choy's brother-in-law wore a bewildered expression and a suit that must have belonged to Mr Fat Choy and was so big it was like looking at clothes on a hanger. I think he'd just arrived on a boat from Hong Kong but, anyway, he followed behind with the trolley, urging me like a goatherd along corridors and down lifts until we reached the car park where he bowed long and low before the red Mercedes with *Emperor's Palace Chauffeurs* sprayed in gold along the sides.

'Haa,' he said, and pressed the button to open the doors as if the little box in his hand was made of magic. Mr Fat Choy's brother-in-law could only say *Haa*, which was a relief because it gave me time to sit and think, and what I thought was that if the twins had been plotting all along with their brother, that wasn't just two-faced, it was four-faced.

The girls were totally blasé about the whole werewolf thing, all shrugging shoulders and Gauloises at every angle, and I came to the conclusion that people eat themselves up with little worries that don't add up to *niente* as Nonno would say. I would pay the girls the £2,000 I owed them when I had the money and decided not to mention it again.

The fruit trees across Kent were wearing new parasols of pale green and the fields were patchworks of yellow rape, which is such a crass name and made me wonder if Henry had been taking liquid ecstasy or whatever it is that's turning everyone into a maniac.

The thrill of being taken by Mrs Scott-Wallace to see her shoes, the collection having grown to 256 pairs, all colour coded with Polaroids on the boxes, turned out to be as anticlimactic as the school trip to see the British Museum, and she disappeared on a boat with Alastair Bloom the day after that night in the chapel and took the dildo and devil mask with her. First Dallas McTee pilfers my sunglasses. Now this!

When I flew home to London, Henry and the twins followed their mother to the Caribbean, and I thought it was dead mean that I had not been invited.

Anyway, I was back in Kent. Old men with hearty strides and jaunty hats were taking dogs on long leads to do their afternoon business and the driver tooted his horn as he passed Mr Fat Choy outside the Chinese restaurant. The lanterns were glowing and I saw two girls in headscarves rushing along as if the wind was caught in their long blue gowns. I glimpsed Mrs Ormsby brushing a brown and white pony that stood as still and as astonished as the two small girls in new tack who were watching. That was me, like a million years ago.

The chimneys lancing the sky above Ickham Manor came into view and the fresh coat of gloss on the door and window frames reminded me that the house hadn't been painted for as long as I could recall and the faded, shabby, lived-in look belonged to another age. The flames hovering about the olive jars turned out to be geraniums in three different shades of red and a new layer of pink gravel carpeted the drive. Esperanza, the maid, hands on hips, was staring owlishly through her big glasses as the car gushed to a halt.

'*Bella, es tanto tiempo. Eres más alta, más guapa.*'

I stepped from the car. '*Gracias,*' I said, and I was determined to put more effort into Spanish.

We touched cheeks and she counted out money from an envelope for the Chinaman.

'Haa,' he said.

'*Si,*' she said.

'Haa,' he repeated,

I ran straight upstairs, avoided the slap of the angry palm, and closed the bedroom door. I kissed Daddy, content and smiling still in the picture frame, and with Sylvester the cat watching with Henry's blue-green eyes, I set off like a spider across the weird wobbly web. I was searching for record companies and found 63, which may sound a lot but it is like a pyramid with a few big ones guarding the high ground where the hits are created, while the further down the sides you slide the more specialised they become and the less likely that they can score airtime on the radio. Bribery and corruption is the secret, but I didn't know anything about that yet.

The computer bleeped and whirred and played sample tracks that were cosmically awful and Esperanza marched in to warn me that I was going to make myself blind if I didn't give my eyes a rest. She was carrying a big glass of milk and I thought it was a miracle that Esperanza was still with us.

My tutor card with its catalogue of Bs, Cs and the D in history would bring a smile to Mother's lips because it proved *she was right* and to cheer me up Simon Daviditz acquired a hundred padded envelopes, stamps and labels as a business expense.

I was always *such* a mystery, *so* cute, such a Tinker Bell, so ... *bella* and he drooled over the shell-embroidered knickers that caught my eye while we lingered in lingerie at Neuhaus & West. I didn't try anything on and I didn't tell him what I wanted the envelopes for. Mother joined us with a ridiculous hat in a large round box that Mr Daviditz carried and, over lunch at Pret, she complained that the stools were too high, too narrow and the mayonnaise on her sandwich too rich.

'You can't be too high, too narrow or too rich,' I said. I was eating sushi.

She gave the gold bangles on her wrist a couple of turns. 'Really, Bella, is that a fact?'

'I read it.'

'Don't believe everything you read.'

'All knowledge is secreted in the written word,' I told her and we both glanced at Simon wreathed in smiles as he chatted up the Italian girl all steamy and bright eyed in a tight T-shirt behind the coffee machine.

He returned with two cappuccinos and an espresso and it occurred to me as Mother's face turned bitter with the first sip of coffee that she was in one of her depressions and I had no idea what she had to be depressed about. Except for being the vice-chairperson of the Conservatives, she had never done anything or been anything, and I suppose that was the problem. She was always complaining that she was tired and when people don't do very much the more exhausting it is to do anything at all.

'We shouldn't really drink coffee, Mummy,' I remarked.

She pushed her cup away.

'Don't tell me we actually agree on something.'

Our gaze turned instinctively to Simon Daviditz, absorbed still with the Italian girl and wiping chocolate dust from his moustache.

'What?' he said with a little shrug and Mother and I shared a rare moment of truce. One day she would need taking care of and, when that day came, I intended to be there for her because Italians are like that.

Now I was anxious to get home and sat in the car wondering if Daisy Bloom had gone to the Caribbean for Easter and if there was a Mrs Bloom, and whether Mr Scott-Wallace was still manning the barricades for the EU in Brussels, and whether the twins knew how exasperating they were?

As I hit the switch on the laptop, I knew without looking that

165

there were lines on my brow.

When you send your demo to the record companies you need a CV and preparing a CV is like inventing the wheel. I mean, I'd hardly had time to discover a new country or a cure for cancer, or writer's block, and that's what I was suffering as I read in the pop magazines about the fledgling stars and their fascinating lives.

Like, this one's *fave* thing is shopping with her mates and she's got like really good mates, and that one just *loves* dogs and shopping and thinks her Mum is *smashing*, and the other one *never* thought about being a celebrity like *ever* and is just crazy about writing songs and saving the planet. And shopping.

This was my work in progress.

Bella is the big voice. Clear and fresh as springtime. Deep and dark as the sea. Bella has been laying licks on the keyboard since she was old enough to walk and all her songs are her own – original, opinionated, inspirational. And totally rockin'.

I added:

When Bella isn't writing new material in her school books she loves shopping with her mates and she has the coolest mates who are all totally real. Her mum is her closest buddy and she is a vegetarian.

The last bit wasn't true because, according to Esperanza, I was an *e-skeleton* and she just adored cooking *pollo picante* Colombian style. I put photos down the side of the fact sheet with me looking pretty, pensive, pouty, punked up and sexy, serene, wind-blown, crazy, determined, shy, schoolgirlish and girl of the world. I'd seen the layout in *Popworld* and thought it was so easy to be a designer because you just borrow stuff you like and sprinkle in your own magic. The CV looked better than it read and I envied Eminem and Christina Aguilera because they had grown up in trailers with bullying fathers to inspire them.

I decided it was time to pay my father a visit and pedalled flat out through the village with a bunch of daffodils I'd picked in the garden. I was arranging them in the jam jar when the mobile played *I'm A Virgin* and I thought it was nice that Daddy would get to hear it that way.

'What? Who is this?'

'You know who it is, Henry, you just called me.'

'Ya. What's happening?'

'I'm in a graveyard.'

'Wow, morose. You should have come.'

'I wasn't invited.'

'Don't bother with all that. Just do what you want.'

'How are your sisters?'

'Boring some Saudi prince. They're all such arseholes. Keep it gangsta.'

His voice crackled into static. The machine whispered trade winds from the Caribbean and I imagined Henry rushing off to molest Daisy Bloom the body slasher with *The Daily Telegraph* under his arm and his Eton tie around his head. I remembered the stab of excitement when I had first seen him by the pool at San Pi, the way he brushed his hair from his brooding eyes and dived across the opium bed. It was a shame Henry had such sharp teeth but I still quite liked him.

When I wasn't planning my campaign, I was rehearsing *I'm A Virgin* and we made the recording the Saturday after I returned to school. It seemed as if I had been waiting for ever for this day and, now it was here, I teetered in my big heels on the edge of a nervous breakdown.

There were 40 members of the orchestra milling about, sucking on cigarettes, and it struck me that they were only doing the recording because they wanted to, because musicians are a special breed, they knew something, or they'd seen something, and you got the feeling as they blew out smoke in long silky streams that they were keeping it to themselves.

The studio piano was battered and scratched but it caught my reflection as I lifted the lid and I thought all these people are here for me. I've done this by myself. Mr Gropius was trembling like he had just caught that shaking disease and wet my ear as he said in an undertone that the kettle drums from the Royal Philharmonic would be sitting in on the session.

At the back of the various nests of unmatching chairs and abandoned instruments, the tall percussionist guarded his drums as if afraid that someone was going to run off with them. He nodded solemnly in my direction and rippled his fingertips across the skins.

My back-up singers consisted of three black girls in strappy dresses. They remained aloofly to one side where they kept glancing at me with rapid eye movements and then going into a huddle. The lead guitarist had toured with David Bowie, who was like *so* famous, and the man on saxophone had once played with Dallas McTee.

'What's she like?' the lead guitarist asked him.

'Standard bitch. Nice tits,' he replied.

He turned towards me and I made understanding circles with my fingers. I was one of the band in blue jeans, a white T-shirt and a red bandana that was holding my rebellious locks in place. The ruby heels were my first Jimmy Choo shoes and I had felt lucky the moment I'd put them on.

We were in a soundproof aquarium with a technician named Dave sliding switches up and down a giant console beyond the glass partition. He was really intense with scary eyes and hair down to his shoulders. On his T-shirt it said BEEN NOWHERE. DONE NOTHING.

'When you are,' came his drawling voice over the speakers and everyone shuffled into position.

Pins and needles prickled my fingers. My hands were white where the blood had fled into my cheeks. Everyone was looking at me and I *really* thought I was going to throw up when Mr Gropius stared at me sternly and tapped his baton on the music stand. The musicians had been tuning up but now everyone was tense with silence. I closed my eyes.

We had cut the first line from *Once In Royal David's City* because you should never state the obvious. I played the hymn's opening bars. The kettle drums pounded as if urging slaves into battle on a Roman galley. The string section was driven by a haunting cello and the sax came in, howling like a wolf.

I breathed into the mike.

> *Everyone wants to be a virgin*
> *Everyone wants a virgin*

168

I'm a virgin
No I really am
I'm a virgin
That's just the way I am
I've done it all
Been everywhere
Climbed the mountain
And I really don't care
I'm a virgin
No I really am
I'm a virgin
As you can see
I'm a virgin

Do you want to play with me?
You can tie me up
You can tie me down
Take me any way
Take me right away
Take me any day
Take me no matter what you say
Take me yesterday
When all my troubles seemed so far away
You can make me kneel and pray
I'll just shake my head and say
I'm a virgin
No I really am
I'm a virgin
That's just the way I am

I'm a virgin
I'm just a teen
I'm a virgin
You don't know where I've been
I'm a virgin
You don't know what I've seen
I'm a virgin
It's just, you know, so obscene

I'm a virgin
No I really am
I'm a virgin
That's just the way I am

I'm a virgin
Take me in your arms
I'm a virgin
Take me, yeah
Give me peace of mind
Give me a piece of time
Give me two words that rhyme
You know I look so fine
I'm only biding time
I'm in the firing line
Cos I'm a virgin
No I really am
I'm a virgin
That's just the way I am
I'm a virgin
Take me now
Take me please
Take me, take me, make me, take me

Dave rattled his cage and the instruments fell away as if the musicians were jumping over a cliff. He shouted over the speakers and pointed at me.

'You, take it easy, you're coming in too fast.'

I bit my lips until they bled. It was the first time I'd sung with the trio of back-up singers and, by the end of the rehearsal, I still didn't know if I'd got it right. My T-shirt was clinging in nervous sweat to my back and the black girls peered at me with long, cautious expressions.

'Solid.'

'Respect.'

'Yeah.'

One after the other they raised their fists and my knees were trembling with relief as I stood away from the keyboard.

Mr Gropius was still shaking but in a nice way. His arrangements were just so cool and after a break we were ready for the off.

'When you are,' came that voice again and I watched Dave's quick fingers running over the levers and dials on the console. He was like a magician and reminded me of Harry Potter.

We did five takes with rests in between and Dave said the second one was best. 'It always is,' he added.

He lit a fag, took a long, concentrated pull on the filter and looked me up and down, but not in a sexy way, but like he was taking me seriously for the first time. 'That should do it,' he said slowly, nodding his head so that his long hair shook like a curtain.

Mr Gropius, when we were driving back, interpreted *That should do it* as *That's brilliant* because Dave was the master of the understatement. I should have gone straight back to school, it was time for tea, but I was hyped up after the recording and felt like breaking the rules for a change. I was totally sweaty from all that nervous energy and told Mr Gropius I just had to have a bath or I was going to die.

'Ov course, ov course,' he said, his English going wonky again.

I followed him upstairs at the cottage and was thrilled because the bath was huge. He turned on the taps, put some crystals into the running water and, while he went to find some fresh towels, I watched the water turn blue. He left, closing the door, and I threw my smelly clothes in the corner.

I laid back in the foamy water and, when I closed my eyes, I could hear a violin slowly growing louder as it approached. I had forgotten to lock the door, not that I minded; in fact it was sweet when Mr Gropius entered and stood on the threshold playing, his mad hair swirling about his head like a snow storm.

'Johannes Brahms, violin concerto, opus 77,' he said when the concert had come to an end.

He sat on the loo and looked at me for a long time lying back in the bath and it felt cosy somehow.

'Mr Gropius, if you had one wish, just one, right now, what would it be?' I asked him.

'Ah, zat is so easy, little Bella.'

'Tell me.'

'The secret ov gut music, like gut stories, is to show. Not tell.'

'Then show me then.'

A little smile crossed his face and his old eyes were twinkling. He placed the violin and bow carefully in the corner, rolled up his sleeves and plunged his hands into the blue crystal water. He ran them over my breasts, down over my tummy and I squealed it tickled so much. He lifted my left leg over the side of the bath and massaged my shin, my knee, my thigh and his clever fingers that danced so quickly over the violin strings danced quickly over the lips of my pussy.

I closed my eyes and lifted myself away from the warm porcelain below my bottom. A finger pushed up inside me, then another, he was playing me like you would play a clarinet, and I could feel oily trickles leaking from my puffy lips. I felt deeply happy and satisfied. This was something special for Mr Gropius. I knew that. How often does a man who looked like he was 70 at least get to play with the perfect body of a girl my age?

Practically never I imagine, but it was strange because Mr Gropius didn't seem old. He had a youthfulness that came from his attitude, from the way he played the violin and conducted the orchestra. I felt safe in his hands. I wanted him to enjoy this, to have something special. He had done so much for me and I wanted to do more for him. I started to come and stopped myself, saving pleasure for greater pleasure. I was getting so mature. I brushed his hands away and pulled myself up.

At first he looked sad and lost, but I bent, cupped his cheeks and kissed his nose. I didn't say anything. I stepped out of the big bath tub, took his hand and led him down the hall until I found the master bedroom.

'Music,' I said.

'Ah, yes, alvays ve must have music.'

He went and got his ghetto blaster and played Brahms, naturally. He turned me round in the subdued light falling through the leaded windows.

'Ah, yes, ah, yes,' he said. 'You have breasts that men dream of.'

He ran his palm over my nipples, backwards and forwards, very fast, and they grew hot with the friction. He leaned forward and took Pinkie in his mouth. He sucked hard and long, then transferred his allegiance to Perky. They were hard now and jutted out like two rosebuds, pink and pretty, flowers about to burst into bloom.

My mouth was swollen and moist. He kissed me and, when I pressed my eyes tight, it didn't feel wonderful like kissing Troy, but it didn't seem vulgar like being kissed by Simon Daviditz. He wormed his old tongue into my mouth and I wondered where else that tongue would be travelling.

South, of course, over my chin, across my neck, which is just like *so* erogenous, into the little triangular-shaped cavities below my collarbones, down on the faint indentation that divides the breasts like the seam on a really good silk dress to my belly button which he licked and licked like he was sucking a boiled sweet. He nuzzled my pussy with his nose and then turned me around. I noticed over my shoulder that he was leaning back and studying my bum like you'd study a Picasso on the wall, like I was the *Femme nue* or something.

'You have ze best bottom on the whole vide vorld,' he whispered.

'Thank you.'

'It is a bottom for spanking.'

'Yes, I thought so.'

He looked up at me. His eyes were shiny. There were tears welling up in the corner.

'Let me get my violin.'

He went off back to the bathroom. He turned off the ghetto blaster and performed one of Bach's Brandenburg concertos. He was playing, not to me, I realised, but to the best bottom in the world, and I dutifully leaned over the wooden baseboard at the end of the bed and pushed it out, all perky and bright like a ball of infinite joy.

He played for like ages and, when the piece came to an end, he placed the violin on top of the bureau and ran his lips over the bow. Our eyes met. I smiled. He smiled. He took up his position like he was about to play a double bass and brought the violin bow down across my pouting cheeks. Smacked. Slippered. And now bowed. I squealed and wriggled about, but I kept my poise and waited for the next one. There is always a next one. Slash. Down it came like a guillotine, slicing into my flesh and sending that odd blend of pleasure and pain through my cute little body.

It's very strange, but the first whack, whatever it's with, hurts like you've been cast into hell, but the second one is never quite as painful. The third is actually the most painful of all. You've decided in your mind that it's not going to hurt, and because you've showed the spanker how resolute you are, the third one comes down much harder. So there are two things at work, you don't think it's going to hurt, then the spank or the slipper or the bow breaks across your flesh like a streak of lightning, burning the surface and turning your knees to jelly. And yes, it *really* hurts.

And again.

Number four.

Wow. I screamed at the top of my voice, but I didn't move. I didn't want to seem like a baby. There were four lines across my bottom. I could feel them like four cuts with a knife. I gritted my teeth, pressed my eyes so tight I could see stars, and dug my toes into the carpet. Then again. The line was laid down in a neat parallel below the other four and it dawned on me that my bottom was now a page of sheet music waiting for the notes of a masterpiece.

I had been thinking that six strokes was traditional, but musicians always do things differently. It was over. I stood up shakily and looked back at my poor little bum. Five bright red lines sat on a sea of pink, my favourite colour, of course, and poor Mr Gropius seemed exhausted. He sat down on the bed panting. His mad hair was wet with sweat and his chest was heaving.

'Come on, you'll be all right,' I said, and I lifted his legs up onto the bed. I pulled the cover over him and tucked the pillow under his head. He was still finding it hard to breathe and I didn't want the poor man to have a heart attack. I soothed his brow. Gradually his breathing became normal and I went back to the bathroom to get dressed.

'Are you going to be OK?' I asked, and he nodded.

I managed to find a taxi on the far side of the harbour and got into school without being seen.

I had the pressings by the end of the week and burnt another bunch in the IT room, just in case. The originals went off with my fact sheet to the record companies and radio stations sealed with a lucky kiss on the padded envelopes in the last post on Saturday.

It was becoming more of a nuisance – life being plotted in Saturdays – but according to my stars the winds of change were blowing. I was about to meet a dark acquaintance from the past who would play an active role in the future and I kept thinking it must be Zach Kessler.

It was just as well that I was busy and didn't have to rely on Saskia and Tara for anything. They had remained cool, as in glacial, since the beginning of term and although they persisted in speaking only French to each other, that had more to do with Daisy Bloom's lack of French than mine. Daisy had been moved into our room and Jack had been moved out. We had no idea why this had taken place but, as Mr Bloom was the convent's major benefactor, I imagined it must have had something to do with him.

I glanced at the twins.

'I said I'll pay you back,' I said and bit my tongue because I'd decided I wasn't going to mention it.

Oui. Oui. Shrug. Shrug. Puff. Puff. And there was something else about the twins that was annoying. They weren't even gossips, and I'm sure they'd started smoking pot because I'd seen the packet of Drum and rollie papers hidden in Tara's sports bag.

From the post office, I dashed straight across the busy road to the sex shop where I found Mr Glick wearing a new suit and those octagonal glasses without frames. He was much younger than I'd thought and even looked excited when I gave him a

175

copy of *I'm A Virgin*. He suggested in a half jokey way that we made a new film called *I'm Not A Virgin* with me sampling a selection of porn stars *famed for size*.

'I can't wait, Mr Glick,' I said and he swallowed his tongue.

'Are you serious?'

'I don't have a sense of humour.'

'Then we should discuss terms ...'

'I want £100,000.'

'My dear, it doesn't work like that.'

'Then there's nothing to discuss.'

I looked back at the cover design for the DVD. 'That should do it,' I said.

'You know, I could get you £10,000.'

'I don't bargain, Mr Glick.'

'It's vulgar.'

'You're quicker than an Italian.'

'Multi-skilling,' he pronounced, and held up the CD in its see-through box as if he'd just won a medal.

For the DVD cover they had taken a still of me with my skinny girl body gleaming and the dildo jutting out like a weapon of mass destruction. The top half of my face was covered by the devil mask but it was obviously me. The twins were bent forwards, unrecognisable with their backs to the camera. *I'm A Virgin* was across the top in shocking red.

I glanced around the dusty room above the sex shop as if I were looking out of a train window at something that was momentarily interesting but the train had moved on and the scene was instantly forgotten.

'You have to think about it,' Mr Glick pressed as I was descending the stairs in my ruby shoes but I wasn't listening.

Jason looked like he'd just been struck by lightning and his little eyes twinkled as he jumped up and rushed out to open the minicab door for me.

'Bugger me, who'd have thought,' he whispered.

'Absolutely,' I replied.

Mr Glick stood behind shaking his head, the new glasses polished by the sun, and the car drew slowly into the traffic. I had to get a taxi everywhere. My bum was still sore from being bowed by Mr Gropius, although the five lines of sheet music were already beginning to fade. Like most pop music, it doesn't last long.

On the estate the boys in their hoodies and baseball caps waved fists and spat at our car and I wondered why Mr Asis, my regular driver, wore the little crocheted hat and sharp beard if he didn't want to draw attention to himself.

Troy was caddying and his sister Mandy was out shopping with her mates. Troy's mum made a nice cup of tea and I don't usually drink tea, but it was delicious in the big Arsenal mug and I didn't even worry about the germs lurking in the cracks.

I kicked off my Jimmy Choo shoes and decided I was only going to wear high heels from this day on and wondered briefly what the twins were doing. I ate two Bourbon biscuits and it was a riot telling Troy's mum all the sordid details of how Henry had tried to rape me in the chapel.

'That's bloody, whatsit, you know, what's it called, you know, in a church ...'

'Sacrilegious.'

'Dirty sod.' She waved a red fingernail at me. 'Don't trust 'em, sweetheart, they're only after one fing.'

'One bloody thing,' I said.

We shook our heads and blew steam from our tea.

'And when they geddit, they fukk orf. Scuse my French.'

She was dressed for a quick getaway in a skinny top with her bra showing and denim shorts that showed little slices of her bottom. Ash fell on her flat tummy and she brushed it away.

'You've gotta good little figure there when you ain't all covered up,' she said. 'If you've got it, darlin', flaunt it.'

I was cross-dressing in tight jeans and my school blazer, my toes wriggling over the unfamiliar texture of the orange carpet, and I watched as she added a nip of something from a miniature bottle to her tea. 'Too bloody 'ot,' she said, and crossed her long polished legs as she looked back at me. 'Here, 'ark at me. Loik I know anyfing.'

'I think it's good to give friends advice,' I said.

'Dead right. I always do. And I'll tell you something else shall I, I always get it wrong.'

We laughed and it was great sitting there with Troy's mum.

She leaned forward with the miniature bottle. 'Here, a little drop won't hurt,' she said and I held my mug towards her.

I had gone to Troy's flat that day on a special mission. I was carrying the original disc from the film of Simon Daviditz pawing me and stored it among the debris in Troy's bedroom. No one would ever find it there. I walked back through the estate, I knew all the shortcuts now, and I don't know what it was that Troy's mum put in my tea but everything in the High Street looked nice for a change, brighter in some way, and I went to check out my future fans at Greens.

Chapter Fourteen

NOTHING.

I'm not one to show off. No way. But the musicians thought *I'm A Virgin* was the best piece of work to come out of Canterbury *since the 60s*. The three black girls had rolled their bottoms and called me Sista, which is like *amazing*, and the kettle drum player bent like a weeping willow to whisper, 'Mmm, operatic'. And he's with the Royal Philharmonic.

When jaded Dave says: 'That should do it,' the master of understatement is merely practising his art, and as Mr Glick is always trying to get one over on me, when he said the soundtrack was too good for porn I didn't know what to think.

Saskia was lying on her bed, kicking her legs back and forth in time to the kettle drums and said *très bien, superb.* Tara stuck her finger between the pages of her Michel Houellebecq, stretched like a cat across the window sill and yawned *no pas mal.* She was dressed in black. Saskia was in sk8er jeans and a T-shirt, and I've no idea what happened in the Caribbean, but I didn't need the little heart-shaped birth mark to tell the girls apart any more because they never dressed the same and Saskia had switched to *Marlboro Lights* because of her cough.

'The absolute first thing I'm going to do is pay you back,' I said. 'Cross my heart.'

They glanced at each other, raised their thin shoulders and, as they glanced back at me in tight jeans and my school blazer, the look in their eyes gave me the feeling we were friends again, and that's what friendship is all about, a little bit of using here, a little bit of using there. There was something in me they needed and something in them that I needed and it was just too

179

existentialist to explain.

'Have you heard anything?' asked Saskia.

I shook my head.

Tara opened her book. 'You will,' she said.

But I didn't.

My script was now a film and, while the CDs and DVDs were crossing the land in dirty white vans, I was limping through the bleak corridors of Saint Sebastian like a mediaeval nun with a stone in my shoe.

'You're very quiet these days,' Sister Theresa said in her nice way.

'I'm thinking,' I told her and she went away feeling as pleased as a Teddy bear.

Sister Mustapha in art was always going on about Marcel Duchamp and the *readymades* and I got a good grasp on the concept when I made my daily calls to the record companies and got the same set of readymade replies.

'I'm sorry, we have not received your package ...'

'I'm sorry, but there is no way of knowing if we have received your package ...'

'I'm sorry, but if we received a package from you it is one of the incalculable number of identical packages that flood across our desks in an avalanche and it will be listened to when Sara or Lara or Farrar get back from Cheltenham or Cannes or Caunes or Calcutta ...'

'I'm sorry, but you have reached the wrong number and the people you are trying to reach have died or gone abroad or gone out of business.'

And I thought, gone mad more likely and someone had once turned down the Beatles, which was a silly name even if they were bigger than Jesus. Apart from sending out 63 padded envelopes to the 63 record companies I'd drawn from the net, I'd sent out another 37 to radio stations and DJs.

Nothing. Nothing. *Niente*.

Call back next week. Write a letter. Phone the Samaritans. It was hopeless. I went to see Mr Gropius and he dug wax out of his ear and sighed because the world was never ready.

'Remember Mozart?'

I did and I don't know why, but I felt so dead with all the waiting there was only one thing that would put some life back into my eyes and Mr Gropius, the old devil, knew just what it was.

'Shall we?' he said.

I sighed. 'I suppose so.'

He followed me upstairs. I took off all my clothes and laid them carefully over a chair. If you are going to do something you should do it properly I always think. I was going to get sweaty and spunky and, anyway, I just adored being naked. I had, as Mr Gropius had once remarked, probably the prettiest bottom in the whole world and, if that's the case, what was the point in keeping it hidden? Old Vlad was fixated, obsessed, possessed by my perfectly round rump and spent like an age running his soft palms over the surface, following the curve into the crack, circling the winking dark sea shell of my back gate, the secret entrance to paradise. I lay across the high bed with my arms and legs stretched out like I was a starfish and felt like a cat being stroked.

'Mmm. That feels lovely,' I moaned.

'It is like practising scales,' he said. 'It's all in the preparation.'

First he softened and warmed my flesh and then he brought his hand down across the surface as hard as he possibly could. I squealed with delight. I wriggled about on the big embroidered bed cover and he aimed the flat of his hand once more across the protruding cheeks, scorching them like two buns in a baking hot oven.

It's a strange alchemy, the heat of those slaps passing up your spine and down your legs, and while your head is buried in the bedclothes and your eyes are pressed tight, it's like jumping out of an aeroplane and waiting for the moment when the parachute jerks you back to reality. You are freefalling between one slap and the next, a tide of agony that drifts inexorably towards ecstasy.

That's what's so weird. Being smacked made me feel alive, human, real, and it occurred to me that my life had really been in so many ways too easy. I was pretty, great breasts, a tiny waist, the best bum in the world, and when you are pretty and young you can get what you want from anyone you want. I just had to say *please* and people melted in my hand.

Mr Gropius laid another spank across my bum and I rocked up and down, and if anyone was watching through binoculars from across the harbour they would have seen an old man spanking a naked young girl and assumed he had enticed or tricked her into this humiliating position. It just shows how appearances can deceive. If I was being chastised, I was chastising myself. The spanking was a big pleasure to old Vlad Gropius. But it was a greater pleasure to me. I needed it.

Down it came again, a mighty wallop that made the ornaments on the shelf rattle off their dust. My bum was burning and, to my eternal surprise and pleasure, I felt little contractions like the stitch when you're running cross country grip my tummy and slither like a snake down to my pussy.

I was sopping wet. Literally sopping. Gurgles of girl juice were slipping over the swollen lips of my vagina like sap from a tree, glossing my thighs, soaking the embroidered bed cover. I gripped the edge of the bed and pushed myself up onto my knees so that I must have looked like a little pony with its rear end high in the air.

Mr Gropius lifted his arm up to the roof of the low beamed ceiling and, as his hand came down, ringing across my flesh like a cymbal, all those ripples and contractions burst like an exploding atom bomb and I screamed through the biggest orgasm I'd ever had.

'Vunderbar!'

Yes, indeed. Wonderful. Do all girls climax when they are spanked? I really had no idea and didn't actually care. I did. And it *vas vunderbar*. I lay there writhing and sweating and the old devil went down on his knees and licked the burnt surface of my flesh, over the cheeks, his plump tongue pushing at the sea shell until he had wormed his way like a clever little creature deep inside.

'I don't have very long,' I said.

I pulled myself further across the bed. I went up on my knees, lowered my head to the bedcover and waited while Mr

Gropius removed his trousers and big white underpants. This is what he really wanted. I knew that.

'Bella,' he said.

He pushed the head of his penis against the tight ring of my bottom and I wiggled about until it wriggled its way inside. Fortunately, I was soaking from that great big climax and with just a couple of good hard pushes he managed to get the shaft right the way in. He was so happy, pushing in and out of my arse, and I thought people take sex far too seriously. It's just fun.

For about a million years people have held back in what is surely the most natural, most human thing in the world, two people having sex, young or old, fat and thin, what did it matter as long as they were enjoying it?

He started to go faster. I rocked with the beat. We were two musicians. And then he started to come, his sperm coating the inside of my anus and sliding down my legs. I collapsed in a heap and Mr Gropius lay there like he'd just run a four-minute mile.

I kissed the tip of his nose and leapt up to get dressed. I didn't bother to take a bath. Like the twins, I had learned the pleasures of being all spunky.

I trotted down the stairs and took a deep breath of salty sea air. I was alive. I will succeed in everything I set out to do, and there was a spring in my step as I crossed the wet cobbles, drawn by the soothing smell of fried food, and discovered how chips dipped in tomato ketchup really do cheer people up. Not that I was miserable, mind you. I was ecstatic. I was just royally pissed that I hadn't heard from those record companies yet.

Anyway, I ate three chips smothered in blood red ketchup and fed the rest to the seagulls before walking on. The junk outside the second-hand shops was arranged as if by the random whims of a hurricane and a gypsy selling heather grabbed my hand.

'Be lucky,' she rasped, and I gave her 50p.

The shop windows carried the usual range of lies like false flags on a pirate ship, SALE, half-price, cut price, deluxe, luxury, best ever, everything must go and I wondered why and to where? M&S had a new display of knickers for S&M and I crossed the road between the racing cars and couldn't imagine where all these people were going and why they had to get there in such a hurry.

When I entered the sex shop Jason raised his arm like he was Che Guevara and his tattooed fist froze midair. There was a collective gasp as if an industrial vacuum cleaner had sucked the breath from the world and the three figures before me moved together like the witches in Macbeth. Bubble, bubble, toil and trouble.

Tabatha Van Deegan stared at Jason, stared at me, stared back at the videos and DVDs and CDs in the new releases display, stared again at Jason, then at me, then at Jack Bennett, who was wearing a clingy pale blue cashmere top with a white pleated skirt, white shoes and pearls (!), then at Daisy Bloom, ditto in lemon (!), then Tabby grabbed a DVD case and shook it as if it were the incontrovertible last and final piece of evidence in a long and complex murder trial.

'You,' she hissed through her braces. She was in pink. Not her colour.

'Hi, Tabby,' I said. 'Hi,' I said to the girls.

'Honey ...'

We all glared at Jason and I shook my head. There are times in life when you should just keep your mouth shut. This was one of them and Jason worked that out all by himself.

It was, in fact, a special moment although how special only time would tell. For now I stood there with my warm and tender bottom, a bit smelly, and looked at the girls all fluffy and full of themselves in spring pastels and couldn't help wondering how Tabatha had lured the Satanists out of their leather.

Jack and Daisy grabbed DVDs from the display, peered down at the artwork and stared back at me with the faces of small children when they first learn to read, their lips moving while they shaped the words, their tiny eyes flooded with joy and changing emotions.

The primordial calm which may have gone on forever was broken by the sound of the plastic strip curtain slapping the door frame as Christian Thomas slid out of the hardcore room with his skin drained of colour from the sickly pink light inside.

'Don't say anything because I'm still not speaking to you,' I said.

He joined Jason in keeping silent.

The little mouths dropped open, the braces gleamed and the curtains settled down.

'You look great,' I told the pastel bunch and they studied me from my wild hair and melancholic brown eyes, down across the white slopes of my undecaled T-shirt, the school blazer with the badge unsewing itself from the pocket (was that a metaphor?) my jeans with the split knee and lucky red heels. They looked and they kept looking as if I were someone they had once seen in a photograph and were seeing for the first time in the flesh.

'Gotta bounce,' and I bounced.

Christian Thomas caught up with me almost immediately and, as I turned, I noticed the girls squeeze out of the shop doorway like striped toothpaste.

'Please let me explain ...'

'Never explain, never complain and never say sorry. That's what Nonna used to say.'

'She's my damn agent, Bella. You don't know what it's like.'

'And girls should learn French and play the piano.'

'She's trying to sell my book. I need this.'

'Has she sold it?'

'No.'

'Well then. Don't make promises if you don't intend to keep them.'

He hung his head. The girls swivelled on their heels and the cross currents sucked them back into the sex shop. The cars raced and we walked back to the cottage where I chugged up the chips and drank camomile tea because it's good for the nerves and *everyone* was getting on my nerves.

I produced *I'm A Virgin* from my bag.

'What's this?'

I rolled my eyes and watched as he slipped the CD in his fancy machine. He listened. He looked at me. He looked back at

185

the machine. His shoulders sort of slumped. He held out his palms as if feeling for rain. He shook his head and, as the strings faded and the echoes slipped away from the saxophone, he stared at me with the same expression he'd worn that day when he found £20 in my knickers.

'You wrote it?'

I nodded.

'You're playing ...'

I nodded.

'Vlad did the ...'

'With no help from you.'

'It's incredible.'

'Incredible as in amazing and unbelievable, or incredible as in it has no credit, it's unworthy.'

'Bella, it's ... it's so good.'

'Do you know anyone at the record companies?'

'I'm not sure ...'

'Or the radio?' I added.

'Not really.'

'Typical.'

We were silent. The Hindu statues on the shelves were frozen in the midst of erotic dance steps and I could hear the seagulls screaming like babies through the open window. He put the CD back in the case and sat cross-legged on the floor. I stretched my legs across the velvet sofa. Specks of mud dotted my ruby shoes.

'You've changed your style, Bella,' he finally said.

'Have I?' I replied. He was slumped forward. I said, 'I read your book,' and his back shot up, straight as the Buddha.

'And?'

'I didn't understand it.'

'Yes, but ...'

'Don't explain.'

The air left him in a depleted gush and I waved goodbye over my shoulder without saying another word.

I wandered around the curving coast with the white tips of the waves licking the cliff face. I remembered Troy calling Saint Sebastian a prison and it was the sort of prison where

186

people are sent for petty crimes like insider trading or corrupting officials, and Simon Daviditz said everyone's at it and the only crime now is getting caught. They had passed the tipping point at Zach Kessler's real estate and the last of the squatters would be out of the flats by summer when the weather's nice.

The Union Jack stirred above the high tower and I remembered feeling so proud in my school uniform and straw hat that day in autumn when I first arrived at the convent to finish my education. It was such a long time ago, over six months, and that may not seem a lot if you're like 50 or something because six months when you're 50 is only one percent of your life, but when you're a teenager it's like forever.

The trees along the drive were in leaf again and an avenue of shade stretched like a carpet over the path and up the stone steps to the entrance doors. The ivy shivered like a shadow on the yellow façade, the flint chips shiny as eyes on the chapel wall and the memory that came to me was Henry staring at me like a wolf across the chapel at San Pi.

In the quiet corridors, the light was sprinkled with motes of dinosaur dust; it struck me that while the Apostles looked darkly mysterious like Mr Asis, they had the irreproachable blue eyes of Christian Thomas.

The TV room was filled with Avril Lavigne lookalikes trying to fill their bras and watching *Buffy* re-runs on video. It killed an hour before tea and Katie Makarios swished along saying Buffy was just *so* cool and she wanted to be *just like her* as we filed back through the dusty light to the refectory. Her wiry black locks with the faint whiff of olive oil had vanished into a pair of perfumed curtains that swayed sulkily from side to side as if her head was balanced on a loose spring and I noticed as she sat down opposite me at the long table that her moustache had gone.

'Your hair. It's like *amazing*,' I said.

'You should do it, Bella. It would look really, really bling.'

'Do you think?'

'You just need like tonnes of conditioner.' Her eyes zipped from side to side. 'Sunsilk,' she added in a whisper. 'I'll give you some,' and a chill ran through me as I recalled Friar Dunstan's warning in his lessons on Troy. *Beware of Greeks bearing gifts*.

Katie Makarios nattered on like we were mates and the pastel trio appeared like a singing group from olden times, teeth sharp as knives, their white bags which they rattled in unison full of magic. When the twins came and sat either side of me I felt better.

'Bonjour.'

'Bonjour.'

'For what we are about to receive.'

'May the Lord make us truly thankful.'

'Amen.'

'Ah, men,' said Tara.

I drank a glass of milk wondering why the Lord should make us truly thankful when really we should be truly thankful without prompting and, at the same time, perhaps a little bit cross that the Lord appeared unaware that in their relentless Pursuit of Happiness, Americans are using like 30 per cent of the world's natural resources and that's just not fair.

Red jam in china saucers and crusty bread in woven baskets made in the art department to a Nubian design passed along the table and being at school was like being in prison, and it was tedious that old people always believe they know best and really everything was moving too fast for them to know what was going on; Mother can't even change the date on the digital watch she wears power walking. The performers were getting younger, the fans were getting younger, and I had to hurry because every day I was getting older. I used to adore weekends but naturally the record companies were closed and I just couldn't wait for Monday when I would be back on the iPhone.

I glanced towards the platform as if in search of the ghost of Sister Nuria and was blinded by three sets of gleaming white teeth in sparkly silver braces.

'The Tabathas are after me,' I said.

'Fuhking oiks,' said Tara and I just know Katie Makarios wished she'd said that.

I was working on a new song. When you have a hit you need

material for an album and that's where young performers get screwed using songwriters and recording covers. *Is It True* was *très* simple, just three chords, and I imagined the black girls wiggling their bottoms and getting their pink tongues round the chorus line.

> *Do you love me?*
> *Is it true?*
> *Yes I do*
> *I know everyone can see*
> *You're the only one for me*
> *Do you love me?*
> *Is it true?*
> *Yes I do*
> *Do you promise to be true?*
> *Am I the only one for you?*
> *Do you love me?*
> *Is it true?*
> *Yes I do*
> *You don't have to look for signs*
> *I'll love you 'til the end of time*
> *Do you love me?*
> *Is it true?*
> *Yes I do*

There was a muted clap and I turned on the piano stool to find Sister Theresa with her hands clasped over her large breasts.

'Bella, how lovely. A song for Jesus.'

Is It True still needed some work.

Chapter Fifteen

THERE WERE DEEP GOUGES across my forehead and bags under my eyes. I changed creams. I went to bed early. I did yoga every day. I swam in the pool with the fat girls and learnt how to meditate from a book. A week later the lines were still there and the numbers had worn off my mobile phone.

I spent like hours sitting on the windowsill and, as I stared out at the choppy grey waves, I thought if I swam out into the bay and just kept on swimming, when I drowned they would listen to my music and I'd teach everyone a lesson.

'Do you think drowning hurts very much?'

Saskia's *doh!* face as she left the dorm showed she was like *so* interested. Tara was writing still in her prep book and was about to follow when she stopped so spectacularly midstep I thought for a moment she'd been picked off by a sniper. She dragged the local paper from her bag and pointed at one of the ads. Jazz P Bang Bang was bringing the *Live From The Street Show* to Canterbury.

'He's quite, you know,' she said and shrugged like she felt awkward about something. 'Influential.'

I read the ad. 'It's tonight,' I gasped.

'Is it Friday already?' she said and wandered off shaking her head as if life was so full of surprises.

I let it sink in for a moment and got straight on the phone to Troy, who acted bored as boys always do and I had to tell him that seeing DJs live was good for his career. 'Jazz P Bang Bang's like *really* influential.'

'You got a ticket for me an' all this time, didja?'

'It's not like Dallas, Troy. We have to pay,' I replied. Troy had never quite forgiven me that Mr Thomas had taken me to the *Bitch Tour*, and of course he didn't know that it was Mr Thomas who had planted his seed in the dark corners of my virgin bottom. It was weird, I adored Troy, but I'd only ever sucked him off.

'Yeah, right,' he said, and I'd almost lost the thread.

'Get the ladder from Mr Thomas. I'll call the cab company.'

'Spud can drive us.'

'Doh?'

'My drummer.'

'Are you mad?'

'Live fast, die young.'

'Forget it. I'll call the cab company,' I said. 'Gotta bounce.'

All my muscles felt young again as I flew along the empty corridors to Latin where Friar Dunstan pretended not to notice I was late and continued with the 12 labours of Hercules, his latest fad.

It was interesting, actually, and I was listening, but the moment I peeked out the window I was mesmerised by the groundsman as he painstakingly followed the white lines on the hockey field with a fresh layer of paint. He was moving so slowly it was like he was searching every blade of grass for something very small and very lost and what I didn't see was the old friar slide down the aisle between the desks. His bony fist pounded the woodwork in front of me and I gagged on the chalk dust rising into the air.

'If you're not interested in acquiring an education, young lady, I don't know what you're doing here.'

'I'm sorry, I've got my ...'

'No more excuses. Just get on with it,' he screamed and I thought, *wow*, when saints lose their cool it's like the Ice Age.

His voice resounded through the open window, the groundsman swerved from the straight and narrow and the class fell about in hysterics.

Friar Dunstan made his way back down the aisle. He composed himself by polishing his glasses and spoke like a holy man. 'Go to your room. Have a good hard think,' he said, and Jack and Daisy swivelled mechanically like those plants that catch flies, mouths gaping, their teeth caged in braces, and I was so glad I had perfect teeth.

I hurried along the empty corridors and I should have felt embarrassed or remorseful or something, but I was just glad to have a spare hour to get back on the phone. I gazed at the old paintings and swallowed the dinosaur dust and thought nothing ever dies or goes away it just reforms and changes and I was glad I would always be able to visit Daddy in the churchyard. Boarding school was just *so* restricting and the sort of school where Troy went was even worse.

I told the twins I'd made plans to go over the wall as soon as they got back to the dorm. Saskia dropped on the bed. 'If you were a Stymphalian Bird you'd be able to fly over,' she said.

'Then Hercules would shoot you with an arrow,' said Tara impatiently and turned to me. 'We're coming, too.' She went straight for her stash and started rolling a fag from a packet of Drum.

'It's too dangerous.'

'Excuse me.' Her little pink tongue darted out to lick the paper.

'If I'm on my own you can cover for me.'

She stuffed the fag in her mouth, grabbed Saskia's retro Teddy with a studded leather collar and held it right in front of my face. She spoke in a mean Teddy voice. 'No one says no to Teddy,' she growled. 'No one says no to Teddy ...'

Talk about *The Night of the Chapel Rape – the sequel*. 'OK,' I gasped.

Tara lit up, and the way she took lots of short, sharp hits on the fag I guessed she was taking it down now. Saskia rescued Teddy and propped him back on the pillow.

'What time?' she asked.

'Half past six.'

Saskia turned to Teddy. 'You be good,' she said, and Tara looked at me and I looked back at Tara and our bottom lips lost all sense of self control.

Troy was waiting with Spud, who was on probation, both wearing hoodies and cupping fags against the drizzle when we shot across the grass and scaled the spars on the old gate.

'Fuck me, free of you,' said Troy as he shouldered the ladder.

Spud was bobbing up and down, poking out his chin, rolling his shoulders and I thought thank goodness he hasn't pinched a car to drive us to Canterbury. Mr Asis was waiting calmly on the promenade stroking his beard and squinting over the pages of a little book. He drove slowly, as always, and I thought he'd probably make a good groundsman at our school.

The country lanes slipped into wet city streets where people were dodging through the rain like demons in the ghostly yellow light. Saskia towed Troy by the tail of his long red belt and Spud's limbs were moving to some manic beat only he could hear. Glazed clubbers in slashed T-shirts were shuffling into The Marlowe and I learned something else about boys: they don't plan, they don't think things through and they never have any money. It was £10 to get in and we didn't have enough. I rushed back to the car.

'Mr Asis, can you lend me £20? I'll pay you back.'

He looked up from his reading and stared into my eyes. 'Why, of course,' he said, and it was a good job he wasn't mean like Mr Glick.

Inside the vinyl whirled, the strobe lights were quicksilver raining over the heaving dancers and you couldn't understand what the DJ was saying and it didn't matter what he was saying because the repetitive rap and the pounding music were champagne bubbles bursting over your skin, gushing through your bloodstream, and it made your legs move and your arms move and my shirt was sticking to my back and I dropped my blazer on the floor. Troy looked like a little bird bursting from its shell and seeing the world for the first time.

'Fuck,' he said.

Spud was studying the abandoned shoulder bags and Saskia rolled her eyes. Tara in her mesh top slid against me and her green eyes flashed and her hair was gelled in points and her long legs were white like ribbons below her black mini. She grabbed the loops on my jeans and our pubic bones rolled together and the beat grew pagan and it was so wild and sexy I

193

almost forgot why we were there.

The music went on and on like a rising tide thrusting against the walls and pulsing in waves across the ceiling, growing louder and louder like something eternal and hypnotic. The lights turned amber like a million tiger eyes staring from the dark and all around me girls and boys were taking off their tops and everyone was wet and young and the heat was rising and the smell of damp bodies made my hormones fizz and it was all so intoxicating I felt like I'd arrived, that I really, really belonged. I was pulling off my T-shirt when Tara stopped me. She held me tight and I wanted to kiss her.

'Let's go,' she whispered, and I reached for my jacket in the pile on the floor, and I didn't know where I was going but I wanted to be wherever it was.

Saskia was dancing between Spud and Troy, the tart, the *tarts*, actually, and I followed Tara up to the platform where Jazz P Bang Bang was protected by two security guards of the black T-shirt and big belly variety.

'Sorry, darling, can't talk to the DJ.'

'Tell him it's Tara Scott-Wallace.'

She spoke forcefully, pushing her nipples forward, and he could hardly pull himself away.

Jazz P Bang Bang was a white Rasta who talked black and had golden hair in springy dreadlocks. He was moving from side to side like a giant insect talking gibberish.

'Dis my brudd, he big bigger dan big, he king, he da king rap wid da sling slap, he bad, he bad, he bad, he da bad bad of de bad.'

The security guy tapped him on the shoulder and he paused, glancing down at us. He was confused for a moment, but then a light sparkled in his blue eyes and he shrugged an OK to security. We climbed up onto the platform and Jazz P Bang Bang put his hands on his hips and stared at me.

'You're not ... hang on,' he said and looked back at Tara. 'Where's the other one?'

Tara yawned. 'Hello, Jasper. What are you doing in Canterbury?'

'Getting ecumenical, what else,' he said and he didn't sound black now, he sounded like Henry.

And Tara sounded like Nena.

'This is Bella. She's made a recording. It's awfully good.'

'But I have a set, Tara. You can't just slip things in.'

'Oh, really.'

'Well, you know ...' He sighed and shook his golden hair. I took the CD from my red blazer.

'What are you doing here?' he asked suddenly, turning back to Tara again. 'Aren't you at school?'

'Bore, actually.'

'Ya. Ya. I haven't seen Lulu since, God, that weekend ...'

'Nor have I.'

They both sounded confused and exhausted and I wondered who Lulu was. Jasper removed the CD from the case. He seemed puzzled, like he'd never seen a CD before, like he didn't quite know where he was and what he was doing there, like life was just one endless series of minor irritations. 'What's it called?'

'*I'm A Virgin.*'

'Oh, jolly good.'

'It's operatic,' I said.

He looked vague as he stuck the disc in the console. 'Bella, ya?'

I nodded. He pressed the play switch, the pounding faded, he dragged the spinning vinyl backwards and became animated as he turned black.

'Dis my sista. She da main girl. She da new chick-a-chick-chick wid da big hit. She da last virgin, I mean da last of the last, yeah. Let's give it up for Bella and da rap opera.'

The kettle drums were beating, the sax was punching out the high notes as he spoke, the cello led the strings from the big speakers and *I'm A Virgin* had never sounded so good. I could see Saskia sandwiched between Troy and Spud. Tara linked her fingers with mine. The whole room was jumping. I looked back at Tara and she smiled and Tara never smiled.

'*No pas mal.*'

'Who is this person?' I asked her.

She threw up her thin shoulders. 'Oh, don't worry about all

195

that rubbish. Come on.'

Tara whispered something to Jasper. We stepped into the crowd like a stone being hurled into a pool and, as we moved, everyone seemed to be moving with us, *I'm A Virgin* cranking up the beat and I felt hot and happy and I didn't even care that Saskia was snogging Troy.

Was Tara the dark figure from the past who would blow the winds of change into the future? It couldn't be her. She was there now. She was always there, her skinny pretty body in pink mesh swaying to the rhythm and like we were twins we both crossed our arms, reached for our tops and ripped them over our heads. It was so liberating. Rasta words sizzled over the sound system, *I'm A Virgin* slid straight into Dallas McTee's new single *Fetish* and the clubbers kept dancing and clapping and, as I swayed like a candle flame, Tara swayed like a candle flame and I remembered the giant shadows following me along the corridors of San Pi.

On the way home they passed endless cigarettes and all you had to do was take a deep breath because the car was full of smoke and Mr Asis had the windows closed and kept nodding and shaking his head like he was back wherever he'd come from.

I was exhausted and relieved because *I'm A Virgin* had made its début and Spud, who didn't say a lot, said it was *awright*. Saskia had her face all over Troy. Tara was holding my hand and the countryside was shifting and mythical like the sea at night and the convent, when it appeared outlined against the dark blue horizon, was like a castle in the Dark Ages and we were travellers bringing the future from places far, far away.

If I kept a diary, which I don't, although Christian Thomas said life is easier when you do, and that's not his real name, by the way, but anyway, if I kept a diary I would have called that Friday Good Friday or D-Day or something because in the following days the siege of Troy began at Saint Sebastian.

Like all sieges it was a slow build up and started with *The Daily Telegraph* being left mysteriously on the prep table in our room after breakfast on Saturday.

On the *front* page was a postage stamp headshot of

me ... *Me!* ... in the devil mask copied from the DVD cover. Above, with a question mark, was the heading *I'm A Virgin?* and below it said: WHO IS THIS GIRL? See page 17.

Saskia riffled through Afghanistan, Pollution, Starvation and Scientists Deny Global Warning Threat until, on page 17, under the heading WHO IS THIS GIRL? we came across another photograph of me bare from the waist up with Pinkie and Perky looking adorable, even if the reproduction was a bit fuzzy.

Saskia read: 'A pornographic film with three teenaged girls indulging in unnatural acts is becoming hot property in sex shops, through mail order and over the internet.'

'That's us.' I said.

'Shush,' said Tara.

Saskia continued: 'Under the provocative title *I'm A Virgin*, the 10-minute film shows two girls who appear to be twins performing lewd acts before another little Jezebel appears with bared breasts and wearing a devil mask. Strapped around her waist is a false penis in black rubber.

'Moving from one to the other, the young woman in the mask, wielding the dildo, performs acts that would be perverse among adults. But these are young women.

'The point that should be made, and made in no uncertain terms, is that whoever made this film has contravened every moral code that guides decent society. There are laws to protect our young people and it is the responsibility of the relevant departments to track these pornographers down and charge them accordingly.

'As for the young women themselves, in spite of their adult bodies and the adult acts I have witnessed, they are still just young people, and I can only assume they have been tricked or threatened by evil men into making this vile, disgusting film.

'It is true that young women are growing up faster, but it is not a question of changing hormones but a sign of changing social norms and values. There has always been teenage culture, if that is the right word under the circumstances, but the marketing men have pounced on indulgent parents in these indulgent times to sell them all manner of products and, indeed, turn our young people into products ...'

Tara yawned. She was yawning like *all* the time, and we scanned the rest of the article but it was all about teenagers being sold low-budget movies by the greed merchants of Hollywood and children being dressed by their mothers in designer trash.

'We ought to get the paper fingerprinted and see who put it in our room,' I suggested.

Tara pushed out her tummy and turned to her sister. 'Does Black Jack still have the key, Mr Holmes?' she said.

'He does, indeed, Doctor. Pass me my pipe.'

The twins are *just* amazing.

We had locks on our rooms because if you put something down for half a second it vanishes. The girls were all rich, with few exceptions, and it must be coded in the genes because rich girls were truly dedicated to larceny. I had a different theory about the locks and was convinced that the nuns knew what went on in the dorms and didn't want to know what went on in the dorms, and like the church since forever just closed their eyes and kept praying. I mean, think about the last war and the Vatican!

We trotted off to Spanish and I did try to work hard but it was never easy on a Saturday and Sister Gilberte with her solitary long eyebrow just wasn't Sister Nuria. Anyway, she was French *not* Spanish and even the twins couldn't understand a word she said.

While we were sitting at our desks like nice schoolgirls, feet crossed at our ankles, the conjugations for the verbs *ser* and *estar* in precise columns on the blackboard, outside in the real world all the pieces of a giant puzzle were slowly slotting together and I would only see the picture much later.

What I didn't know then was that when Jazz P Bang Bang wasn't being black he was Jasper Bryant Browne and reads *The Daily Telegraph,* obviously. He must have recognised the *I'm A Virgin* title on the front page and started playing *I'm A Virgin* on his radio show *Sounds Like The Street* like every five minutes.

Something else we didn't know, or actually we probably did know but had never given it any thought, is that apart from the royal family, the number one fixation in tabloidland is teenage girls with bare breasts, and while *The Daily Telegraph* was moving on to loftier subjects, the bottom feeders of the gutter press were grubbing about in sex shops buying up *I'm A Virgin* DVDs and beginning a manhunt, well, girlhunt, anyway.

We strolled into town, past the broken things in the grimy shops, Saskia loyal to her new look, sex on a stick with her black bra riding over a skinny white top and white hipsters, Tara in the black mini she liked so much and copying me in a school blazer, and me in Police shades and my lucky shoes. We went to see Jason for something to do and when he told us he'd sold every *I'm A Virgin* DVD in stock I felt a nice little zing.

''Ere, an' I'll tell you what, that blonde tart, the Yankee one, came and got one of them devil suits, didn't she.'

'I don't know, did she?'

'Yeah, right an' all.'

We crossed the road and, as if guided by a divine hand, coming towards us in the High Street were Bubble Bubble, Toil & Trouble all polished in pastel and it was like we were meeting for a shootout at the OK Corral or wherever it is. They stopped. We stopped. They reached for their white bags and we pushed back our jackets, reached for our hips.

'I happened to read the newspaper this morning, don't you know,' Tabatha said, and I thought she looked so old now she'd applied to Cambridge and was finishing her A-levels *for the third time*.

'Fuhk off, Tabby. Don't be such a prig,' Tara said and we marched on without a shot being fired.

'They know who you are, *Tara Scott-Wallace*,' Tabatha yelled and we didn't look back. We strolled into Greens where Tara gave the pimply boy a CD of *I'm A Virgin* and told him to put it on.

'Rye, rye, right,' he said, and Tara kissed him because she's nice like that.

I watched all the plump things wobbling about to the music and I wanted to tell them it was me singing but it was sort of nice being incognito like a celebrity behind dark glasses. Then Spud walked up, pointing at the speaker.

'Oi, that's you,' he said.

'No, I'm me,' I told him.

'Was on the radio this morning, wannit.'

We did the big doh!

'No?'

'Heard it, didn't I.'

He sniffed. I was gobsmacked, or over the moon. One of those things and when I looked at Tara she just shrugged.

''Ere,' Spud continued, turning to Saskia. 'Got a message from Troy. He's finishing his round caddying. He'll be 'ere in 'alf hour.'

Saskia blushed, Tara squeezed my fingers and it was just so weird that I'd always been closer to Saskia, and now it was Tara, and I thought it was totally cool that Troy fancied Saskia because that's what happens and, anyway, I'd been on the radio.

I walked back up the High Street with Tara and, as we queued at the chip van, I could hear piano music through the open windows at Mr Gropius's cottage.

'I'm going to quite miss it here,' Tara said, and the tide washed over the harbour wall while we fed the seagulls.

Chapter Sixteen

I'VE HAD *ANOTHER* BIRTHDAY. I'm five feet, eight-and-three-quarter inches in bare feet, exactly 101 pounds and the other day I found a grey hair. I almost had a heart attack, and it wasn't exactly cheering when my publicist decides it's time for me to write an autobiography.

'Are you *like* snorting Tiger Balm?'

'We need it before we go to America. They like all that bullshit.' She pauses to draw air. '*Sowwy.*'

So Lucy finds this journo, like the *best* in the world, her sister or something, it's so nepotistic, whatever that means, and she was just useless and I said I'll use my own writer or forget it.

'Like *you* know a writer?'

'Like *I'm* not paying *your* wages?'

Lucy sucks more air through her designer teeth, I get on the phone, and I thought what's the point in having a publicist when you have to do *everything* yourself.

The blonde tart with the silver Audi never did sell Christian's book and now here we sit with his little tape machine whirring like Chinese whispers. Lucy has piles of newspaper cuttings and a mad look in her green-almond eyes. Gabriella, my stylist, must have learned hairdressing at Braille school and is busy massaging her CV with my Spanish tutor, who's kind of cute if you can tolerate the rainstorm on the soft cees.

'Ouch!'

'*Por favor, repite: Bar*the*lona es una* thi*udad con muchos* thi*nes ...*'

'*Bar*the*lona es una* ...'

'Doh! Gabriella. I think he means me.'

'*Pardone*.'

'Ouch! You did that on purpose.'

Christian looks up and smiles.

That's not his real name, by the way, and I know I've mentioned this before, and I may just mention it again, but anyway, Christian is wading through the cuttings and don't ask me how the newspapers work because I don't know how they work, and all I do know is that it's a dance to the death and you have to use them because they're only using you.

'There are a lot of loose ends, Bella.'

'Excuse me?'

He holds up one of the front pages: me, naked from my tiny toes to the devil mask, the babies just gorge, the dildo so *out there*.

'That's a body double,' snaps Lucy.

Actually Lucy Mikimoto is Japanese and what she snapped was *Aghh, that a bodi-doddle*. You get used to it.

He holds up another newspaper, and another, pages and pages of the stuff, the tabloids screaming just look at those saucy young tits, it's absolutely disgusting, and there's eight more pages of saucy young tits inside, oh dear oh dear and isn't it immoral, you can even see their pubic hair: *full spread inside*!

Yawn. While the big presses were rolling that Saturday night after the Friday night disco, men with cameras were following the M2 out of London to the Kent coast and that woman from New York whose 44DD enhanced breasts have been so enhanced it's like *ughh!* and I can't recall her name ...

And, anyway, she received a tip-off from her London contact and was flying the redeye from JFK. Sara, Lara and Farrar had finally returned from Cheltenham, Cannes, Caunes and Calcutta and *I'm A Virgin* was playing on 37 different radio stations across the land and Rupert said if you kept twirling the dial that day you could find it somewhere.

Sometimes when you look back you kind of realise that you knew all along that something amazing was about to happen because you had a sense of déjà vu or you glimpsed yourself standing outside yourself and it always seems obvious later that the signs were there. I can recall so clearly feeling the first breath of the coming wind that Sunday morning when Tara slipped into the shower wearing the dildo that had vanished from the chapel at San Pi. Nena had stolen it from me and Tara had stolen it from her. It's in the genes.

She started kissing and biting my neck. She ran her tongue over my breasts, around my nipples, down into pussy. 'Mmm, honey,' she murmured. She sucked my bottom lip and slowly, forcefully, pushed the dildo up inside me.

'You're doing me,' I said with a little cry.

She opened her eyes wide and didn't say anything. She just pushed and pushed and kept on pushing. The breath caught in my throat and I closed my eyes and let the moment of pain carry me on its thin shoulders to that other place and it was romantic and magical under the warm shower and so beautiful my insides turned liquid and I was glad I had saved it for Tara. I will always remember her and wherever she is we will always in some way be together.

I don't know why it happened that morning of all mornings but I felt the future drawing at me like a magnet and it was time to start moving on. When I wrote *I'm A Virgin* I was a virgin, probably the last girl in the world still a virgin at 18. I had some vague plan of saving my little prize for my husband, for some special thing, a honeymoon or something. But I had a feeling that when you do that you end up disappointed. I'd already had my bottom pierced a few times and losing my stretched little hymen to Tara in the dildo was poetic. It was the dildo; after all, that was the making of me.

We dressed in our uniforms for Sunday service and, as I slid with flaming cheeks into the front row of pews with the twins, all the girls in their scarlet jackets couldn't have been more attentive if Mary Magdalene had walked down the aisle.

There was no feet shuffling, no coughing. The girls weren't lusting over Saint Sebastian, still young and sexy on his wooden plinth. They were waiting, quietly waiting, and were rewarded for their patience immediately after chapel when Sister Theresa hurried towards us with bowed shoulders and the look of someone whose doctor has just told them they have leukaemia.

She said in her soft voice that Mother Superior wanted to see all three of us, *immediately*.

Sister Theresa followed as we crossed the quad to the tower. Two hundred pairs of schoolgirl eyes turned glinting like the chips of flint on the chapel wall. Still none of them spoke and I know what was going through their little heads: I'm glad it isn't me but I *wish* it were me.

Standing outside the tower door like a guard with Jack and Daisy was Tabatha Van Deegan. I smiled and the look of triumph she wore slowly faded from her wan features. Her triumph was the key to my triumph and it was only dawning on her at that second.

We climbed the spiral stairs that curved up through the tower like strands of DNA and I felt a knot tighten in my tummy. The sea beyond the leaded windows was blue and calm and I suddenly felt calm too because when you try to make something happen and something happens you have to be ready for it.

The tall arched double doors were open. Summer had arrived and the light crossed Mother Superior's severe office in silver stripes. We stood before her with our buttons buttoned and she produced the first of the many newspapers and magazines that would pass through my hands in the following days and which Christian Thomas was fingering like the perfect perv even now.

I gasped but the twins remained glazed and vaguely disinterested.

'I cannot understand why girls like yourselves would do such a thing?' she said and collapsed into her chair.

'For the money, Sister,' Tara answered, and I was just *so* impressed.

Mother Superior sat there sighing. 'What will your grandfather say?'

Tara raised her thin shoulders. 'I don't suppose he'll mind that much.'

My iPhone vibrated in my blue skirt pocket and I had a funny feeling that it was important.

'I can't understand what the world's coming to.' She sighed before turning to me with bloodshot eyes. 'As for you, I have always had my doubts. You are clearly the ring leader.'

'It's true,' I said, and felt really good about myself for saying it. 'I just wanted to make a record, that's all.'

I was standing in the middle. Tara and Saskia both turned to look at me and Tara took my hand.

'That will be quite enough of *that*,' said Mother Superior, and Tara let go.

Mother Superior had shrunken into her chair like a deflated dinghy and took a big gasp of air that pumped her back onto her feet. On the window behind her there was a blind with wooden slats which she raised. She stood to one side and we approached like little birds to breadcrumbs.

Even the twins gasped.

Outside the convent walls were the massed batteries of the press, cameramen with mile-long lenses, reporters with fat wallets, crowds of sightseers from the grey tower blocks eating chips and spitting, TV crews with blondes speaking into microphones, and you knew even across the distance that what they were saying was rubbish. The Italians were there and the French, the Germans, the Japanese, of course, the American woman with the 44DD whoppers, the BBC, Sky and that nice man from Channel 4. It was *amazing*.

'You've done this Isabella di Millo.'

I turned to look at Mother Superior. 'Have I?' I said, and Tara gave one of her rare smiles.

I felt the phone vibrate again and couldn't stand the suspense a moment longer.

'I have to go to the lavatory,' I said.

As I went by Sister Theresa, I paused for just a second and kissed her cheek. 'Thank you,' I whispered, and clicked on the mobile the moment I turned the first curve on the spiral.

'Bella. Thank God. It's Rupert.'

'Doh?'

'Rupert. I got your number from Christian Thomas.'

Pause.

'Dallas McTee.'

Pause.

He switched to his Jamaican voice. 'The black man,' he said and through the missing pane of glass in the window beside me I felt the winds of change begin to blow. 'I'm outside,' he added. 'It's like a cup final. They're animals. Listen, Bella, listen.'

'I am listening.'

'I have offers from *nine*, N I N E, nine record companies to redub and release *I'm A Virgin*.'

'How much am I going to get?'

'Bella, that has to be negotiated.'

'Am I going to get screwed, Rupert?'

'No. No. No way.'

'My stepfather's a lawyer, you know.'

'Good. You need representation. You need good people. '

I remembered that night when he'd said everyone was going to want a piece of my *ass* and I thought: everything is falling into place, I'm a woman, I have intuitions and I have to go with them.

'What do you want me to do?'

'Bella, listen: I want to see you coming through the school gate. You can't pay for that kind of publicity.'

'I'm your man,' I said and he laughed as the line went dead.

I slipped my mobile in my skirt and the tight feeling in my tummy unwound as I spiralled down the stone stairway. The girls were standing outside the tower like a sea of red poppies. Then, in slow-mo, Katie Makarios took off her straw bonnet.

'Way to go,' she yelled and all but the Tabatha *clique* threw their hats in the air.

Like a soldier picking my way through land mines I wove a path through the straw bonnets to the gate where Mr Gibson was standing guard.

'I have to go, I'm afraid. I've been sent down.'

'I'm sorry about that,' he said. 'I'm going to miss you.'

'I'm going to miss you, too, Mr Gibson.'

As he pulled the gates open, and the press pressed forward, he leaned close to my ear. 'I always knew you sneaked out through the boiler room.'

'Don't tell anyone,' I said.

''Course I won't.'

But of course he did. I mean, wouldn't you for £2,500 and lunch at The Ivy?

This was my first taste of paparazzi mania and I loved it and it was amazing and incredible and now it bores me to tears.

They think they *own* you.

Everyone wants *something* and when they get their teeth into you they chew you up and spit you out *like* school dinners. The photographers are so pushy and the blondes are the worst with their sharp haircuts and sharp accents and sharp shoes.

They called me a nymphomaniac, a sex maniac, a sex goddess (honest) and they said I was decadent and a pervert (*me* a pervert!) and what they all wanted to know was what went on between the sheets and behind the walls at Saint Sebastian.

I saw Rupert's shiny head as he eased his way through the throng towards me. I don't know what the blanket was all about, but he waited until I had been photographed about a million times and then bundled me into the back of Christian Thomas's green Jaguar where Lucy Mikimoto was waiting with a flask of hot soup. I kid you not.

Aghh, I ate da press. That's my publicist.

Fists were hammering on the roof and I felt like a murderer or something as the car nosed through the flashing cameras, the people spitting and throwing chips, the blondes screaming, *Are you a lesbian*? and Rupert going on about how he'd heard Jazz P Bang Bang playing my song and couldn't believe it, and he couldn't believe it when he saw the article in *The Daily Telegraph,* and he must have believed it because he packed his laptop and said adios to Dallas McTee.

Rupert had traced Christian Thomas through the press cutting in the local paper, and that's all boring because from the moment we drove away from the convent gates everything, *everything* I've done has been reported, twisted, exaggerated, inflated, embellished, embroidered, blown up, spat out, managed, spun and stuck in the press and I did start out keeping cuttings for a scrapbook, but really with concerts, rehearsals, recordings, dance lessons and writing new material who has time?

You get so exasperated with the lies the autobiography began to make sense, and if Christian Thomas, or whatever he calls himself, can type out what he plays back on his little tape machine, what appears on these pages is the un-inflated, un-embellished, un-embroidered truth.

To continue:

Aghh, no. No is Bella, is bodi-doddle.

'Ouch. Gabriella.'

'*Pardone.*'

I don't think I'll ever forgive Thames Bridge Records for not investing the teeny weenie extra bit of bling it needed to nudge *I'm A Virgin* just two more places up the Christmas charts from number three, although Rupert said it could work to our advantage because the fans root for the outsider and you make your money on album sales.

Is It True, incidentally, will be out in the spring, so *please, please* order a copy.

My contract ties me to Thames for three years and I only signed it after Zach Kessler took it to America to have *his* lawyers read it. He's the only person I truly trust, I mean, Rupert de la Rue found Lucy Mikimoto, so he needs watching, and that's Simon Daviditz's job.

Simon almost had a heart attack, I mean he *really* almost had a heart attack, when I got my junk back from the convent and showed him a copy of my secret film disc. It's our little secret, and I keep meaning to get back to the coast before Troy unearths the original and goes rushing off to the press. One thing the newspapers did get right is that new young stars *don't* make millions overnight and it's only now with the American tour organised that I can seriously start planning my future.

'*Cuando era joven vivía en Granada, una thiudad bonita.*'

'*Cuando era joven vivía en Granada, una thiudad bonita.*'

'*Perfecto.*'

My Spanish tutor turns like I'm a ventriloquist and I'd thrown my voice into the open doorway where Tara appears in a black blazer, black jeans, Jimmy Choo points and a red bandana like she's a communist or something. She's growing out her hair and it looks *really* good.

'*El coche ya está*,' she adds, yawning and lighting up as I untangle myself from Gabriella's grasp.

'Ouch.'

Christian Thomas clicks off his machine and Lucy sucks air through her perfect teeth.

U have re-ersal four o'clock.

Yeah. Yeah.

There's a miniature bottle of champagne and two glasses in the fridge and I collect them before chasing down the stairs behind Tara, who's puffing away as fast as she can and lets out streamers of smoke through the open window as the car gets sucked into the creeping metal snake pumping out pollution as we cross London.

At Blackheath there's a little Romanian man selling flowers in bunches and it's nice not having to worry about money because I bought them all and sent him home early with a smile on his face.

I didn't manage to get to see Daddy over Christmas or New Year because there were concerts *like* non-stop. On my birthday I had to do 11 exclusive interviews, *Desert Island Discs* (and I'll never live it down choosing *I'm A Virgin* as record number 6) and then we rushed off to do a live performance on that ghastly gay chat show. I wore my school blazer with the badge long gone and told Rupert I would not dress in the devil costume even for the £50,000 they offered. *I'm not just a pair of tits, you know.* He's negotiating *Playboy* but that's different.

'Tara, you never stop yawning.'

'I know.'

I turned with a smile and Tara didn't smile and it's great that Nena relented and let her become my PA, and I finally learned what PA actually means and it's a job that someone does where they don't actually do practically anything at all. PA: Practically Anything. *geddit!*

After I got sacked from Saint Sebastian, the twins in September went to some private American university in Monaco. Tara, for something to do, borrowed the Solex belonging to the caretaker and drove the little bike over the Pyrenees to Spain where she lived in a cottage below San Pi and sold heather in pouches in the square at night.

The girls like all girls need to find their own way and I understand that. It was a bore for them always being lumped together as twins but as twins they are never far apart. Saskia is joining us on the world tour, as a PA, naturally, and plans to run away when we get to Hollywood. You're nothing, says Rupert, until you make it in America.

Oh, yes, and there's something else about Saskia and Tara Scott-Wallace. The fact that I'm getting rich and famous doesn't faze them at all. My every whim is catered for and that gets so boring. Tara supposedly works for me and when I ask her to do something she usually says nothing or she says, 'Why don't you do it yourself?' It's like, so refreshing.

We zipped through the village. We passed the Chinese restaurant and crested the hill.

'Look. Ickham Manor.'

Yawn.

There was snow on the roof and smoke hung in frozen spirals on the pale blue sky. Esperanza would be preparing lunch and I wondered if there were Christmas trees in the olive jars. Mother still thinks it's her house and, in a way, it is because if anything happens to me, and that like happens *all* the time in my business, then she is my beneficiary.

Mr Asis was slowing down.

'No, I want to go to the church first,' I told him.

'Thank you very much.'

He waggles his head and keeps going. Mr Asis has shaved off his chin beard, he's stopped wearing that little crocheted hat and people don't spit at us when we're stuck in traffic. You just have to pay people properly and they stop being fanatics. Tara's learning Arabic for something to do and starts practising the moment the car reaches the church.

You have to do *everything* yourself, champers in the little backpack, bouquets leaping from my arms as I cart them to the graveside where the plastic flowers in the aluminium vase *must* have been left by Mother. I fill the glasses and, after taking a tiny taste because you should never say no to champagne, I give the rest to Daddy a sip at a time. I just know he's so proud of me.

The flowers are *everywhere* and as I make them neat because that's the way I am, I remember all the loose ends Mr Thomas wants to tie up like Troy sending me his first demo, and it's not bad, and Mandy's pregnant, and her mum's going to let her keep the baby at home.

They did arrest Mr Glick and the Scott-Wallace clan had to pull in all the favours at the *Bloody* Vice Squad before they let him go. He took his fortune to Cambodia. What else? Tabatha Van Deegan didn't get into Cambridge. She returned to Texas where, through family connections, she got a job at the Bush Research Institute, which sounds like totally pornographic.

Katie Makarios runs the Bella Fan Club and just a little reminder, *Is It True* will be out in the spring and it's like *really* amazing.

Oh, yes, and one more thing.

Christian Thomas, my *ghostwriter*, wants to call my autobiography *A Girl's Adventure*, but I think I'll go for something more literary like *The Secret Life of Girls*.

Look out for it.

THE END

Also by Chloë Thurlow

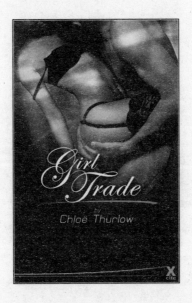

She feels wicked, liberated, daring. And bored. But her adventure begins on holiday in La Gomera, when a rugged beachcomber removes the leather thong from his neck and binds her hands behind her. Crossing oceans and continents in a nether world of smugglers, arms dealers, and pirates, she becomes the adored but captive jewel of the tough inflexible men who make a living in inhospitable landscapes. On hot afternoons on long days without number, she dedicates herself to the pleasures of sex in all its shapes and forms. She learns subservience. She becomes the perfect concubine. The perfect lover. She becomes *Chengi* – Girl.

ISBN 9781907016417   £7.99

When a mysterious stranger gives failed actress Greta May his phone number, she dreams of adventure and plucks up the courage to call him, but the moment she enters his flat he rips off her knickers and spanks her bottom. At first shocked and humiliated, Greta grows bewildered as the pain turns to pleasure, and after being tied to the bed for a thrashing, she agrees with rising excitement to play a game where she will win a prize if she does everything Richard demands.

It is the beginning of an erotic journey of self-discovery, where Greta meets Dirty Bill, the water sports specialist; Vanlooch, who uses oils from unusual places to highlight his portraits, and the moody Count Ruspoli who, after bedding 10,000 women, has taken a vow of chastity. Can Greta save him?

Under Richard's firm hand Greta finds her true nature through discipline and seizes the elusive prize: the chance to play the role that will change her life and put her back in the spotlight.

ISBN 9781907761119   £7.99